100 PROOF MURDER

100 PROOF MURDER

Mary Ellis

SEVERN
HOUSE

First world edition published in Great Britain and the USA in 2021
by Severn House, an imprint of Canongate Books Ltd,
14 High Street, Edinburgh EH1 1TE.

Trade paperback edition first published in Great Britain and the USA in 2022
by Severn House, an imprint of Canongate Books Ltd.

severnhouse.com

British Library Cataloguing-in-Publication Data
A CIP catalogue record for this title is available from the British Library.

ISBN-13: 978-0-7278-9100-6 (cased)
ISBN-13: 978-1-78029-793-4 (trade paper)
ISBN-13: 978-1-4483-0532-2 (e-book)

ONE

Louisville, Kentucky

The moment she spotted her videographer in the hotel lobby, travel writer Jill Curtis signaled the bartender. 'We'll take two of your famous cocktails,' she said.

'Hey, Erickson, over here.' Jill produced the broadest of smiles since her videographer and partner looked like he'd just eaten a dozen lemons.

Dragging his suitcase behind him, Michael pushed his glasses up his nose and shuffled to the barstool she'd saved.

'Quick, sit down,' she ordered. 'I practically had to arm-wrestle two women who wanted your seat.'

Michael glanced around the elegant interior with mild interest. 'Why are we here?'

'Because this is one of the hottest bars in the coolest hotel in town. Did you know that Al Capone and his cronies hung out here during Prohibition? So did F. Scott Fitzgerald. In case you weren't paying attention in English lit, he wrote *The Great Gatsby.*'

'Fascinating.' Michael's sour expression didn't change.

'Plus this bar makes a cocktail for lightweights like me who can't handle bourbon straight-up.' With impeccable timing, the bartender set two lemon-garnished flutes in front of them.

Michael's left eyebrow arched. 'Why on earth is a bourbon drink fizzing?'

'Because it also contains champagne. If you don't like it, I'll drink both of them.' Jill took a sip of hers and grinned.

He studied the bubbles and then drank. 'It's not bad. Now tell me why we're in Louisville. The last time we talked, I said Mr Fleming wanted us in Lexington to tie their distillery tour with the Kentucky racing industry. Anyone who's driven down Interstate 75 has seen those impressive thoroughbred farms.'

Jill took another sip. 'Oh, my, that is so good.'

Michael pushed her glass beyond reach. 'No more bubbles until I get answers. I didn't appreciate you changing the destination when I was halfway through Illinois. And by sending a text, no less. Did you forget Mr Fleming is still our boss at the syndicated news service?'

'I didn't forget. That's why I called him for approval before switching cities for our next bourbon tour travel log. Louisville is home to the granddaddy of horseracing, the Kentucky Derby, along with their famous drink, the mint julep. Louisville also has four stops on the state's tour circuit and a new urban circuit of bourbon bars and restaurants, including where we're sitting now. It didn't take long to convince the boss that this would be a better location.'

'Here you are, miss. My name's Ray, by the way.' The bartender, who'd been eavesdropping, pushed Jill's glass within reach. 'Besides, we're closer to Illinois and we're more chic than Lexington.'

'Thanks, Ray,' Jill said with a wink. 'See what I mean, partner? Best of both worlds.'

'OK, fine. At least I didn't have to smooth things over with the boss like last time.' Michael relaxed on the barstool. 'Let's finish these and head to our hotel. I'm starving and exhausted. There was nothing but road construction and fender-benders the entire trip from Chicago.'

'This is home-sweet-home for the next week, the beautiful Thurman House Hotel.' Jill flourished her hand around the room. 'And we're very close to the famous Whiskey Row.'

'No way can we afford this place on our expense account.' Michael downed the rest of his drink. 'Did you drive your Uncle Roger's pickup to Louisville? The valet here would love getting behind the wheel of that old relic.'

Jill shook her head. 'I did not. Parking is too expensive in the city. My aunt dropped me off and went home. During the drive from Roseville, I negotiated a corporate discount with the manager. Plus, this hotel is part of a chain where I have tons of reward points. If we're here longer than a week, you can use your points for the second week. I also made reservations for our first tour at Parker Estate Distillery tomorrow and lined up an interview with the manager of operations.'

Michael's expression improved considerably. 'I thought the infamous Whiskey Row burned down.'

'It did, but their historic façade survived intact and they have since rebuilt.'

'Not bad, Curtis. For once, you did good.'

'Ray, let's have another round.' Jill sang the words like a radio jingle. 'I've got something to celebrate.'

'Absolutely not, Ray. Knowing her, she hasn't eaten anything since breakfast and it's almost suppertime.' Michael hooked his thumb at her.

Filling a bowl with mixed nuts, Ray set it in front of her. 'Have a snack, Miss Jill. I'll have those drinks up.' His smile could have charmed a snake.

'How long have you been here?' Michael asked under his breath.

'Not very long, maybe fifteen minutes. I make friends fast.' Jill poured nuts onto a napkin and started to eat. 'Did you buy new equipment so you can video our tour stops?'

'I replaced everything with top of the line. I hope Fleming's insurance covers the full cost. And you better hope no more ex-boyfriends take their animosity out on my car.'

Jill almost choked on a cashew. 'That guy was not my ex-boyfriend. He turned out to be a murderer, remember?'

'Yeah, but I also remember you went out with him a couple times.' Michael grabbed a handful from her bowl.

'Hey, use a napkin,' Jill hissed. 'Who knows when you last washed your hands?'

Ray returned with two fresh drinks. 'For the record, plenty of people have dated psychopaths. At least you didn't marry the guy.' He moved the nuts in front of Michael and produced a fresh bowl for Jill.

'You're right, Ray, I didn't.' She lifted her glass in toast. 'Unfortunately I have a bad habit of judging books by their cover, if you get my drift.'

Michael waited until Ray walked away to serve other customers. 'You've been here fifteen minutes and you already have another admirer,' he whispered.

'I can't help it if I'm irresistible. You better be careful, Erickson. Bartenders have extraordinarily good hearing. It's part of the job description.'

Michael glanced down the bar. 'How are things in Roseville? Can your aunt Dot handle the bed and breakfast by herself?'

Jill ate another handful of nuts since getting tipsy was the last thing she wanted on their first night in Louisville. 'Other than missing Uncle Roger, she seems to be OK. Of course, summer is the busy season at Sweet Dreams and that's over with. She'll soon have someone to help her – my grandmother – long before spring rolls around. Those two patched up their differences.'

'How much help will another old lady be? Mrs Clark needs someone young and strong working for her.' Michael flexed his bicep.

'I'll recommend you if we get fired. In the meantime, don't discount my grandmother. She's a great cook and no longer needs assisted living now that her knee has healed. My parents kept her there so they didn't have to worry about her.'

'That must have made Granny mad.' Michael gobbled another handful of nuts. 'What happened to her house?'

'It was just sitting empty, but with all the bedrooms upstairs, it was no good for her. After a little encouragement from her favorite granddaughter, Granny sold the house and invested the proceeds in mutual funds.'

'You talked her into *what*?' Michael's eyes grew round.

'I sent her the best real estate agent in Chicago and then hooked her up with a reputable stockbroker. Granny will soon be on a Greyhound bus on her way to Louisville.'

'Your mother will pull your hair out.'

'Not if I never go home again.'

Michael shook his head. 'You better hope things work out in Roseville. Those two women didn't speak for over forty years. What happens if they have another fight?'

'I honestly don't see that happening. Even if they argue, Dot's house is so big they can stay out of each other's way until things cool down.'

'Aren't all the bedrooms upstairs at Sweet Dreams?'

'No, there's a small bedroom and bath off the library. It was for Uncle Roger when he snored too much.'

'Sounds like you've got life tied up with a bow.' Michael sounded unusually snide.

'What do you mean by that?' she asked, her hackles rising.

'First, you took care of lonely Aunt Dot and your underutilized Granny in one fell swoop, while making sure your new romance with the Kentucky state cop will have another two weeks to see if anything comes of it.' Michael pulled his stool closer. 'I'm not stupid, Jill. I know Nick Harris works out of the Louisville post whereas Lexington would've been three hours away.'

She furled her lip. 'Do you lie awake at night figuring me out? Or do these brilliant insights pop into your head without warning?'

'You, Jill Curtis, are as complicated as a hamster on a wheel.' Michael finished his second drink and hefted his duffle bag to his shoulder. 'I want to check in, change clothes, and walk to Whiskey Row. We can find a place for dinner along the way and eat here another night. I'll meet you in the lobby in thirty minutes.' With the matter settled Michael strode from the bar.

'Sure, Mikey, whatever you say,' Jill muttered under her breath.

Like magic, the attentive bartender materialized. 'Pushy little man, isn't he?' Ray tossed Michael's nuts in the trash and wiped down where he'd been sitting.

'Oh, he's all right,' Jill said. 'We usually take turns being a pain in the backside.'

Ray's expression deepened his substantial number of wrinkles. 'That's how life should be. If I may be so bold, what are you two – casual friends, former lovers, ex-spouses? If you say boyfriend and girlfriend, my heart will break.' He placed his hand on the center of his chest.

Jill chuckled. Despite his extraordinary sense of hearing, Ray had to be seventy years old. 'Michael and I are best friends besides co-workers. We write travel articles for syndicated news-papers and several internet sites, while he usually shoots the video. But unfortunately, I have a boyfriend. We just met a few weeks ago.'

Ray topped off her bowl of nuts. 'Ah, yes, the Kentucky state cop. I was hoping I heard wrong. Sometimes this bar gets so noisy.' He frowned at three women who were unwinding rather vocally. 'If that cop doesn't live up to expectations, you let me know. In the meantime, try Doc Crow's Southern Smokehouse for dinner tonight. You won't be sorry.'

'We'll look for it. Thanks. Can I take this drink up to my room for later?'

'You, Miss Jill, can do whatever you please while a guest of the Thurman House.' Ray reached for her hand and air-kissed the back of her fingers. 'Take these nuts for later too.' He emptied the bowl into a takeout box.

'You know the way to a girl's heart.' Jill started to walk away then hesitated. 'Goodness, I almost forgot to pay my tab.'

Ray was already refilling beer mugs for a group of men. 'Would you like me to add it to your room?'

'Sure, but I haven't checked in yet.' She dug for her credit card.

'That's no problem. You just run along, Miss Jill.'

Just run along? I'm sure not in Chicago anymore. But she had no time to ponder flirtatious bartenders in a gorgeous land-mark hotel. By the time she checked in and found her room – a two-bedroom suite to be exact – and washed her hands and face, Michael was tapping his toe in their shared living room.

'Did I *not* mention I was starving?' he whined. 'What in the world takes women so long?' Opening the door, he waved her through.

Jill pressed the button for the elevator. 'You should have eaten more nuts. I took my bowl to my room.'

'You did *what*? Oh, never mind.' Down in the lobby, Michael scanned nearby restaurants on his phone. 'Any idea where we should eat?'

'I have my heart set on Doc Crow's Southern Smokehouse.' Jill applied lipstick using her reflection in the window.

'That one and Merle's Whiskey Kitchen were highly rated in my search. Let's head down Main Street and see which one we come to first.'

Unfortunately for Michael, they reached Whiskey Row first, which was still under construction after the fire four years ago. Jill studied each giant photograph along the brick façade to gain perspective. 'Until I saw a news video of that warehouse fire two years ago, I couldn't imagine liquids burning. Forty-five thousand barrels destroyed at Jim Beam. What a shame.'

'Haven't you ever had Cherries Jubilee?' Michael asked, studying the chronology of photographs. 'It's the rum that burns, not the ice cream. Anything eighty proof or higher will burn, and most bourbon is one-hundred proof.' Michael pulled her away from the display by the hand. 'Food, Curtis. Or I'll start gnawing on your arm.'

Following the prompts from his phone, they soon found Doc Crow's and were seated, Monday not being a busy night for dinner out. Their menu was extensive, the list of bourbons and other whiskeys long. After a short perusal, Michael ordered a smokehouse sampler with ribs, pulled pork and beef brisket. Jill selected blackened tilapia with fried okra, pickled vegetables and hush puppies. The food was delicious, but neither of them came close to finishing their meal.

'Happy, now?' Jill asked, slurping her iced tea.

'I am, but we're not going back to the hotel until I have a real Kentucky bourbon, straight-up. People don't come to Louisville to drink iced tea.' He pushed away their glasses.

'Some do, but all right. Let's sit at the bar where we can breathe in the atmosphere.' Jill found two seats at the far end. On her left was a young couple on a date, judging by their attire. On Michael's right was a group of multi-aged women, who had just left a business conference, judging by their nametags. The group was well along in the wind-down process.

'What'll it be, folks?' The female bartender's gaze roved from one to the other.

'We'll each have a shot of Parker Estate,' Michael said. 'What's with the black armband?'

She gaped at him. 'Since you picked Parker's, I assumed you'd heard the sad news.'

Jill spotted two other bartenders wearing black armbands. 'We just arrived in Louisville. What happened?'

'William Scott, the master distiller at Parker Estate, passed away this afternoon. Most bartenders in Louisville are wearing black bands to show respect.' She poured a goodly amount into two snifters, pushed them over, and the tiniest amount for herself.

'Oh, dear. We scheduled a tour at Parker's Distillery tomorrow.'

'I'm sure it will be cancelled. The family is in mourning. To Mr Scott, cheers.' She raised her glass and downed the contents.

When Michael lifted his glass for a hearty swallow, Jill felt obligated to take a small sip. The liquid tasted delicious but burned a trail down her throat. 'Was the master distiller, Mr Scott, murdered?' she asked.

This time the bartender stared at Jill. 'Why on earth would you say that?'

'Don't pay any attention to her.' Michael motioned for a refill. 'My partner sees murder around every corner.'

The bartender refilled his glass, gave them an odd perusal and wandered away, not to return any time soon.

'We scared her off,' Jill whispered.

'Not we, you. There went your big plans for tomorrow. What now?'

She checked her messages. 'No one has cancelled my appointment with Miss Scott, the operations manager, so I plan to show up. We can take the distillery tour with tourists anytime, but this could be my only chance to meet her.'

'You can't invade the family's privacy during a time like this!'

'I don't plan to,' Jill snapped. 'Most likely I'll express my condolences and leave a business card.'

Michael shook his head. 'The last time you were in a distillery, you tripped over a dead body and became the sheriff's number one suspect.'

'I didn't *trip* over anyone. And how was I supposed to know Roger Clark was dead? I was trying to help.'

'We both know how that works out. This Miss Scott is undoubtedly related to the deceased, William Scott,' Michael hissed between his teeth.

'I've done my research. The master distiller was the operations manager's father.'

'Then pick another operation for tomorrow and stay away from Parker Estate. You said there were four distilleries in Louisville.'

As Michael turned his attention to his phone, Jill sat there fuming. Sometimes her partner could be so unimaginative. In Roseville, she had ended up helping the distiller's widow, Dot, who turned out to be a distant cousin. She had also assisted law enforcement, including Lieutenant Harris, whom she was now dating. So why did Michael believe her incapable of tact and decorum?

Jill took another sip and pushed away the glass, preferring her bourbon mixed with the bubbly stuff. She planned to show up for the appointment with Miss Scott on time and dressed professionally, pretending not to know someone had died. If the appointment gets cancelled, so be it. But she'd gained a lot of insight in Roseville while helping Aunt Dot with Uncle Roger's murder, so she might prove useful in this town too.

At eight the next morning, Jill crept silently from her bedroom into the kitchen area of their suite. Loud snores coming from the other room told her Michael was still asleep. She slipped her tape recorder into her purse and headed straight for the door. She would grab coffee in the lobby or on the way, instead of chancing a litany of questions from Michael, or worse, his wrath.

Her appointment was only several blocks away. By the time her giant cup of java cooled enough to drink she had arrived at the corporate headquarters of Parker Estate Distillery. A sign on the front door indicated all distillery tours were suspended until further notice due to a death in the Parker family. The sign mentioned nothing about appointments with the operations' manager.

Jill marched up to the receptionist's desk with the air of someone in control. 'Good morning. I'm Jill Curtis with an appointment with Alexis Scott.' She stretched to her full height of five-foot-seven in heels.

'Your appointment was for today?' asked the blue-eyed blonde.

'Yes, miss, at nine o'clock.'

'Didn't anyone call you, Miss Curtis?'

'No, no one did.' Jill let the tiniest bit of pique invade her tone.

'Forgive me, but our president and master distiller passed away yesterday.' The receptionist dropped her voice to a whisper. 'I'm sure Miss Scott is busy making arrangements for her father.'

'I'm so sorry to hear that. I was unaware of Mr Scott's passing, but are you certain Miss Scott isn't waiting for me upstairs?' Jill glanced at her watch.

'No, I'm not certain.' The woman glanced around nervously. 'Let me try her extension.' Jill crossed her fingers behind her back and waited. 'She must have stepped away from her desk. I'll keep trying. In the meantime, you may go up to the fourth floor, suite eleven, and have a seat in the outer office. Although her secretary won't be in today, if Miss Scott wishes to keep the appointment, she'll come get you. This key card is for the elevator. Return it when you're done.'

'Thank you. I will.' Jill scurried to the elevator as fast as her legs would carry her, fearing a security guard would block her path at any moment. On the fourth floor, the door to suite eleven stood ajar. Jill peeked inside, spotted the secretary's desk and a reception area devoid of people, and sat down to wait. Hearing a female voice beyond the door, she assumed the operations manager, Alexis Scott, was in.

After twenty minutes of reading magazines, Jill heard something which filled her with shame: a woman sobbing. Michael had been right about her. This was nothing but an invasion of privacy. Jill dropped the magazine on the stack and rose to her feet. But unfortunately, the magazine triggered a mini landslide of periodicals to the floor.

'Is someone out there?' A voice called from the inner office. 'May I help you?'

Jill crept sheepishly to the inner door and opened it a crack. 'It's me, Miss Scott. Jill Curtis. We had a nine o'clock appointment. This must be a bad time, so I'll call to reschedule.' Head down, she turned and shuffled away.

Suddenly, a dark-haired woman appeared in the doorway. 'Didn't my secretary call you to cancel?'

'No, ma'am, no one called.' At least that part wasn't a lie. 'But it's OK. Everyone has bad days and deserves a break.'

'I'm so sorry! Come in, please . . . Jill, did you say? Alexis Scott, Operations Manager at Parker Estate.' She extended her hand.

'Yes, Jill Curtis.' After shaking hands, Jill followed the well-dressed executive into her office.

Medium height, early thirties, and other than a mottled complexion, Miss Scott was very attractive. 'Yes, here it is.' She tapped a long nail on her desk calendar. 'Jill Curtis, syndicated travel writer. We were supposed to discuss how the bourbon industry has changed over the years, along with its impact on Louisville. But my father unexpectedly passed away yesterday. Someone should have called you to reschedule our appointment.'

'I'm so sorry for your loss,' Jill said, her expression horrified. 'I hadn't heard.' Regretfully, that was the second time she told that lie.

Alexis blew her nose in a tissue and crossed her arms over

her suit jacket. 'Although no one's ready to lose a parent, my dad's death came as a total shock to me.'

'He hadn't been sick for a long while, giving you time to prepare?'

'Oh, no, Dad was the picture of health. He still ran a mile before breakfast every morning and worked out at the gym three times a week.'

Jill crossed her arms too. 'Maybe his doctor can shed some light and help you to find closure.'

'I doubt it. Dad just had a physical two months ago for insurance purposes. His physician gave him a clean bill of health. So either the doctor missed something, or all the healthy eating, sufficient exercise, and getting enough sleep is a pack of hooey.' Alexis drummed her fingers on the desk. 'I think I'll have a greasy burger and fries for lunch.'

'I should let you get back to it since I personally know all you have to do. Recently I helped my aunt bury her husband in Roseville. He was the master distiller at Black Creek.' Jill backed toward the doorway.

Alexis's eyes grew round as saucers. 'You're related to Roger Clark? I had never met the man, but I've tasted his excellent product.'

'Dorothy Clark is my grandmother's first cousin, but she insisted I called her "Aunt Dot". Same as your dad, Roger's death came as quite a shock to her and the rest of the family.'

Reaching for another tissue, Alexis wiped her eyes. 'Please, Jill, we will reschedule the interview for your article, but can you stay for a moment now?'

'Of course.' Jill walked back to the chair and sat down primly, but kept her tape recorder in her bag.

'First, my sympathy for the loss of your uncle. I'll send a card to Mrs Clark and mention that you and I met.' Alexis rolled her chair up to the desk. 'I'd been following the story in the Louisville newspaper. The article reported Roger Clark had been murdered and the police have arrested a suspect. Is that true?'

'It is.' Jill chose not to mention she'd dated the alleged suspect who then subsequently had tried to kill her.

'How awful. At first the paper reported Mr Clark's death as an accident.'

'Yes, then a state investigator discovered something suspicious that had been missed, so law enforcement took a closer look at the case.'

For a long moment Alexis sat quietly, as though processing the information. 'We might have the same situation here.' She stared down at her hands.

Unsure if the operations manager had been talking to herself, Jill remained mute.

'How do you know if someone dies of natural causes or not?' Alexis looked up, meeting Jill's eye.

'That's for the coroner or a medical examiner to determine. Someone in charge must sign the death certificate.'

'My mother thinks Dad died of a heart attack and that's how it appeared to the deputy coroner who examined him at the scene. Most likely that's what will end up on the death certificate. But Dad had no family history of coronary artery disease and as I mentioned, he recently passed his physical.'

'I'm no doctor, but I heard that heart disease can remain undetected for years.'

'I understand, but I want Dad's death looked into, just like your Uncle Roger's. Things aren't always how they first appear.'

Jill shifted uneasily in her chair. 'Do you have any reason to suspect foul play?' When the executive hesitated, Jill sprang to her feet. 'Sorry, Miss Scott. This is *so* not my business. I'll call your secretary to reschedule once this funeral is behind you.'

'Wait, I made it your business when I questioned you about Mr Clark. I just need you to point me in the right direction. Right now, my only "reason" for suspicion is a bad feeling in my gut. And the fact that everything is happening so fast.'

Jill sat back down. 'Did your father have any enemies?'

'I imagine he made a few along the way. There's plenty of competition and jealousy in the bourbon business.'

'I can certainly attest to *that* after living in Roseville for two weeks.'

'Unfortunately, I run the production end of the company with my head in the sand regarding other facets of Parker Estate.' Alexis tossed her pen across her desk.

Jill chose her next words carefully. 'Forgive me . . . but is your dad still happily married to your mom? Or are they in the midst of a nasty divorce?'

'They're still married, but I don't know whether they're happy or not. Another example of my head-in-the-sand personality.'

'Don't be so hard on yourself. That's how everyone handles life until something comes along to wake us up.'

'Now that I'm awake, I don't know what to do.'

'In my Uncle Roger's case, once the cause of death was changed from accidental to murder, the police began interviewing everyone with a grudge against him or who stood to benefit from his passing. That should give you a place to start.' Jill felt less invasive and more useful as Alexis jotted notes on a tablet.

'But first I need to make sure *natural* isn't listed as the cause of death.'

'Absolutely, otherwise your mom can proceed with the funeral. And it would be much harder to exhume the body for an autopsy than to stop the burial now.'

A flood of tears ran down Alexis's face.

'I'm so sorry,' Jill said. 'I must sound callous when I refer to your beloved father as "the body".'

Alexis shook her head from side to side. 'That's not why I'm crying. In keeping with my parents' wishes, my father will be cremated and not buried. Only immediate family will be present. The memorial service will be this weekend with an urn of ashes.'

'When will this cremation take place?' Jill leaned forward in her chair.

'Soon, if my mother gets her way.' Alexis sobbed. 'I've never felt so out of control in my life.'

This time it was Jill's turn to sit quietly and consider the consequences. 'There is no way around this – you must stop the cremation from taking place. Talk to your mother or her attorney, or whoever is in charge.'

'Mom has already made arrangements with the funeral director. If I insist she stop the cremation, she'll want to know why. I don't have a single concrete reason other than my gut feeling.' Alexis's wrapped a stray lock of hair around her finger.

'The deputy coroner must first talk to your dad's doctor to see if he or she agrees with a finding of natural causes. If the doctor agrees, demand that Dad's body is sent to the state medical examiner for a full autopsy. Tell your mom you need another opinion to have closure. You're his daughter, not an uninterested bystander. If necessary, make up a reason to your mother.' Jill realized she was being over-the-top pushy. 'That is if you want to. I'm a complete stranger. I don't want to tell you what to do.'

Alexis flattened her palms on the desktop. 'Believe me, you're not. I'm so glad you showed up today. If I'd spilled my guts to anyone here, they'd think I lost my mind.'

'My videographer and partner, who goes everywhere I do, thinks that about me all the time,' Jill said.

'Well, I don't. Could I call you if I have more questions? Then whenever you're ready to do the article, I'll give you full behind-the-scenes access or anything you wish in return.'

Jill handed the woman her card. 'Call me anytime you want. No bribery necessary, and I'm truly sorry about your father.'

'Thank you. I know it's silly, but I feel much better after talking to you.' Alexis jotted a second number on her business card. 'Here is my cell number. Feel free to call me if I can open any doors while you're in Louisville.'

The two women shook hands, then Jill marched to the elevator before considering the myriad of doors she might need opened.

TWO

J ill entered Alexis Scott's phone number into her cell directory in the unlikelihood the operations manager for Parker Estate would call. Never in a million years did she think Alexis would get in touch later that day. She and Michael had just finished a trolley tour around Louisville to familiarize themselves with the city and were back in their suite about to choose a restaurant for dinner when her phone rang.

'Hello, Alexis?' Jill asked.

'Yeah, it's me. Bet you didn't think you'd hear from me so soon.' Her voice sounded raspy, as though she'd been crying.

'I told you anytime and I meant it. What can I do for you?' Jill motioned to Michael to lower the TV volume.

'I know this is a major imposition since you're traveling with a videographer, but could you possibly swing by my place tonight?' Alexis asked softly. 'I need to talk more about what we discussed this afternoon, plus we can begin the preliminaries for our interview.'

Jill took less than a second to decide. 'Of course. It would be no imposition whatsoever.'

Inferring the gist of the conversation, Michael frowned with his hands on his hips.

'Thanks. I'm still at the office but I prefer to do this at home. You never know who could be listening at work. Got a pencil to jot down my address?' Alexis recited the number and street. 'My apartment is the top floor of the old carriage house behind my parents' house. I'll order pizza or anything you like. Can you be there in an hour?'

Jill gave her assurance, hung up and turned to Michael. 'I know we planned to eat out, but Alexis Scott, the operations manager, wants to prepare for our interview. This is a once-in-a-lifetime chance to get the inside story.'

'I've heard those exact words before and they almost got you killed.' Michael's frown didn't falter.

'I know, but this is different. Since the death of the master distiller, Parker Estate has suspended tours—'

'So we head to one of the other three distilleries and come back to them,' he interrupted.

'Alexis said if I pointed her in the right direction, she would give us full access to the distillery, not just what the tourists see, plus whatever else we want.'

'Point her in *what* right direction?' he asked.

Jill shifted her weight between hips. 'Miss Scott doesn't believe her father died of a heart attack. She thinks there could have been foul play.'

'Oh, no, not again.' Michael closed the distance between them in a few strides. 'You need to stay away from her, before you end up in jail. I'll go to the interview in your place.'

'No way. I want to do the narrative while you shoot the footage.' Jill resisted stomping her foot. 'You're overreacting. Alexis isn't asking me to investigate. She wants to know how to get the police to take another look at his death. Plus she has some questions about funeral decorum. She's aware I'm only a travel writer.'

Michael's brows knit together over the bridge of his nose. 'But do *you* know that?'

'I do, Mikey.' Jill glanced at her watch. 'I need to change and leave. Can I borrow your car?'

'Sure.'

'If you don't want to go out alone, order a burger and fries at the bar downstairs.'

'Don't worry about me. Just don't let this woman drag you into something time-consuming. We have four distilleries to cover before we move on to another town.'

'Don't worry your pretty little head about a thing.' Jill grabbed the keys to Michael's car, made her way to the parking lot, punched the directions into the GPS, and soon left the city behind. In an area of rolling cornfields and green pastures, she paused at the lane marked Parker Estates. If the founder had named his whiskey after his ancestral home, *estate* hit the nail on the wooden head. A white split-rail fence enclosed acres and acres of land, far as the eye could see. At the entrance, a speaker mounted on a pole controlled whoever came and went through the iron gate.

Jill pulled up to the intercom and pressed the red button. 'Jill Curtis, here to see Miss Alexis Scott.'

'Did you come by yourself, Miss Curtis?' asked an unseen voice.

'I did.'

'Please circle around the main residence to the carriage house in the back. Miss Scott is waiting for you at the top of the stairs.' After a moment the gate swung wide. Jill drove up a tree-lined driveway usually seen only on television. Cameras mounted in trees verified her claim of traveling alone.

The imposing main house had four floors, chimneys at both ends, and a wide, wraparound porch held up by tall columns. Jill would have loved a tour, or better yet, ramble through the house at night with friends and a flashlight. But with Alexis waving from the balcony, Jill cut short her fantasy and parked next to a sleek BMW, undoubtedly belonging to Alexis.

'Can I leave my car here?' she asked, hurrying up the steps.

'Of course, anywhere you like. I'm so glad you're on time.'
Alexis motioned her into a tidy apartment with a kitchen, living,
and dining room combination and two closed doors, most likely
to a bedroom and bath. Overhead, several skylights flooded the
space with plenty of natural light.

'I love your apartment,' Jill said.

'Thanks. I told Mom I'd stay here until I got married. Now
I'm not sure if that was a wise promise.' Alexis pointed to the
overstuffed sofa. 'Make yourself comfortable. What would you
like to drink: coffee, iced tea, glass of wine?'

'Iced tea would be great.'

Alexis poured two drinks from a pitcher on the coffee table.
'Tell me which angle you will pursue for your travel story.'

Jill placed her glass on a coaster. 'The boss wants to tie the
Louisville distilleries to the horse racing industry, so I'm thinking
a Kentucky Derby angle.'

'Good choice. I have several friends connected with racing at
Churchill Downs, including the beverage manager for the race.
Although Parker Estate wasn't chosen to be this year's official
bourbon for mint juleps, we have been in the past and patrons
can request our bourbon or any other by name.'

'Too bad your friend didn't pick your brand.'

'There's much to consider with a Derby sponsorship and
plenty of traditions that must be honored.' Alexis sipped her
tea. 'Would your partner like to video my friend mixing a batch
of juleps? The beverage manager could provide a behind-the-
scenes look inside Churchill Downs and answer any questions
he has.'

Jill's mouth dropped open. 'That would be awesome – more
than I'd hoped for. Michael will soon be getting antsy since your
tours are temporarily suspended. I want Parker Estate to anchor
my Louisville article, so I don't want him moving on to the next
distillery.'

'In that case, I'll see if Paul can free up some time
tomorrow for Michael. That would figure nicely into what I
have planned for us.'

A slight frisson of unease snaked up her spine as Jill remembered Michael's parting words: *Don't let this woman drag you
into something time-consuming. We're here to do a job.* 'What

did you have in mind for tomorrow?' she asked, shaking off her discomfort.

'First, let me bring you up to speed.' Alexis took a sip of tea. 'I called my father's doctor shortly after you left. After the standard niceties, I asked him why my father died suddenly after passing his physical with flying colors.'

'That had to make him fearful of a lawsuit,' Jill murmured.

'You would think so, no? But Dr Cribbs didn't sound afraid of getting sued. He seemed genuinely flummoxed by Dad's death. He told me about several markers for coronary artery disease that were all negative in his bloodwork. And according to the calcium artery test, Dad's score was a zero. Zero . . . which meant his likelihood of having a heart attack was extremely low.'

'Is he willing to write a statement to that effect?'

'Yes, the deputy coroner already contacted him. Dr Cribbs' refusal to sign was enough for the corner to change from "natural" to "unknown causes, pending autopsy" on the death certificate. Even if he had signed, Dr Cribbs said since I'm a close family member, I have the right to demand an autopsy by the forensic pathologists in the medical examiner's office.'

'Good, have you stopped the cremation? That's first and foremost.'

'I have.' Jill saw Alexis smile for the first time. 'I told the funeral director I didn't agree with my mother and that no cremation should take place. Mr Shea will hold my father's . . . body until he receives official instructions.'

'Whew, that had to be tough for you.'

'It was.' Alexis peered up with watery eyes. 'But I can be persuasive when I need to be. Now that there will be an autopsy and the medical examiner's office is involved, how do we prove . . . or rule out foul play?'

'To the best of my knowledge the police or sheriff's department will go to work once the autopsy indicates homicide or suspicious circumstances based on forensics.'

'So the police department should be our next step.' Alexis inhaled a deep breath and blew it out. 'I need something stronger than iced tea. Will you join me in a glass of wine?'

'All right, but just a small amount. I'm driving.'

Her hostess crossed the room to the kitchen, expertly opened a wine bottle, and returned with two glasses. One containing slightly less than the other. 'I hope you like Pinot Noir. All I have is red.'

'It will be fine.' Jill took a sip. 'What did your mom say about tomorrow's change of plans?'

'I didn't tell her. Instead, I went straight to Mr Shea.' Alexis whooshed out another breath. 'I wasn't up to one of Mom's tirades earlier. But like you said, I'm not a casual bystander. I'm William Scott's daughter.'

'And who are *you* to be offering advice in a personal family matter?'

Even though neither of them had heard the door open, a middle-aged woman marched into the apartment and stopped in front of Jill. Dressed from head-to-toe in black, with deep circles under her eyes, Jill knew immediately who she was. She opened her mouth to speak but emitted not even a squeak.

'Mother, this is my friend, Jill Curtis. And I've asked you several times to knock before barging into my home. Jill, I'd like you to meet Rose Parker Scott.' Alexis tucked her hair behind her ear.

'How do you do, ma'am?' Jill asked in a voice usually reserved for animated mice.

'I've just lost my husband of thirty-five years. How do you think I am? And you haven't answered my question.' The perfectly coifed, perfectly made-up Mrs Scott sat down, no longer looming over her.

Alexis was first to reply. 'Jill is here because I asked her to come. You're not the only one affected by Daddy's passing.' Her voice cracked as tears streamed down her face.

Rose Scott's expression softened slightly. 'I realize that, dear. That's why I thought expediting the process would relieve stress on us all. Why on earth did you call Ken Shea to stop the cremation?'

'"Expediting the process"?' Alexis snapped. 'We're talking about Dad, not a new way to add barley to the mash.'

Jill picked up her glass and drank. Mrs Scott was right – she had no business here. This was a personal family matter.

'I hope you don't mind if I help myself.' Rose strode to the kitchen counter and poured a glass of wine.

'Since you don't stand on decorum with front doors, why would you bother to ask now?' Alexis glared at her mother.

'Forgive my poor selection of terms.' Rose sat back down and crossed her legs. 'But it was your father's wish to be cremated, not buried, so I don't see any reason to drag this out. We'll have a small service at the crematorium and the funeral service in church.'

Alexis wiped her face. 'I don't believe Papa died of a heart attack and neither does his doctor. He refused to sign the death certificate, so the coroner ordered an autopsy.'

This might have been the last thing Mrs Scott expected. 'You talked to Dr Cribbs?'

'Yes, this afternoon.'

'I've known Patrick Cribbs for many years. Why didn't he say that to me?'

'Because you didn't ask him. You were all set to take the deputy coroner's assessment of a flushed and perspired face as a heart attack.' Alexis reached for another tissue.

Rose's confusion only increased. 'But that's the coroner's job, for goodness' sake, to determine the cause of death.'

'Everyone makes mistakes. How many determinations does a deputy make in a year? He views a sixty-one-year-old man who distills hard liquor for a living, and assumes Dad was a heavy drinker. Which he wasn't,' Alexis added, looking at Jill.

Jill took another swallow of wine.

'Did you know that Dad had a calcium artery test?'

Rose shrugged. 'No, what's that?'

'It's a blood test which determines the evidence of heart disease. Dad scored a zero, which means *no* evidence of the disease, which indicates a low likelihood of a heart attack.'

'But it still could happen?' Rose asked.

'I suppose so, but don't you want to know the truth?'

'What difference does it make?' Rose shouted, her composure finally cracking. 'It won't bring your father back and I miss him so much.'

'I do, too, but for me, it makes a difference. I want to make sure there was no foul play.'

One of Rose's thinly drawn eyebrows arched. *'Foul play?* What are you talking about? What kind of garbage is this new friend filling your head with?' Rose's venomous glare fastened on Jill. 'Do you think I murdered my husband, young lady? I loved William.'

'I certainly don't think that,' Jill said. 'Even though we just met, I'm sure you're a very nice lady.' She wasn't sure of that at all. But since this woman had a bad temper and fingernails like claws, Jill wasn't taking any chances.

Alexis jumped to her feet. 'Stop accusing Jill of things she had nothing to do with. This is just like when I was a child. You always assumed someone else put me up to something.' She marched to the kitchen and returned with a new bottle of wine and the opener. 'I'm an adult who thinks for herself. So I'd like you to apologize to Jill.'

'Oh, that's not necessary. Everyone's under—' Jill began, but was soon interrupted.

'It is necessary. My mother taught me good manners, yet she seems to have forgotten hers.' Alexis refilled her glass and her mother's.

It was another statement Rose hadn't expected. A bright flush spread across her cheeks as a muscle tightened in her neck. 'My daughter is correct, Miss Curtis. I'm under a lot of stress and searching for someone to blame. I apologize,' she added after a pause.

'No problem.' Jill wished she could vanish into thin air.

But Rose had already refocused on her daughter. 'Do you think I somehow hurt your father?'

'Of course not, but someone else might have. Dad had enemies. Everyone in the business world does, if you stop to think about it. Maybe it *was* natural causes. Maybe Dad did die of a heart attack. But I want to know for sure and that won't happen if we quickly shove Dad's body . . .' Alexis stopped, the horror of her words hitting home. She dropped her face into her hands.

Jill slipped an arm around her shoulders and squeezed – after all, they were now friends – while Rose Scott rose to her feet with the dignity of a queen. 'Proceed with whatever you feel you must, but please keep me posted.' She marched out the door, still ajar as she left it, and down the stairs.

'May I get you something?' Jill asked when Alexis finally lifted her head.

'Will you stay for a while? I'm going to call for a pizza and I don't want to eat alone. Will you have another glass of wine?'

'All right, but if it's OK with you, I'll leave my car here and call Uber later.'

'Of course it is. That will make things easier in the morning. If you have time, I want you to visit the chief of police with me.'

'If Michael spends the day at Churchill Downs, I've got all the time in the world.'

Jill awoke the next morning to a mild headache and incessant ringing in her ears. 'OK, already, I'm coming.' She threw back the covers, staggered to the door, and found a crabby face on the other side.

'Do you have any idea what time it is?' Michael asked.

'No clue.' Jill padded straight to the coffee machine.

'It's almost nine o'clock. Isn't Wednesday still a workday? What's going on with you? You stayed out late and came home in an Uber. Where is my car?'

Gulping some coffee, Jill slumped into a chair. 'Golly, Erickson, for a minute I thought my mother came down from Chicago.'

Already showered and dressed, Michael sat down across from her. 'Are you hungover? Where is my car?'

'One question at a time, please.' She emitted a gasping, strangled sound. 'I slept in because I was talking to Alexis Scott until late. I am *not* hungover, but I did have two glasses of wine, so that's why I called Uber and left the car. Alexis asked me to stay because her mother dropped in and caused a nasty scene.' Jill slurped some coffee. 'And since the wine was red, I have a headache, so I would appreciate you calming down.' She laid her head on the table.

'You were there during the argument? That must be great for background information.'

'Yes, but I don't know how much I can use.' Jill sat up, carefully considering how much to reveal. 'Alexis is friends with the beverage manager at Churchill Downs. You know, where they run the Kentucky Derby every year. As a favor to me, she asked him to give you a behind-the-scenes tour of the racetrack and mix up a batch of their official mint juleps. You'll be able to video Paul Broadhurst creating the juleps and narrating your tour of Churchill Downs. Then you can ask whatever questions you want. I have his name and number in my purse.' She walked back for a refill, already feeling the caffeine's effects.

'Are you joking? That's exactly what we need for a Louisville angle.' Michael had a spring in his step as he followed her to the coffeemaker.

'I know. Alexis was kind enough to set this up for today at ten o'clock.'

'At ten o'clock?' he wailed. 'But you're still in your jammies.'

'You are going alone. Your video camera picks up sound and you can record any interview you do off-camera.' Jill filled her cup to the rim.

'Where are you going to be? I thought we were partners.'

'We are partners, but Miss Scott needs my help today with details with her father's . . . funeral. Since I just had experience with Uncle Roger, I said yes. It's the least I could do since she set this up with Broadhurst.' Jill pulled a slip of paper from her purse. 'Here's his number, the address for the racetrack, and which entrance you are to use. Can you handle this alone?'

Michael rolled his eyes. 'Of course, I can, with pleasure. But how am I supposed to get my car? Will Miss Scott's limo driver pick us up?'

'She has a BMW, not a limo. Call for an Uber while I get ready. Then you can drive your car to the racetrack from Parker Estate.' Jill carried her coffee into the bathroom with a sigh of relief. She'd explained the situation without using the word 'murder' once.

Luckily on the way to Parker Estate Michael busied himself listing questions to ask the Churchill beverage manager, which was fine with her. The fewer inquiries about what Mama Scott and Alexis argued about the better.

Alexis yanked open the door the moment Jill reached the top of the steps. 'You must let me reimburse you for Uber. After all, I'm the one who kept you here so late.'

'Nothing doing. I'll turn the receipt in on my expense report. Is the coffee ready?' Jill headed straight to the kitchen.

'Of course, and there's freshly baked zucchini bread.'

'You know how to bake?' Jill filled her mug and carried it to the table.

'No, but Mom's housekeeper does and she makes everything from scratch.' Alexis cut two large slices. 'I should get some perks in exchange for a total lack of privacy. Sit, we have time before our appointment.'

Jill did as instructed. 'You made us an appointment with the chief of police?'

'I did, at eleven. How did things go with your partner?'

'Michael should be arriving at Churchill Downs right about now. He's very excited about interviewing and videoing Paul Broadhurst. And I'm grateful to you for setting this up.' Jill slathered a piece of cake with butter and took a bite.

Alexis sliced the air with her hand. 'No, I'm in your debt. Without you, I would never know the truth about my dad.'

Jill swallowed her mouthful. 'You're really convinced he was murdered?'

'I am, now more than ever. You told me to consider any enemies my father might have made in the business world. Well, I thought of one.' She laced her fingers together. 'Another Louisville distillery recently sued Parker Estate for corporate espionage and lost. After one of their employees came to work for us, the competitor claims he divulged certain trade secrets, despite having signed a non-disclosure agreement.'

'With so many distilleries around here, I would imagine employees change jobs a lot.' Jill cut another sliver of zucchini bread.

'They do. That's probably why the judge ruled against our competitor. They couldn't prove we financially benefited from information the employee brought with him. If the employee simply broke his non-disclosure agreement, the lawsuit must be against him, not us. That made Dennis Donagal, the distillery's owner, hopping mad.'

'Parker Estate's pockets would be much deeper. How much was he suing the company for?'

'Five million.'

'That could be a motive for murder.' Jill dabbed crumbs from her mouth.

'Let's see if the chief of police agrees with us.' Alexis wrapped a slice of zucchini bread in a napkin to eat along the way.

Jill climbed into the BMW and off they went, downtown. Not only did the operations manager drive well above the speed limit, she steered with one finger while merrily eating her breakfast. 'Ah, could you slow down a tad?' Jill asked. 'I get carsick at warp speed.'

'Sorry, I learned to drive on wide open country roads.' Alexis reduced her speed considerably. Once they reached the city, she was forced to crawl along in traffic.

As it turned out, their appointment was not with the chief, as Alexis had thought, but with one of his homicide detectives, which in Jill's estimation was a better choice. After a thirty-minute wait, they were shown to a conference room surrounded by a warren of cubicles.

'Hi, I'm Lieutenant Grimes,' greeted a thirtyish female officer. 'The chief thought I might be more helpful. Which one of you is Miss Scott?'

'I am,' Alexis said. 'This is my friend, Jill Curtis. I asked her to come along.'

Grimes nodded and sat down. 'First of all, my sympathy on the loss of your father. Now, let's go over the details from the police report. Your father died two days ago inside the study at his home at Parker Estate. He was found by his wife, Rose Parker Scott, who called nine-one-one. Is she your mother, Miss Scott?'

'She is.' Alexis shifted on the metal chair.

'Does she work for your dad?'

There was a small hesitation. 'Not really, but as a major shareholder Mom likes to stay somewhat involved. I believe they were planning to go to dinner downtown that evening.'

Grimes glanced back at the report. 'Police and an ambulance arrived approximately sixteen minutes later. But unfortunately, paramedics were unable to resuscitate Mr Scott after several attempts with a defibrillator. Is this also your understanding, thus far?'

Alexis nodded agreement, while Jill jotted down a few notes of her own.

'Paramedics pronounced your father dead at the scene and called the coroner's office. A deputy coroner arrived twenty minutes later to examine the body. No signs of foul play were observed by either the police or deputy coroner, while several physical indicators pointed to death by myocardial infarction – a heart attack. The coroner listed probable natural causes on the death certificate and had his body transported to a funeral home under the care of Mr Ken Shea at your mother's request.'

The detective looked up at Alexis, then down again at the report. 'When there's a death, a specific procedure must be followed. The coroner's office must contact the attending physician to see if the doctor concurs with the presumption of myocardial infarction. If so, the death certificate remains as is and no autopsy is performed unless specifically requested by the next of kin, which in this case is your mother.'

'And she would say "no,"' murmured Alexis.

But in your father's case, the attending physician wasn't willing to sign the certificate, so a full autopsy will be performed at the medical examiner's office, courtesy of the commonwealth.'

'My dad had no heart disease, that's why Dr Cribbs wouldn't sign anything.'

Grimes flipped through her notes. 'Normally, the body stays at the coroner's office pending word from the doctor. Apparently that wasn't done.'

'My mother insisted he be transported to Shea's Funeral Home.'

Shaking her head, the detective consulted her phone directory and jotted a number. 'I will call Mr Shea and contact the coroner. They will arrange transportation to the state medical examiner's office.' Grimes leaned back in her chair. 'You realize an autopsy will hold up the burial or cremation.'

'It won't hold up anything. My mother plans to have his funeral service this Saturday, with an empty urn if necessary.' Alexis's voice cracked, betraying her emotions.

Grimes set down her notes. 'I'm not sure why you're here, Miss Scott. Do you have reason to suspect foul play in your father's death?'

Alexis cleared her throat. 'For starters, Dad had at least one enemy. Anybody who works in a competitive industry like bourbon usually creates a few. Secondly my dad just had a complete physical and there were no signs of heart disease. None,' she repeated.

'Then that's all you can do at this time.' Grimes stood and picked up her tablet. 'If the medical examiner finds something suspicious, she'll notify the homicide department. I will person-ally take the case and contact you, Miss Scott. Again, my sympathy on your loss.' She bobbed her head at both of them, then retreated into the world where civilians cannot go.

'You did well,' Jill said, grabbing Alexis by the arm. 'Now let's get out of here before they discover my unpaid parking tickets.'

Alexis bought them lunch in a fancy restaurant before driving her back to the hotel. Jill was eager to get to their suite and call Nick, preferring to talk to her boyfriend while Michael was out. *Her boyfriend.* Jill giggled at the sound of it. It had been a while since she'd had a beau. A romantic entanglement. A significant other. No matter what she chose to call him, Jill loved having someone who cared about her.

Nick Harris was patient, kind, and an all-around nice guy, besides tall and rather handsome. And the fact he worked for the Kentucky State Police as an investigator assigned to the Louisville post might just come in handy with the investigation of William Scott's death.

Unfortunately, it only took Nick five minutes after the 'I miss you's' and the 'I can't wait to see you's' for him to say 'no'.

'Sorry, Jill, as much as I'd love to help, my hands are tied,' Nick said in the husky voice she'd come to adore.

'But Mr Scott had no history of heart disease. Don't you think someone should look a little closer at his death?'

'I certainly do.'

'And he had an enemy in the bourbon world. One of his competi-tors just lost a lawsuit and the five-million-dollar settlement that went along with it. And doesn't it sound a tad suspicious that Mrs Scott didn't request an autopsy? Why would she have gone along with the idea of a heart attack if he was as healthy as Alexis told me and had no history of disease?'

'It could be suspicious. But at the risk of annoying someone who I've missed very much, it could also be Mrs Scott was suffering terrible grief and wanted to get the ordeal over with.'

'You're lucky you prefaced that statement, Buster.' Jill dropped her voice to an ominous tone.

Nick chuckled. 'It's not that I don't want to help you *stick your nose* into this master distiller's death, but I can't. Considering your recent history, aren't you worried about becoming a suspect?' His chuckle turned into an all-out laugh.

'Not worried in the least. And what do you mean you can't? You're an investigator for the state of Kentucky. Of course you can.'

'We're a commonwealth, but regardless. Louisville isn't a small town like Roseville where your Uncle Roger died. It's a big city with homicide detectives, a major crimes unit, and forensic pathologists. If there was foul play, a team of professionals will get to the bottom of it. I have no jurisdiction and won't be called to assist with the investigation. That only happens when a county sheriff or small police department has limited resources.'

'Is that your final word on the matter, Harris?' she asked.

'Of course not. I'm here to advise *you* every step of the way and hopefully, keep you out of jail.' Nick hesitated before continuing. 'How did you get so tight with Alexis Scott anyway?'

'That's a story for another day. Do you have any advice for me right now?'

'No, but I have a question. Isn't your job creating a travel log of bourbon tours around Kentucky? I think you should concentrate on that and have dinner with me as soon as possible.'

'What do you mean by soon? I'm free tonight as long as I can bring Michael along. I don't want him to eat by himself again.'

'As appealing as that sounds, I can't tonight. I got a call from my mother's next-door neighbor. She needs to talk to me and it doesn't sound good.'

'Did something happen to your mom?' Jill asked. 'I'll go with you to Lorraine.'

'I asked Mrs Diaz and she said nothing is wrong. But it's time she and I talked. So I'm taking a week's vacation, maybe more. The next time I go home, I'll take you with me.'

'Lorraine is less than two hours away. Why do you need that much time off?' Jill's anxiety was all too apparent.

'I probably don't, but I have so many accrued vacation days I might as well burn off a few.'

'Will you keep me posted?'

'Of course I will. Just do your job while I'm gone and don't make trouble for the Louisville police. And try not to worry about my mother. I'm sure everything is fine.'

Nick signed off with a smooch, but despite his assurance, Jill couldn't relax. On one hand he'd promised to take her to meet his family. That was a good sign in a romance. But now that she was in Louisville for a week or two, where Nick supposedly had a perfectly fine apartment, she didn't want him two hours away in a town the size of a postage stamp.

Selfish. That's what she was. And tomorrow she planned to wake up a nicer, more generous person. But it had been so long since she had a real relationship, she decided to feel sorry for herself for the rest of the day.

THREE

Since he had no idea how long he'd be gone, Nick Harris watered his two houseplants and asked the lady across the hall to feed his cat. The neighbor didn't mind because he reciprocated each time she visited her children in Somerset. Getting time off from his job as a state investigator hadn't been difficult either. It was what lay ahead in his old Kentucky home that made him worry. How long had it been since he visited his mother – a month? Two? Although he called her on a regular basis, Nick couldn't remember going home since his father's funeral six months ago.

What kind of son did that make him?

None of his three older sisters, all of whom were married with children, lived in Lorraine. Despite the fact Nick worked long hours and traveled all over the state, the responsibility of checking on his mom fell to him since he lived the closest. In that category he certainly hadn't distinguished himself.

The moment Nick exited Interstate 264 he switched off the AC and rolled down the window. Bardstown Road through Nelson and Larue Counties was twisty and potentially dangerous, but the scenic vistas also soothed and relaxed. Instead of inhaling exhaust fumes from Louisville traffic, he breathed in the smell of fresh-cut hay and Japanese honeysuckle, which seemed to be spreading across Kentucky like kudzu in the Carolinas.

As the clean air cleared cobwebs from his brain, Nick realized he should have invited Jill to come along. She could have met his mother and forgotten about whatever was happening at Parker Estate. How could another master distiller have been murdered, the second within a month? Apparently whenever Jill searched out a story, she riled up one hornet's nest after another.

As he ticked off the miles to Lorraine, Nick tried to imagine what he would find. Considering her generous nature, maybe his mother had rounded up homeless people and brought them home to live. Maybe she'd adopted thirty cats from the shelter or had started hoarding more newspapers than the recycling plant. How could a sixty-two-year-old woman possibly frighten her neighbor? By the time Nick entered a town of shady streets, two traffic lights, and no jobs, and parked in front of the bungalow where he'd been born and raised, he still had no idea.

Unfortunately the long overdue reunion would have to wait a few minutes longer. Refusing to be ignored, Mom's neighbor and lifelong friend waved frantically from her front porch.

'Hello, Mrs Diaz,' Nick called as he approached. 'How have you been?'

'I'm fine, Nicky. It's your mom I've been worried about.'

Dread churned his gut as he climbed the front steps. 'Is she sick? You should have called nine-one-one before calling me.' Nick pulled out his phone.

'No, no, she doesn't need an ambulance. But she sure hasn't been herself since your father died.'

Nick sat down on the stoop and blew out a breath. 'Could you be a bit more specific?'

'Julie is getting forgetful. Maybe we all are, but your mom more than the rest of us. Just last week, I told her to watch *Masterpiece Theater* and she plum forgot.' Inez kicked her feet to get the porch swing moving.

He tamped down his impatience. 'Maybe she liked another show better and didn't want to hurt your feelings. You know how she refuses to use the DVR.'

Inez peered at him over her reading glasses. 'Maybe, but the next day she hung out laundry and didn't fetch it from the line

until three days later. I would've brought it in for her but sometimes she gets funny when people try to help. Then there's the
matter of the electric bill . . .' Inez let the words hang ominously
in the air.

'What about the electric bill?' Nick's stomach took a turn for
the worse.

'She hadn't paid it in months. It's a good thing the utility sent
somebody out before cutting off the power. I heard Julie arguing
with their representative, so I hurried over. Julie kept insisting
she'd paid the bill, but when I looked at her check register, she
hadn't paid *any* bills in weeks.' Mrs Diaz shook her finger at
Nick. 'Before you accuse me of snooping, your mother told me
where she keeps her checkbook years ago in case of an emergency. And we have keys to each other's homes.'

'I'm not about to accuse you of anything. I'm very grateful
you've kept an eye on her.'

The older woman relaxed before his eyes. 'Well, I caught
her utilities up, but that made her mad. Julie insists they are
now overpaid.' She stopped swinging. 'Honestly, Nicky, they're
not overpaid, so that's why I called you. Maybe you can put
her utilities on auto-pay?'

Nick smiled at the neighbor who once made him coquito
cheesecake and coconut pudding. 'I'm glad you called me. And
I'll look into signing her up for auto-pay tomorrow. Thank you,
Mrs Diaz. How's your husband?'

'Carlos is fine. He's sleeping in the recliner now, but if you
wake him he'll swear he was watching the ballgame.' Her laughter
revealed two gold crowns.

'I'll stop in to see him before I head back to Louisville. But
right now I'm eager to see Mom.' Nick stretched to his full height.

'You know where we live, kid. Don't be a stranger.' Inez
smiled and went inside, letting the swing bang against the wall.

Nick crossed the lawn to his mother's front door as fast as
legs could carry him. He knocked twice and after a decent interval,
pushed open the door and walked inside. 'Ma?' He swallowed
a taste of panic in his mouth. 'Mom, where are you?'

'Nicky, is that you?' Julie Harris, tousled-haired and sleepy-
eyed, shuffled down the hall from her bedroom. 'What a nice
surprise! Did your boss give you the day off?'

'Yep, I took some vacation when I realized how long it had been since I was home.' Nick wrapped his mother in a bear hug, her head barely reaching his shoulder. Maybe it was his imagination, but she felt thinner, smaller. And when did she stop dying her hair? He held her at arms' length. 'Are you all right? Your hair looks different and you've lost weight.'

'Pooh with my hair. I'm tired of coloring it. I'm going natural – gray, white, whatever. All the old ladies like me are doing it.' Chuckling, Julie lowered herself into the recliner. 'And no, I haven't lost a pound. Now, what's new with you, son?'

As much as Nick wanted to grill her about utility bills and laundry day, he didn't want to spoil their reunion with an argument. So he launched into an abbreviated version of the last six months, including how he'd met travel writer, Jill Curtis.

'My son has a serious girlfriend? That is wonderful.' Julie clapped her hands.

'Don't get too excited. We're still in the early stages, but yeah, I really like her. In fact, I'll bring her along the next time I come home.'

'Woo-hoo! In that case, don't wait another six months!' She hooted just like in the past when happy.

'I promise I won't. Tell me what's going on with my sisters. Sometimes I see pictures of the kids on Facebook, but I'm not on social media very often.'

His mother delivered an hour-long narrative of minor medical troubles for his sisters, job changes for his brothers-in-law, and updates on which nephew or niece excelled in which sport. Nick enjoyed every minute. It had been a long time since he'd felt part of a family.

When she finished, Julie leaned back and grinned. 'Soon you'll have personal news to share with your siblings.'

Nick felt himself blush. 'Like I said – still the early stages. But hopefully someday I will.'

Julie pushed to her feet. 'Goodness, what kind of mother am I? I haven't offered you a single thing to eat or drink. What would you like? Can you stay for dinner?'

'I would love a cup of coffee, but instant is fine. And yeah, I plan to stay for dinner and spend the night if my old bed is still upstairs.'

'Where else would it be? I'll put a set of clean sheets on the steps for you to take up. I go up and down stairs as little as possible these days.'

Nick rubbed the back of his knuckles. 'I've not been the best son lately, but I aim to change that. Anything you need, just call me. Anytime,' he emphasized. 'Louisville isn't that far away. I can be here before you know it.'

'You're a fine son. I just haven't needed anything.' She walked toward the kitchen door. 'Let's get a pot of coffee going, while I start something for supper.'

Nick ran a hand through his hair, relieved by her reassurance. But that reassurance lasted only until he reached the kitchen. Plastered over every cabinet door and appliance were yellow Post-it notes with a variety of reminders. Take out the garbage on Tuesday. Turn off stove before leaving kitchen. Bring in wash Monday night. Don't use garbage disposal. There were dozens of them, some regarding chores to be done, others for long ago medical appointments.

'What are these, Ma?' he asked softy.

'Oh, that was Inez's idea.' Julie rolled her eyes as she filled the coffeemaker with water. 'Inez thinks I'm getting forgetful. She's the one who forgot to send her goddaughter a birthday card.'

'What kind of things have you been forgetting?' Nick set out two mugs and the jug of milk.

'Once I forgot to bring in the laundry. One time. Yet Inez acted like I went to Kroger in my underwear.' Julie pulled a package of cookies from the shelf and shook half the bag onto a plate. 'Sorry about store-bought sweets. If you'd told me you were coming I would have baked.'

'Store-bought is just fine. Let's get back to the laundry. Didn't you notice it hanging on the line the next day?'

She screwed up her face. 'No, I didn't. I was fall cleaning that week and had plenty on my mind with the church bake sale.' Surreptitiously, Julie glanced out the window.

Checking to see if the laundry was still there? Nick thought it wise not to press her too hard. He filled their mugs as soon as the machine stopped gurgling and opened the lid on the milk. The sour smell almost knocked him flat, yet Julie didn't seem to notice. Nick turned on the faucets and poured the contents down the drain, trying not to breathe. 'Do you have non-dairy creamer?' he asked.

'Sure, honey, but I thought you'd sworn off preservatives.' She pointed at the top shelf of her cupboard.

'We'll make an exception for today.' Nick added a tablespoon to both mugs. 'How are the Post-its working? Have you missed any doctor appointments?'

'Not to my knowledge. Sit down, son, and stop wandering around. Have a cookie.'

Dutifully, Nick devoured an Oreo in two bites. 'What's wrong with the garbage disposal?'

Mom's face went blank. 'Nothing, why?' Julie added two spoonfuls of sugar and carried her mug to the table.

'You have a reminder not to use it.'

Julie scanned the kitchen surfaces until she found the note. 'Oh, yeah. Once when I was doing dishes a fork slipped down the drain. Now the disposal makes an awful racket if you use it.'

'I'll turn the breaker off in the cellar and call a plumber. Lots of people would switch on the disposal out of habit.' Nick studied her over the rim of his mug.

'Would you stop worrying about me? There's nothing wrong with my memory. Inez is the one going batty.'

'I'm glad you two are neighbors. You can look out for her and Carlos, and she can keep an eye on you.'

Julie took a small bite of cookie. 'I'm glad we are too, but don't you think these notes are over-the-top?'

'I don't know, Ma. If they help, you should leave them.'

'I plan to, if for no other reason than to make you and Inez happy.' She leaned over to pat his hand. 'Now, while I figure out something for dinner, you run upstairs with those sheets. Take your coffee and cookies with you.'

Just as if he was twelve instead of thirty-two, Nick did as he was told. In his old room he found everything as he had left it, including *Star Wars* posters on the walls. But the room looked smaller and shabbier than he remembered and smelled faintly like mothballs. He found his high school jacket still hanging in the closet with proud letters for football, track and baseball.

Hopefully his mother wouldn't insist he take it home with him. He didn't want it anymore, yet he wasn't ready to pitch it in the trash either.

For a while Nick sorted through the clothes he'd left behind in the closet and drawers and the stack of CDs next to the bed. He should have packed everything up for the Salvation Army long ago instead of leaving it for someone else to deal with. Before he returned to Louisville he would take care of the eluvia of his youth. But right now he had bigger problems on his mind: the laundry, the milk, the unpaid bills, the Post-its. His mother was denying anything was wrong with her memory, yet there were too many instances to be a coincidence. One thing was for certain – he needed to talk to his sisters right away.

That evening for dinner his mother served hot dogs without buns, coleslaw with Italian dressing instead of mayo, and frozen French fries without catsup. He had no idea how much was forgetfulness or how much was because he dropped in without calling first. Few people who lived alone kept a well-stocked refrigerator. He certainly didn't.

After they ate and he'd washed the dishes, Nick told his mother he wanted to drive around town and reminisce. But instead he drove straight to the Nelson County Sheriff's Department. After introducing himself and flashing his badge, Nick got straight to the point.

'I know your deputies have a large county to patrol, but whenever one happens to be in Lorraine, I would appreciate them driving past 1815 Hickory Street. My mother, Julie Harris, lives alone and, for the first time, I've noticed memory impairment. If your deputy sees anything out of the ordinary, I would appreciate a call.' Nick laid his card on the desk.

'We'd be happy to check on the welfare of Mrs Harris. I'll send a message out, Lieutenant.' The sheriff tucked the card in his shirt pocket.

'My mother doesn't believe she has a problem, so until my family figures out how to handle this, let's keep these drive-bys under the radar.'

The thin, rawboned officer nodded. 'I understand. We'll maintain discretion unless the situation demands immediate intervention.'

'I appreciate it.' Nick shook hands and left, feeling somewhat relieved. At least he'd made law enforcement aware of the situation and provided contact information. On his way home, he bought a fresh gallon of milk and entered a tidy kitchen with all burners off, dishes done, and countertops sparkling. When he peeked into her bedroom Nick found his mother snoring softly. Maybe Inez Diaz had exaggerated the situation. Everyone gets a little forgetful as they age. One or two incidents might not mean anything.

Nick climbed the steps to his room, stretched out on his bed and pulled out his phone. He still had one thing left to do that day . . . something that had him smiling before Jill even picked up the phone. Maybe Jill could shed some light on his dilemma, maybe not. But at least she would leave him with a sweet image to dream about.

When Jill returned to the hotel after lunch with Alexis Scott, Michael still wasn't back from Churchill Downs. That was a very good sign. Her partner occasionally annoyed the people he video-taped, but hopefully that hadn't happened at the most famous racetrack in the country. Jill had time to shower, change into comfortable clothes, and learn all she could about Lorraine, Kentucky from the internet, which turned out to be not a whole heck of a lot. Her new boyfriend was from a town which made Mayberry look like a metropolis. Jill hoped whatever was wrong with Mrs Harris wasn't serious and he would soon be back in her arms.

Before she began seeing her life as a succession of song lyrics, Michael strolled in and dropped his equipment bag on the couch. Thanks to Nick's impromptu trip she wouldn't have to cancel dinner with her partner two nights in a row. 'Hey, Michael. How did it go?'

'Fine and dandy, missy. Just like you, I might have a new best friend.' He grabbed a Coke from the mini fridge.

'Really? Paul Broadhurst liked you?' Jill rocked back on her heels, feigning shock.

'Don't sound so surprised. Once I'm around men of my own ilk, not moonshiners like your mountain kinfolk, I relax and get along well. No offence,' he added.

'None taken. I'm happy for your newfound success. Did you take plenty of video?'

'Tons. Paul let me interview him for over an hour while we shared a pitcher of mint juleps. Then he put out a sandwich tray and made us a pot of coffee. With the time it took to tour the grounds, I was there almost five hours.' Michael grinned like a cat that fell in a bowl of cream.

Five hours? Either Broadhurst and Alexis were really good friends, or the beverage manager had owed the distiller a serious favor. Either way, Jill was happy for Michael. 'If you have no plans, let's have dinner together. I want to hear the whole story, plus I might have a tidbit or two to share with you.'

'Great, but I'll pick the restaurant. We're in bourbon country and I want to leave no stone unturned.' Michael headed straight to the bathroom for another shower, which also rarely happened, so today was a red-letter day all around.

After much vacillation they ended up dining at the hotel bar, where the food was wonderful and the conversation . . . lively. Michael couldn't stop talking about the week-long festivities and elegant parties that led up to the Derby. Jill absolutely knew they would come back to cover the event in May.

Michael was on his second drink before he finally came up for air. 'So how did things go with planning the funeral?'

'*What?*' she asked. Unfortunately, Jill forgot she hadn't told him the whole truth.

His forehead furrowed with wrinkles. 'So why *did* you go see Miss Scott?'

'As it turned out, her mother already took care of the funeral details. The memorial service will be on Saturday. Alexis needed my help with another matter.'

Michael's gaze rolled up to the ceiling. 'Spill your guts, Curtis. I knew this morning you were up to something.'

'I am not, but she asked me to go to the police department with her. After she'd been so helpful, how could I say no?'

Michael set down his roast beef sandwich. 'And she just *happened* to hear about Roger Clark's murder?'

'Roger was another master distiller, same as her dad,' Jill said defensively. 'Of course I mentioned that I helped my aunt make funeral arrangements.'

'Did the police believe your theory about Mr Scott being murdered?'

'It was Alexis's theory, not mine. They're not buying anyone's theory. They're waiting for the results of the autopsy. Homicide will jump in if and when the medical examiner finds something suspicious.'

Michael took another bite of sandwich. 'How could someone fill out the death certificate without an autopsy?'

'Ahh, now you're asking the right questions!' Jill shook a French fry at him. 'Several physical signs indicated a heart attack, so based on that, his age, and a stressful career, the deputy coroner thought myocardial infarction at first until he talked to Mr Scott's doctor. He asked Mrs Scott if she would want an autopsy but she declined. Doesn't that sound suspicious?' Jill gave the fry another shake, then popped it in her mouth.

'Hmmm, maybe, maybe not. Let's hope for Alexis's sake Mrs Scott had nothing to do with it. It's hard enough to lose your dad, but sending your mother to the Big House would be a tough load to carry.'

Suddenly Ray, the charismatic bartender with an incredible sense of hearing, dropped a glass into the sink. The ruckus drew everyone's attention and a round of applause.

Jill frowned and narrowed her eyes. 'Ray and I need to chat after dinner. He'd better not be writing a gossip blog or they'll find his body floating in the Ohio River.'

'Shush,' Michael warned. 'Never issue death threats in public, not even in jest, especially with your track record of being in the wrong place at the wrong time.'

Jill swallowed another forkful of fish and pushed away her plate. 'I can't eat another bite. What do you want to do now? Walk the streets of Louisville? Have a bourbon nightcap in some hole in the wall?'

Michael stretched and motioned for the check. 'Nah, I've had enough bourbon for one day. I'm going up to transcribe my interview with Broadhurst while details are fresh in my mind. And you're not walking the streets alone.' He scribbled his name and room number on the bill. 'Play nice somewhere inside the hotel. Maybe you can find a haunted attic or a tunnel beneath the river.'

The moment Michael left the bar Ray appeared in front of her. He removed her glass of iced tea and replaced it with a sparkling cocktail. 'I thought your partner would never leave.' Grins didn't get any wider than Ray's.

'Thanks for this, but I've got a bone to pick with you, mister.' Jill took a tiny sip of her drink.

'Where would you like to begin? An arm? One of my legs? My jawbone seems like a good starting point.' Ray ran a finger along his chin.

'You were eavesdropping while Michael and I were discussing a very private matter. What exactly do you do with the info you glean from customers?' Crossing her arms, Jill offered her meanest expression.

'Nothing!' he exclaimed, dropping his voice to a whisper. 'Honest, dear woman, I would never repeat a word of it. Listening is simply a harmless hobby for a lonely old man.'

Jill leaned forward. 'How could you be lonely with all that flirting you do?'

'In deference to my late wife of forty years, I only flirt with women I have zero chances with. I intend to remain single until I meet Jenny on the other side of the pearly gates.' Ray placed his hand over his heart.

'Are you really a widower?' she asked as her phone began to buzz.

Ray stared at her. 'No one who's been happily married would lie about that. Answer your phone, Miss Jill. Your secrets are safe with me. Maybe it's your handsome state cop. That drink's on me.'

'Thank you.' Jill picked up her glass and carried it to a table beyond Ray's earshot. One glance at the screen told her it indeed was her handsome cop. 'Hey, Nick. How's life in Lorraine? How's your mom?'

'Lorraine hasn't changed a bit except for new green recycle bins for each house. The situation with my mother isn't so simple an answer. She looks OK, maybe a little thinner, and she insists she's fine. But the next-door neighbor alerted me to some memory issues, like hanging out the laundry and forgetting about it.'

'Sounds like something I would do,' Jill murmured.

'I know. We're all forgetful at times. It's hard to draw a line.

For supper tonight, Mom served hot dogs without buns and made coleslaw with Italian dressing.'

'Ahh, I might not be the best person to discuss "normal kitchen practices".'

Nick's laugh lifted Jill's spirits. 'You're the right person for me. I also noticed Mom put Post-its all over the kitchen, yet still forgot to pay her utilities.'

'Does she have money in her account? Maybe she's broke.'

'I checked. She has over ten grand in her checking account, thanks to my dad's pension and social security.' Nick released an exasperated sigh. 'If it wasn't for the neighbor's intervention, Mom's utilities would've been turned off.'

'What are you going to do?' Jill asked.

'Nothing until I talk with my three sisters. In the meantime, I plan to make myself useful. Rake leaves. Clean out the gutters. Have the garbage disposal fixed. Bag up everything I left behind. And put her bills on auto-pay.'

'You're a good egg, Harris.'

'No, I'm not, but I want to be.'

'Not to change the subject, but could you check into Dennis Donagal, if you have time, under the radar, of course. He owns a small distillery that sued William Scott for stealing trade secrets. Donagal lost his five-million-dollar lawsuit, which made him hoppin' mad. That could be a motive for murder, according to Alexis, William Scott's daughter.'

'Sure, as long as you realize I'm not getting professionally involved in this case, even if it turns out to be murder.'

'I understand.'

'Right now I hear Mom stirring around downstairs. Let me call you tomorrow when I have a better idea when I'm coming . . . back to Louisville.' Nick hesitated as though about to say more but then didn't.

'The sooner the better, big man. Sleep tight and dream only of me.'

'That goes without saying. Goodnight, Jill.'

When Nick hung up, Jill was left with an uneasy feeling. He had started to say 'coming home' but changed his mind. Did that mean Nick no longer considered Louisville his home? What a fine how-do-you-do after she'd snagged a two-week assignment here.

Jill chugged her champagne cocktail, stifled an unladylike burp, and headed to her room. She'd lost her desire to snoop down employee-only passageways or find the hidden staircase to a rooftop garden in the grand old hotel. Would she become just another romance novel cliché? A woman kept from the man she loved by life's obstacles? *Perish the thought.*

The next morning when Jill awoke in a tangle of bed clothes, she had only one thought on her mind. And it wasn't the AWOL state investigator. Today was Thursday, meaning it was time to get some serious work done on her bourbon tour article. But how does one tactfully approach a grieving daughter who'd just lost her dad? *Say . . . I know you're down in the dumps, but can I get inside Parker Estate Distillery to see what makes them tick?*

Michael had already advised her to write off this distillery and take tours of the other three. But the introduction Alexis made with Mr Broadhurst had been worth its weight in gold to a journalist. Who knew what other contacts Alexis had up her sleeve? Besides, Jill refused to move on to the next distillery when Alexis needed her . . . or at least needed someone objective outside the family. Once the matter was settled with William Scott's untimely passing, Alexis could get back to work at the company her grandfather started. And Parker Estate might benefit from Jill's positive slant on bourbon in general and their brand in particular.

Michael, who'd fallen asleep at his keyboard last night, was hard at work on his Churchill Downs segment. So Jill headed down to the hotel's coffee shop for breakfast alone. After two eggs fried in butter, country ham, and toast with strawberry preserves, she dialed Alexis's cell number. 'Good morning, Alexis. This is Jill Curtis.'

'Are you kidding me? I was just about to call you.'

'How fortuitous.' Jill heard chomping in the background.

'Mr Shea, the funeral director, received a directive from the M.E.'s office and transferred my father. His autopsy will be next in the queue. I'm so grateful.'

'I didn't do anything.' Jill sipped her coffee.

'You told me to stop the cremation and went with me to the police. Without you giving me courage, I would never know the truth.'

'You still might not.' Jill bit her tongue as soon as the words were out.

'I know, but at least I tried. What can I do for you?'

'First of all, thanks for paving the way with Mr Broadhurst. Michael thoroughly enjoyed interviewing him yesterday. He was especially thrilled because he loves bourbon and loves horseracing.'

'I'm glad I could help.'

'Can I help you with your father's funeral?'

'That's very sweet, but everything is done – the church service, the flowers, the organist, the catered luncheon. I even have my dress.' A hitch in her voice revealed her raw emotions. 'Whatever happens with the medical examiner won't change anything on Saturday. I hope you and your partner can come.'

'Of course we will.' Without thinking, Jill answered for both of them.

'Good. I know you have other distilleries and your time in Louisville is limited. Would you like to tour Parker Estate today? You'd have full access, as I said.'

Jill's mouth dropped to her chest. 'According to your website, tours have been suspended until sometime next week.'

'This won't be a public tour. You'll be on your own, but free to ask all the questions you want. Production was suspended yesterday and our employees given the day off with pay. The same will be true on Saturday, but production resumed today and will continue tomorrow since our company has obligations to meet.' Alexis punctuated her sentence with a sigh.

'I'm sure that's how your father would have wanted it. But with everything you have to worry about, I don't want you—'

Alexis didn't let her finish. 'No, Jill, the arrangements have already been made. You can enter the distillery at entrance B, which is used by employees. The security guard has been briefed and knows you have *carte blanche*. He has a badge waiting for you.'

Given *carte blanche* to research her story? This was another journalist's dream-come-true. 'Thanks, and if you need me for anything, just call.'

'I will. Enjoy your tour.'

When Alexis clicked off, Jill considered going upstairs to get Michael. But since she was uncertain how much Alexis would want videotaped, Jill hurried to the distillery alone, before the magical door closed before her eyes.

Everything at the distillery was exactly how Alexis said it would be. The guard, who'd been expecting her, handed Jill a map and a VIP guest badge. Then he reiterated Alexis's words precisely: 'Feel free to wander anywhere you want and ask questions. If the employee you ask doesn't feel knowledgeable enough to answer, he or she will direct you to someone who is. Whenever you're hungry, follow the arrows to the cafeteria where your lunch will be on the house.' With that, the guard tipped his hat and walked back to his wall of security monitors.

Jill stepped into a corner to study the map. Since starting at the beginning made the most sense, she headed to the room where workers ground the corn, rye and barley. Next, she watched the mash cooking in limestone well water, where it would then be mixed with malted barley and sour mash from a previous fermentation. This started fermentation in this particular batch. Jill moved from the area where huge tanks boiled the slurry mash twice, evaporating the water from the mash to give a smooth bourbon in preparation for aging in oak barrels.

'What on earth are you doing here?' a hostile voice demanded.

Jill slowly turned to face Alexis's mom. Rose Parker Scott wore track shoes instead of high heels with her business suit, her only concession to being inside the plant.

'Hello, Mrs Scott. Alexis gave me permission to take a quick tour of the plant on my own, since public tours were cancelled,' Jill added unnecessarily.

Rose arched her neck and glared down her nose. 'My daughter had no business doing that. Production facilities can be hazardous environments. That's why only employees covered by our insurance are allowed in here.' Rose yanked the VIP badge from Jill's lapel. 'I'll have security escort you to the nearest exit.'

'I beg your pardon, ma'am. I didn't mean to create trouble for you or Alexis.' Jill slipped her notebook into her tote.

'If you truly mean that, Miss Curtis, you'll stop butting your nose into our family's business.' With that, Rose turned on one heel, which didn't work very well with sneakers, and stomped off.

Jill had no choice but to the leave the plant and the red-faced security guard, wondering what the widow had to hide.

FOUR

When Nick awoke Thursday morning, he momentarily didn't know where he was. Then he spotted the *Star Wars* poster on the wall. His mother's house in Lorraine, two hours and a world away from Louisville. But for now, his responsibilities as a son needed to take precedent over everything else. At least the smell of coffee brewing and bacon frying got him out of bed and into the shower.

'Good morning.' Nick bussed his mother's cheek with a kiss on his way to the coffeemaker.

For a moment, Julie Harris looked confused. 'I had forgotten you were upstairs.' She laughed with good humor. 'The bacon's almost done. Do you still like your eggs over-easy?'

'Sure do, but let me cook the eggs.' He poured fresh milk into his coffee.

'Where did that come from? I thought we were out.'

'I picked it up when I was driving around Lorraine.' Nick took out the toaster, along with the bread and butter. Unfortunately, the butter had been stored next to the bread in the pantry.

'Did you run into any of your old friends?' Julie carefully transferred the bacon onto paper napkins with tongs.

'Nope. Everyone in town must go to bed early.' Nick fried her egg in butter and his in bacon grease. 'When did you last talk to my sisters, Ma?'

'Oh, it's been weeks,' she said after a short ponder. 'They must be busy with their kids. What are your plans for today? Will I have my favorite son for dinner again?'

That jest never failed to make him smile. 'You will. I thought I'd clip hedges, clean out your gutters, and pull out the dead plants in the garden.'

Julie glanced up from the newspaper. 'Didn't your father do that at the end of summer?'

Not knowing which summer she meant or even if she knew Dad was gone, Nick chose a simple answer. 'He did not.'

'Well, your father became very weak at the end.'

She did remember his passing. 'I'll take care of it,' he said, exhaling with relief. 'And I'll call a plumber about the disposal and have your furnace serviced.' He slid her egg onto a plate like an adept chef.

'Thank you, Nicky. I'm not used to taking care of those kinds of chores.'

After breakfast Nick tackled one yardwork project after another, while his mother washed dishes. When he reached the Diaz side of the hedges, Carlos dragged over a chair to watch him work. Mr Diaz didn't seem as concerned about Julie's memory loss as Inez. Then again, maybe he wasn't as observant as his wife.

'Don't worry,' Carlos said, glancing at his watch. 'I promise to be just as nosy as Inez in the future. We'll make sure nothing happens to your mom. Your parents have been good neighbors for years.' He pushed to his feet. 'It's time for lunch. Inez sets a ham sandwich and chips on the table every day.'

Nick paused mid-cut. 'Doesn't she ever fix you anything else?'

'She'd better not. I like ham.' Carlos folded up his chair. 'If you get bored, come over at seven and watch the ballgame with me. I have a six-pack of beer to share.'

Nick watched him lumber back to house with sadness. Carlos used to play catch with him in the backyard. The man had gained at least fifty pounds since those days. When he finished the hedges and gutters, Nick called a plumber and an HVAC serviceman, instructing both contractors to contact the Diazes if they had trouble getting inside his mom's house. After lunch, he took his mother to the grocery store and bank, then helped her put everything away in logical places. When his mother laid down for a nap, Nick spent his free time tracking down Jill's new suspect, the irate bourbon competitor of William Scott. Hopefully the M.E. would confirm death by natural causes and put the mystery to rest.

Nick found plenty of information about the lawsuit Dennis Donagal filed against Parker Estate in Jefferson County Circuit Court. The story appeared in the *Louisville Courier Journal*, along with several internet news outlets. According to business insiders, the lawsuit lacked credible evidence of propriety theft and appeared doomed from the start. One unnamed source went so far as to suggest Donagal simply wished to discredit William Scott, without any illusion of winning his case. In the highly competitive world of distilled spirits, image was everything. Yet damaging the competition's bottom line didn't necessarily boost your own. And with the passing of Parker's master distiller, Donagal's lawsuit might have had the opposite effect.

Whether or not the court's decision had angered the plaintive, Donagal couldn't have murdered William Scott. According to his wife's Instagram, he and his family had been on vacation in Tuscany for the past eight days, with numerous pictures to prove it. So unless Donegal had hired someone for the job while his family toured Italy's hill towns, Alexis and Jill's suspect number-one was off the hook.

Although Jill might not be happy with the news, Nick couldn't wait to talk to her. But first he needed to make the calls he'd been dreading – to his sisters. As he did most things in life, Nick tackled the list logically and called his oldest sister first.

'*What?*' Sarah exclaimed once Nick dispensed with niceties and described the situation. 'It hasn't been that long since I was home, Nicky. I saw nothing out of the ordinary.'

'How long, exactly?' he asked.

'Three months,' she answered after a short hesitation. 'And there were no yellow Post-its all over the kitchen.'

'Inez came up with that idea when Mom stopped paying her bills.'

'Oh, no,' Sarah moaned. 'Last time I was there I asked if she needed help financially and she said no. I never thought she would forget to pay them.'

'I checked her account and she has plenty of money, so I set up three utilities with auto-pay. I'll take care of the water and sewer bills in person before I drive back to Louisville.'

'That's a great idea. I'll check her bank balance each time I'm there. Is her checkbook still in the kitchen drawer by the stove?'

Nick cleared his throat. 'It is, but don't you think it's time to discuss the next steps?' He could feel tension emanating from the phone.

'What next steps? You said you caught up her yardwork and fixed the disposal and furnace.'

'Her pantry and fridge were practically empty of food. I took her shopping and stocked up, but what about next week and the week after? I had to pour half a gallon of sour milk down the drain.'

'That happens to everyone occasionally. Maybe I'll talk to her about having groceries delivered and remind her about the sniff test for dairy products. She's the one who taught me.' A definite note of nostalgia laced Sarah's words.

'Maybe it's time to discuss a durable power of attorney or have one of our names added to her back account.' Nick sucked in a breath. 'Or maybe we can look for assisted living near her church or, better yet, close to one of us.'

One might have thought he'd suggested blasting Mom into outer space.

'Give it a rest, Nicky! You just spotted some minor lapses in memory and you're ready to stick Mom in an old people's home?'

'Mom is old and maybe she shouldn't live alone.' He tried to remain as non-confrontational as possible.

His sister snorted like an angry bull. 'This is the first any of us have heard about the problem. I'll admit I haven't visited as often as I should.'

'Look, I'm guiltier than anyone on that count since I live the closest. But if we could just discuss—'

'We can't discuss anything until I see for myself. I'll pack up the family on Saturday and we'll be there by noon. Don't tell Mom we're coming,' Sarah insisted. 'I don't want her to fuss. Plus I want to see the house realistically.'

'Sounds good,' Nick said, mildly relieved. 'In the meantime, I'll call Susan and Bobbie.'

'No. I'll call our sisters. You'll only cause a panic.' She paused for a moment. 'I appreciate what you've taken care of with the furnace and plumber, but don't do anything else without us coming to an agreement. Susan and Bobbie will probably want to see for themselves too. Understand?'

He did. 'OK, call me next week. In the meantime, I'll ask Mr and Mrs Diaz to keep an eye on things.'

'Fine, as long as they don't upset Mom. Inez means well, but that woman is the definition of "nosy neighbor".'

The siblings hung up, leaving Nick bewildered. Denial was

the last thing he'd expected from the eldest Harris daughter. But Sarah was right. He'd dropped this on her without warning, so she had every right to assess the situation for herself.

With the first phone call made and relieved of duty regarding the other two, Nick emptied out his closet and bureau drawers. He made a small pile of items he would take back to Louisville, two large piles to bag for charity, and a fourth pile headed straight to the trash. He hung his high school letter jacket back in the closet to deal with another day.

Downstairs he found his mother chopping celery in the kitchen, while potatoes simmered on the stove. 'What can I help with?' he asked.

Julie turned around, her eyes sparkling. 'I defrosted chicken drumsticks and thighs. Could you barbeque them on the grill like your father used to?'

'Of course, I can. Anything else?' Nick reached for a bottle of sauce from the pantry.

'I can't think of anything. We'll have potato salad, sweetcorn and barbequed chicken. I defrosted both packages so there'll be plenty of leftovers.'

After a thorough cleaning, the gas grill was soon sizzling with chicken. Luckily, the tank still contained propane. The two of them ate dinner on the patio as memories of happier times drifted back to haunt them. Later, when the kitchen was clean and his mother was watching her favorite show, Nick settled in the old hammock to call Jill.

'I'd been wondering when you'd call, Magic Man,' Jill said the moment she picked up. 'How did things go with your sisters?'

'Fair to middlin'. I am to make no decisions regarding Mom until they can assess the situation for themselves.'

'That makes sense. You four have hard choices to make.' Jill spoke up as though she was in someplace noisy. 'Did you have time to look into Dennis Donagal, Alexis's suspect?'

Nick noticed Jill didn't call Donagal her suspect, which was a good sign. 'I did, but one source in the media felt the lawsuit was nothing but a publicity stunt for his brand, while trying to discredit Parker Estate.'

'Donagal might have killed Mr Scott when he lost the case.'

'Photographs posted to social media show Dennis and his family in Europe the entire week. So most likely, you and Alexis can rule him out.'

'He could have hired a hitman before leaving town,' Jill said more to herself than him.

'You said it seemed the guy had a heart attack. That doesn't sound like a hitman's standard MO.'

'With your sisters demanding time to assess your mom, does this mean you can come home? I've missed you madly.'

Nick laughed. 'I have a few errands to run, then I'll hit the road and be home tomorrow. How did you spend your day?'

The noise in the background ratcheted up a level. 'Ah, I'm sorta in the middle of something here. Could we catch up during your drive to Louisville?'

'Sure, no problem.'

'Sweet dreams, Trooper.' Jill made a smooching sound and hung up, leaving Nick with nothing to do. Reluctantly he walked next door, where he watched a ballgame and drank two beers, while Carlos, his host, slept like a baby in his recliner.

Funny how life works out, Jill thought. After getting kicked out of the distillery by Mrs Scott, she'd spent hours in her hotel room, hoping that the man of her dreams would call. But he hadn't. So she typed up everything she'd seen inside the plant, concentrating on what made the Parker Estate process different from the two distilleries she featured in Roseville, Founders Reserve and Black Creek. Then she brewed a fresh pot of coffee and studied everything she could find online about the distillery started by Alexis's great-grandfather, Robert. Jill also made a list of questions to ask Alexis after the funeral, since not all information found on the internet could be trusted as accurate.

While waiting for the call from Nick with an update on his family, along with a pledge of his undying love, Michael suggested they visit a famous hangout for bourbon-lovers and interview a few aficionados. Jill agreed, as long as Michael agreed to remain relatively sober. Even though they arrived by Uber, Jill stuck to Coke all evening, because she would be conducting interviews. Unfortunately locals were holding their annual dart competition in Jerry's Bar and Grill that night, so the noise level ranged from general commotion to ear-splitting cacophony. Of course, that's when Nick got around to calling her.

Jill managed to hear most of the news about his mother and the fact his sisters were getting involved. But Nick's conclusion that Dennis Donagal wasn't a suspect seemed premature and careless. Why wouldn't a potential murderer pay someone while he was out of the country? All those photos posted on Instagram seemed like orchestrating an alibi. At any rate, Jill chose not to argue the point while surrounded by twenty-somethings chugging beer and throwing darts. Besides, no point in arguing anything until the medical examiner amended the cause of death to homicide. Jill couldn't wait until Nick was home tomorrow. Hopefully, they would have more important things to talk about than whoever killed William Scott . . . if someone actually did.

Jill returned to her partner and the raucous festivities inside Jerry's. People loved talking about their favorites and everyone had strong opinions about the best bourbon. Price seemed no object to some young professionals who bought rounds for their friends in the forty-dollar-per-shot range. *Whatever happened to dollar draught night like her college days?*

After another hour and four more interviews, Jill thought her head might crack wide open. She paid their tab and dragged Michael out the door to their waiting Uber. Jill had had enough of loud bars and louder patrons competing for attention. All she wanted was her soft bed, two aspirins, and a soothing cup of peppermint tea.

A steady rain drummed against the window as Jill climbed out of bed on Friday. It would be a good day to stay indoors and visit another Louisville distillery. Michael was all for the idea, even though his morning headache rivaled hers from last night's noise.

After a pancake breakfast at a coffee shop around the corner, Jill climbed behind the wheel and drove four blocks to the visitor center of one of the national brands. Along with a busload of tourists, they watched a video in the theatre and wandered around distillation mockups in the display room. Since they would never learn interesting tidbits at generic presentations, Jill drove to the outskirts of town to the real distillery, which bustled with activity at midday.

After waiting nearly two hours for the next tour, Michael bought their tickets and they joined the throng. Since this was the fourth distillery Jill had observed, besides having distant cousins who made moonshine in the hills, there wasn't much new to be learned. Proprietary recipes were closely guarded secrets, so tours never included the subtle nuances in process which made bourbons unique. Michael videotaped what they allowed him to, while Jill jotted down the sights, sounds, and smells of the production plant. In the tasting room, she recorded a few amusing comments made by tourists.

After they drove back to the hotel, Michael went to the fitness room to work out, while Jill stretched out on her bed for a nap. Three hours later, the phone on the bedside table jarred her awake. 'Hello?' she mumbled into her cell.

'Jill? Alexis Scott. Oh, goodness, did I wake you?'

'Yeah, but I'm glad you did. I laid down for a short nap and slept for hours. Thanks.' Jill scraped her palms down her face.

'I can't tell you how good a nap sounds right now. I just spent the entire day with my mother, finalizing details for Dad's funeral, along with the luncheon afterwards. Mom was furious that the urn will be empty during the service. As though a single mourner in the congregation will know or care about that!'

Jill paced across her room to the window, which had a wonderful view of the parking lot. 'It sounds like you got through it OK. I'm proud of you.'

'I was shaky in the morning, but Rose annoyed me so often and so badly, I rallied to the cause. Who knew that rage trumps sorrow in a battle of emotions?'

Jill turned up the AC to perk her up. 'I'll keep that in mind for the future. Where are you now?'

'Back at my apartment. I just received news that I want to share, but I don't want to do it here or on the phone. I know how crazy this must sound, but I don't trust my mother. She might have bugged this place or tapped my phone.'

'You're joking, right?'

'I'm not, but I hope I'm exaggerating Mom's capabilities.' Alexis took a sip of something. 'I know you need to spend time with your partner, but could you possibly meet me for dinner? I have news I can't share with anyone but you.'

It didn't take an Einstein protégé to guess Alexis's news. 'I just spent the entire *day* with Michael. First we had breakfast, then spent hours in a visitor center, and finally toured the production plant of one of your competitors. He wore me out. Enough time with Michael.'

She laughed. 'So you'll meet me?'

'Wild horses couldn't keep me away. Tell me the time and the place and I'll be there.' Jill tried to sound as dramatic as possible.

Alexis rattled off the name and address of a restaurant. 'Thanks, Jill. I'm very grateful. See you at six.'

Jill splashed cold water on her face and redid her make-up. After changing out of the outfit she'd slept in, she grabbed her purse and strode through the living room. 'I'm taking the car tonight, Erickson. You can walk, take a bus, or have food delivered for your supper.'

Michael glanced up from the TV. 'On a special errand for the Bourbon Queen? Why doesn't Alexis pick you up in her BMW convertible?'

Jill narrowed her eyes into a glare. 'Be a good boy while Mommy's gone and don't make a mess.' With that, Jill stomped out the door. But she hadn't even left the parking garage when her phone rang.

'Hello, Magic Man,' she drawled after noticing the screen. 'Are you on the long and winding road from Lorraine?'

'Yep, almost back to Derby City and I can't wait to see you!'

'Lovely, but we have one tiny fly in the ointment. Since I didn't know when you'd be back, I promised my new best friend I'd have dinner with her. She has news that can't wait until tomorrow.'

All Jill heard was silence on the other end. Then Nick asked, 'Is your new BFF Alexis Scott?'

'One and the same.'

More silence. Jill thought she heard him let out a deep breath before he said, 'I probably should've mentioned this before, but one or the other of us was always in a hurry on the phone. I knew Alexis in college. We both went to the University of Kentucky at the same time.'

'Splendid. Since you two already know each other, there's no reason you can't join us. Alexis might appreciate a professional lawman's opinion. Off the record, of course. We're dining at Maxwell's at six o'clock.'

There was another significant silence on the other end.

'What's up, Nick? Are you mad about sharing me for part of the evening?'

'No, but if Miss Scott has news to share, she might not want anyone else around. Why don't you stop by my apartment after dinner? You still haven't seen my incredible décor yet.'

'I'd love to, but I insist you join us for dessert. By then she will have revealed her news and I would love to introduce my new boyfriend to your old college acquaintance. What a small world.'

'Indeed, it is,' he murmured. 'If you insist, I'll stop by around seven thirty.'

A wave of unease swept through her, but Jill had no time to figure out the complexities of the male mind. Instead she set the GPS for Maxwell's and arrived right on time. After the hostess led Jill to a booth in a corner, far from other diners, Alexis jumped up to hug her.

'Forgive this cloak-and-dagger stuff, but my parents have tons of friends. You never know who might be listening in.'

'Eavesdropping seems to be a favorite hobby in this town.' Jill slid into the booth across from her.

'You catch on quickly.' Alexis waved her hand and a waiter materialized with a wine list and menus. 'I believe you like wine, so please select your favorite.' She handed the list to Jill.

Jill passed the list back. 'I'm not much of a drinker at all, but I'll have one glass of whichever one you pick.'

'Maxwell's specialty is beef, so I'll order a bottle of red. Why don't we select our food to minimize interruptions later?'

Jill gave her order to the waiter, then folded her hands on the table. 'All right, enough drama. Tell me your news.'

'I heard from Dad's doctor who was contacted by the medical examiner this afternoon. Although certain signs might indicate a heart attack, the M.E. also found a small puncture wound behind Dad's left ear similar to those made by a hypodermic needle, hence the call to his doctor. Dad didn't have diabetes or any medical condition requiring injections. The M.E. has sent a blood sample and the contents of his stomach to the lab for a full tox screen.' Alexis met her gaze. 'I did a little research, Jill. There are several drugs that mimic a heart attack when ingested or injected.'

'When will they have the results?'

'Since tomorrow is Saturday, maybe not until Monday. The M.E. will contact the police and the homicide department.'

'With your father's funeral tomorrow, it's probably best you don't know.' Jill leaned back as their waiter poured the wine.

Alexis considered this. 'You're probably right. Otherwise I might demand an alibi from everyone who shows up at the service.'

Jill reached for Alexis's hand. 'Tomorrow will be hard enough. You should concentrate on saying goodbye to your father. They'll be plenty of time to seek the truth later.'

'You're right. I will see that Dad gets the send-off he deserves. Too bad you couldn't have met him.' Alexis took a sip of water. 'He was a good father. He always made time for me, despite his responsibilities at Parker Estate.'

'How long had he been the master distiller?'

'Not long, maybe eighteen months. My grandfather, Robert Parker II, had to step down because of health concerns. Since no one thought I was ready, including me, my dad took the helm.'

'Don't you have any brothers or sisters?'

The corners of her mouth turned down. 'Unfortunately, no. And most of my friends from high school and college followed their dreams away from Louisville. That's why I'm glad you and Michael are coming to the memorial service. I'm eager to meet your partner at long last.'

'At least one of your pals from long ago hasn't left town.' Jill picked up her fork as salads were placed in front of them.

'Really, who would that be?'

'Nick Harris. He's a state investigator now assigned to post number four. He's on his way back from visiting Lorraine.'

'Yes,' she drawled, blinking several times. 'I remember he came from a small town in Nelson County. You said you were from Chicago. How do you know Nick?'

'We met a few weeks ago when he came to Roseville to

investigate the murder at Black Creek Distillery. We got off to a rocky start because Nick considered me a suspect for a while.' Jill wiggled her eyebrows. 'But once he ruled me out as a murderer, we found we had many things in common.'

'Are you two dating?' Alexis asked, picking up her wineglass.

'We are as much as our schedules will allow. He was called to Lorraine for a possible issue with his mother.'

'Julie . . .' Alexis murmured.

'Wow, good memory! I'll say the same thing I said to him earlier – small world.' Jill took a bite of salad.

'You talked to Nick today?'

'Yes, he called me while driving back to Louisville. I asked him to join us for dessert, since we'd be done discussing your news by then. Won't it be nice to see an old acquaintance?'

'Yes, it will, but we better start eating.' Alexis dug into her salad as though she hadn't eaten in days. When their steaks arrived, Alexis continued to devour food at a ridiculous pace.

Jill couldn't remain silent for another moment. 'Slow down, girl, before you choke to death.'

Blushing, Alexis met her eye. 'Sorry, that must have appeared very rude.'

'Rude? No, but it does seem like you're trying to finish your food quickly so you can leave and avoid seeing your old *friend.* Did you and Nick have a falling out?'

Alexis wiped her mouth with a napkin. 'Not really, but if I hurried and left, you two could have some time alone.'

'Too late to worry about that,' Jill said, grinning. 'Nick Harris is headed our way.' She waved him over, then tapped the side of her face with her finger.

'Hi, Jill.' Nick kissed Jill's cheek and sat down between the two women. 'Nice to see again, Alexis.'

'Is it?' she asked. 'I would think after the horrible way we broke up you'd never want to lay eyes on me again.'

Nick paused as the waiter delivered a third wine glass. 'College was a long time ago. I'm not holding any grudge or resentment toward you.' He picked up the glass as soon as it was filled. 'I'm sorry to hear about your father.'

'That's nice of you to say. Dad always liked you, Nick. It was my mom and grandparents who . . .' Alexis let the rest of her sentence hang in the air, unspoken.

Jill's head swiveled back and forth as though watching a tennis match. 'Holy cow,' she muttered, scrambling to her feet. 'I sure didn't see this one coming. I'll let you two catch up in private.'

'Please, Jill, sit down,' Nick pleaded.

'You haven't finished your dinner yet.' Alexis stated the obvious.

Jill pointed her index finger at the plate. 'That overpriced steak is too rare for my liking. I'll stop for a burger on my way home.' Feeling on the verge of tears, she marched from the restaurant with her head held high.

FIVE

Jill had almost reached her car when Nick grabbed her arm.

'Wait up, Jill. I told you I knew Alexis in college.' He held her by both shoulders.

'There's a big difference between knowing someone and being sweethearts.' She tried to pull away but he held tightly.

'Just let me explain.'

'There's nothing to explain. I get the picture. You were college sweethearts until someone in Alexis's family intervened and broke you up. My money's on Mommy Dearest. Rose Parker Scott would scare off Dracula himself. How am I doing so far?'

Nick tucked a strand of hair behind her ear. 'Alexis and I dated in college for almost a year. When her parents found out, her mother freaked. Rose wanted her daughter to marry a doctor or a lawyer, certainly not someone who aspired to a career in law enforcement.'

Jill stepped back. 'The Alexis I know wouldn't have allowed anyone to tell her who to love.'

'That's just it – Alexis and I were just really good friends. We enjoyed the same things, so we spent more and more time together. In many ways we were going through the motions, living up to the expectations of being a couple. But we were never *in love* with each other. If Rose would've just stayed out of it, we would've come to that realization on our own and parted as friends. Unfortunately, I got into an ugly confrontation with her parents, and horrible things were said on both sides.' Nick's face filled with pain. 'I'm sure Alexis is as embarrassed and uncomfortable to see me as I am her.'

Jill placed one hand on a hip. 'I gotta admit, neither of you seemed overjoyed to reconnect.'

'That's putting it mildly.' Nick forced a smile. 'But I'm glad you're helping her through this. Truly, I am. Alexis doesn't make friends easily, and with a mother like Rose she needs all the support she can get.'

'So I'm not worming my way into a love triangle?'

'On my honor, you are not.' Nick lifted his hand as though testifying in court. 'My heart belongs to someone, but it's not Alexis Scott.'

'Is it some red-haired siren you met in the third grade? I want no surprises when I visit Lorraine.' Both hands now rested on Jill's hips.

Nick shook his head. 'The only redhead I remember hated my guts. Something to do with sticking a worm down her shirt.'

'All right, Harris. You and I are still tight.'

Nick slipped an arm around her waist. 'Since I ruined your dinner, let me buy you a burger. I'm starving. All this romantic drama worked up an appetite.'

Jill laughed. 'Sounds good, but first I'm going back inside to tell Alexis I overreacted. Like you said, she needs friends right now, not a jealous woman defending her territory.'

'Have I been reduced to a territory?' he asked, smirking.

'Live with it. That could've ended so much worse.'

'I'll wait here, but ask her if I can come with you to the funeral.'

Jill waved, indicating she'd heard. Inside she found Alexis still at the table, staring into space.

She flinched with surprise as Jill approached. 'Jill, I don't know why I didn't tell you about Nick before he arrived. I am so sorry.'

Jill lifted her palms. 'No apology necessary. I'm the one who behaved badly. The last thing you need right now is a jealous female overreacting to the past.'

Alexis threw both arms around her and hugged her. 'Nick is the past. I swear it.'

'That's what he said too, but he would like to come to your dad's funeral if it's OK.'

'It is with me, if it's OK with you.'

Jill extracted herself from the embrace. 'Are we going to dance around, politically correct, from now on?'

'You could pull out a handful of my hair first.' Alexis sat back down.

'No, instead I'm going to stay while you finish your expensive supper. Then I'll let Nick buy me a burger and fries.'

Alexis swallowed a bite of steak. 'I'm glad Nick will be at the funeral since he's a state cop.'

'He has no jurisdiction here, but he will keep his eyes open.' Jill finished the wine in her glass. 'All right, Nick, Michael and I will meet you at St Andrew's Episcopal Church on Woodbourne at ten. That way if you faint you'll have at least three people to catch you.'

Alexis cut another piece of cold steak. 'I'm not the fainting type, but I'm glad you'll be there, that you'll all be there. Thank you.'

'You're welcome. But next time we meet for dinner, let me pick the place. I prefer my food cooked before serving.'

Nick took Jill to his favorite burger joint, famous only with the locals. They feasted on burgers and fries with malt vinegar, then split a chocolate shake. Jill didn't stop until she thought her stomach might explode, but Nick finished all of his and picked at what she left.

'What are you grinning about, Harris?' she asked.

'I finally figured out who you reminded me of, temperament-wise.'

Jill pondered, then brandished her fork like a weapon. 'No way. How could I possibly be like Alexis? She grew up on an estate. I grew up in a small three-bedroom bungalow in the Chicago burbs.'

'Wealth doesn't define a person. Money might influence the

clothes you wear or the type of car you drive, but it does not determine your heart and soul.'

Jill pulled over the milkshake. 'Well said, Sigmund Freud. I think Alexis has a big heart too. That's why if someone had killed her father, I want to help her find the murderer.'

'I'll assist as much as I can, as long as I fly under the radar. If you need me, I'll take a few more vacation days next week.'

Jill pushed away her plate. 'Such an interesting offer.'

'I have an even better one. Want to come by my apartment for chocolate cake? I picked up dessert on my way home from Lorraine.'

'As intriguing as that sounds, I'll pass. I can't eat another bite. Plus I need a good night's sleep before William Scott's funeral tomorrow. I want to spot any guilty faces in the crowd of mourners.'

Nick walked her to her car and kissed her softly on the lips. 'Goodnight, Jill. I'll pick you and Michael up at nine thirty. And thanks.'

'For what?' Jill clicked open her car.

'For being far more patient and understanding than I deserve.'

'Wait until you see my bad side. You're in for a real shock.'

As promised, Nick picked her and Michael up early on Saturday. 'Here, you can eat breakfast on the way.' He handed them both tightly wrapped napkins.

Michael peeled back the paper. 'Is this really chocolate cake?'

'It is. I got stood up last night. No way can I eat an entire cake myself.' Nick winked at her from the corner of his eye.

While her cake remained wrapped, Jill concentrated on how to approach Mrs Scott should their paths cross. Unfortunately, they arrived at St Andrew's Church long before she reached a conclusion.

Nick parked half a mile down the street, and the threesome joined a throng of black-clad people entering the church. It was a good thing Jill had purchased a black dress for Roger Clark's funeral so she had something to wear. Although they had arrived fifteen minutes before the service was to begin, they had to squeeze into a row two-thirds of the way back. Residents of Louisville rose early for a funeral, even on Saturdays. With so many people in attendance, Jill couldn't fathom how to discern guilty faces from sorrowful ones or from those who attended because it was expected. The crowd surpassed the number of mourners for Roger Clark. Then again, Parker Estate was a major bourbon producer, not a micro-distillery, and Louisville was a big city compared with little Roseville. Just as people filled the last seats within the church, the giant double doors swung shut. Soon a distinguished older gentleman escorted Rose Parker Scott up the aisle, followed by Alexis on the arm of the funeral director, Mr Shea. An ornate urn rested on a pedestal at the front of the church. Only Jill and a handful of others knew it to be empty of ashes.

Suddenly organ music erupted from the balcony while the Episcopalian priest appeared at the lectern to lead them in an opening hymn. Following two Scripture readings, another hymn and the priest's homily, several co-workers of William Scott delivered eulogies. Even Jill grew misty-eyed during the tributes, while Mrs Scott sobbed on her daughter's shoulder in the first row. Poor Alexis. Not knowing the circumstances of his death had to weigh heavily as she bore the emotional weight of her mother.

After a soloist delivered a beautiful rendition of 'Amazing Grace', the priest invited everyone to the social hall for lunch. Mourners exited the church in an orderly fashion, front rows first. When it was their turn to leave, Jill noticed Detective Grimes near the doorway and elbowed Nick in the ribs as they filed past. Since most people had already headed into the hall, only immediate family and the funeral director remained on the steps, thanking those who'd attended.

'I'm surprised to see you here, Miss Curtis,' Mrs Scott said through gritted teeth. 'I wasn't aware you knew my husband.' Without waiting for Jill's response, she moved onto Michael. 'Since I have no idea who you are, I'll move on to your companion. Hello, Mr Harris. Thank you for attending William's memorial service. He was always fond of you. However, I hope your presence doesn't indicate a rekindling of a relationship with my daughter.'

'Only friendship has been rekindled, nothing more,' Nick murmured. 'My condolences on your loss.'

As the couple talking to Alexis walked away, their group was left alone. 'I already explained to you, Mother, Jill and her videographer' – Alexis gestured to Michael – 'are in Louisville to do a travel feature on bourbon distilleries, including Parker Estate. They are here today because I asked them to come. If you can't be polite, please don't talk to my friends at all.' Alexis hooked arms with Jill and tottered down the steps to the church hall. Michael and Nick followed dutifully behind, leaving Mrs Scott alone with Mr Shea.

Alexis stayed with them during the luncheon, although she barely ate two bites of her food. Jill, also, had little appetite as she scanned the room for the Louisville detective.

'Try the little sandwiches,' Nick whispered in her ear. 'Some are smoked salmon, some are beef tenderloin. Don't worry, everything is fully cooked.'

Jill picked one up, studied it curiously, and took a small bite. 'Better than your average ham and cheese, I suppose.'

'Why did you elbow me in the ribs in church?' Nick asked. 'I don't know that woman.'

'She's a Louisville homicide detective. In my estimation there's only one reason she would be here.' Jill looked at him from the corner of her eye.

Nick waited until Alexis was engrossed in conversation before replying. 'Not necessarily. She might have known the deceased or his charming widow. Don't get ahead of yourself,' he warned.

When Alexis ate a forkful of food, Jill tried her second tidbit sandwich. Michael brought them cups of coffee, so at least they had something to sip until the interminable luncheon was over. Finally Mrs Scott left the hall with Mr Shea and Alexis breathed an audible sigh of relief. 'I thought that would never end,' she said.

Jill tried to think of something appropriate to say. 'I thought the service was lovely and the food was delicious.'

'Magnolia Catering does a great job, should the need arise, and yes, our pastor did an amazing job.' Alexis dropped her napkin on her plate. 'But I want to apologize for my mother's behavior.' Her gaze roved from Jill to Michael to Nick. 'I don't know how my father kept Mom's behavior in check.'

'No one should ever apologize for their mother,' said Michael. 'Mine can be a doozey at times. I'll get us more coffee.'

'Mine, too,' Jill added. 'Is there anything else we can help you with today?'

A large tear ran down Alexis's cheek. 'Did you notice Detective Grimes in church? I cornered her outside the ladies' room and demanded a bit of news.'

Jill held her breath when Alexis paused.

'Since the M.E. found a needle mark on Dad's neck his death has been ruled suspicious while they wait for the full toxicology report. His case has been assigned to Detective Grimes in the Louisville Homicide Department.'

Jill cleared her throat. 'Although it's not exactly good news, it's what you expected. I hope you don't mind, but I told Nick your theory about who might have done it.'

Alexis shook her head and turned to Nick. 'Of course, I don't mind. I would've contacted you myself if my family hadn't treated you so atrociously.'

'All that is ancient history. If you or Jill want my advice, I'll give it. But keep in mind, the Louisville police department has well-trained investigators.' Nick reached for Jill's hand. 'They won't need to call me or anyone else to assist with the case and I don't wish to interfere.'

'We'll keep this low-key around Michael too,' Jill added. 'If my partner hears the words "murder investigation" in the same sentence as my name, he'll make the boss call me back to Chicago. And I prefer to stay as long as possible.' She said this to Nick and squeezed his hand.

Alexis slumped in her chair. 'I can't believe I'm hearing "murder investigation" in the same sentence with my dad.' She covered her face and sobbed.

'What can we do?' Jill put a hand on her shoulder. 'Find you something stronger to drink than coffee?'

'No, just help me figure out who killed my father. I honestly don't trust anyone other than you two. Who knows who my mother has on her payroll?'

'Our killer might not be Dennis Donagal,' Jill said. 'He's been in Europe with his family for a week. Of course, he might have hired a hitman, but you need to think harder about your father's enemies.'

Nick frowned. 'Hold on. Alexis is a grieving daughter and you're a journalist, Jill. The police have opened an investigation, so I suggest you let them do their job. I doubt any Louisville detectives would be on Rose Scott's payroll, no matter how conniving she is.'

'Of course, Nick. What Jill and I need to do is finish our interview before Michael wants to move on to the next distillery,' Alexis said, getting herself together.

'Whenever you're ready, give me a call.' Jill rose to her feet. 'It's time for you to go home and rest. Would you like us to drive you?'

Alexis smoothed down her dress as she stood. 'No, I'm sure the limo is back after taking my grandfather home. Why don't you walk me out?' With supreme dignity Alexis left the church hall with Jill and Nick on either side.

Michael soon caught up with three cups of coffee. 'What am I supposed to do with these?'

'I'll take one.' Jill took a coffee as the limo pulled away with Mrs Scott, Mr Shea and Alexis wedged between them in the backseat. Looking so small and forlorn, the image of Alexis wasn't one Jill would soon forget.

Nick felt a surge of relief when the limo pulled away with Alexis inside. Not that he didn't have pity for a woman who just lost her father. And not that he didn't have special compassion for anyone born to a mother like Rose Parker Scott. But Alexis was definitely part of a past he had no desire to resurrect. She was also part of the reason he was gun-shy about forming romantic relationships. Alexis had been quick to dump him when Rose pulled up her nose about his prospects. He couldn't imagine what Jill had in common with Alexis. But for some reason those two had become friends, and he loved Jill enough to not interfere.

'Ready to get out of here?' Nick asked, taking one of Michael's cups.

'I sure am.' Jill peered up at him. 'Monday will be soon enough to finish my interview with Alexis. I want to spend time with you, Magic Man.'

'Hey, guys, remember me?' Michael was all but forgotten in

the background. 'If you drop me at the hotel, I'll spend an hour in the weight room before heading to the room.'

'Sounds good,' said Nick. 'I want to show Jill some of Louisville's attractions other than distilleries. Then tonight we'll have dinner together, my treat.'

After driving Michael back to the Thurman House Hotel, he took Jill to see the locks on the Ohio River, which allowed pleasure boats and freighters to move down to Owensboro and the Mississippi River beyond. He had planned to take her back to his apartment, but Jill asked the lock-tender so many questions they had no time to go anywhere but back to the hotel to collect Michael.

They decided upon Doc Crow's Southern Smokehouse for dinner, where they all ate too much and talked about subjects from college sports to the difference between Chicago and Louisville winters. While Michael nursed his last snifter of bourbon, Jill practically fell asleep at the table. When Nick dropped the two journalists off at their hotel he received the to-go box with everyone's leftovers, along with one sleepy kiss from Jill for his trouble. But he didn't mind. Jill would be in town for another week, and he planned to take another week's vacation. Hopefully by the time she finished the assignment, she would realize she belonged in Louisville with him . . . or at least in Roseville with her family where they could see each other often. Anywhere but in Chicago, so many miles away.

The moment Nick entered his apartment his cat howled for both attention and his dinner. Bending down to scratch Elmo behind his ears, he swept the giant ball of ginger fur into his arms. 'Did you miss me, buddy? How about salmon pate for supper?'

Elmo purred in response.

He emptied a can of cat food into Elmo's bowl, watered his two scraggly plants, and turned on the nightly news. Nothing like a litany of rape, robbery and murder to guarantee sweet dreams. He wasn't five minutes into the local update when his phone buzzed with a voicemail.

Nick read the message and returned the missed call. 'Hi, Sis, I didn't think you would call so late. Isn't everything OK? How's Mom?'

'I wouldn't have if you had left your phone on.' Sarah sounded mildly annoyed.

'Sorry, I turned off my phone at a funeral this morning and forgot to turn it back on. I spent the day with Jill, the girl I'm dating.'

'Mom is fine,' Sarah said, not bothering to ask who had died. 'She was overjoyed to see us and remembered Bob's and each one of the kid's names. People with dementia don't usually remember names well.'

'That's true, but did you see the yellow notes all over the kitchen?' he asked.

'How could I not? Those were Mrs Diaz's idea and she put up most of them. Mom said she doesn't need them but didn't want to hurt Inez's feelings.'

'What about the laundry hanging for days on the line in all kinds of weather?'

'For goodness' sake, Nick. Once I left a load of clothes in the washer for a week when we went to Disney World. I had to wash that load twice to get the smell out. Busy women occasionally forget stuff.'

Nick pushed Elmo off his lap so he could pace the room. 'Did you look at her fridge and pantry?'

'Yes, you did a great job of organizing so she should be fine for a while. I found some out-of-date bottles of salad dressing and mayo in the fridge, but those things happen when you live alone and don't cook that much. Heck, I'll bet I have a few of them too. You buy something on sale; nobody likes it, and it sits forever in the fridge until you move.'

'So you think we've got nothing to worry about?' Nick didn't try to hide his disbelief.

Sarah sighed. 'I'll admit it's worrisome her electricity almost got shut off, because she wouldn't know who to call to turn it back on. Dad always paid the bills, balanced the checkbook, and took care of the business side of life. Mom cooked, cleaned, and raised the kids. Now that he's gone she had to take over those duties without much training.'

Nick felt a twinge of shame. Why hadn't that occurred to him?

'I talked her into putting everything on auto-pay, not just utilities, so that will take care of insurance premiums and her one credit card bill.'

'We just have to make sure she has enough money in the account.' Nick switched off the TV and headed down the hall.

'Exactly. Dad's pension check and her social security check are deposited around the first of the month, so one of us needs to check her account balance around the fifteenth to make sure she's on track and won't run out of money.'

'Should we set up a rotating schedule?'

'Good idea,' Sarah agreed. 'Since you and I were just there, I'll tell Susan to show up around mid-month. Then Bobbie can take the beginning of the month. Both of them have kids involved in sports, so they'll have to plan for this.'

'I think Mom is more important than elementary school sports.' Nick cringed as soon as he spoke.

'I agree, but there's no reason to panic right now. I see no need for a power-of-attorney or joint checking accounts, and Mom certainly doesn't need assisted living. She won't like us micro-managing her life.'

'What about having groceries delivered or setting up meals-on-wheels?'

'I'll have Susan discuss those with Mom on her next visit.'

'How was the supper she cooked for you and your family? Did everything make sense as a meal?'

'I didn't want to make a lot of work for her. Bob and I picked up a bucket of fried chicken with side dishes before we showed up.'

'Let me know what breakfast is like tomorrow. Mom put strawberry jam on her fried eggs while I was there.'

Sarah snorted. 'This from the guy who used to put peanut on baked potatoes? Stop worrying, Nicky. Bob and I and the kids are already on our way home so she didn't have to cook breakfast for us. With such short notice, Bob couldn't find anyone to replace him as an usher in church. Next time we go, we'll stay longer and I'll watch Mom's every move.'

When Sarah laughed, Nick did too. What else could he do? He had sprung this on his sisters without warning. 'I might have overreacted, so I'm glad you observed for yourself.'

'Me too, but right now I need to hang up and deal with the brats in the backseat. How on earth did I get such whiney teenagers?'

'Thanks, Sarah, I know it's easier for me to drive to Lorraine than you. And don't forget to send new pictures of your two angels.'

'I'll get those in the mail next week. We'll talk soon.'

She hung up leaving Nick nostalgic and yearning for a family. It wasn't often that he longed for a houseful of kids, running, screaming, fighting over the remote. But when it happened, it hit him like a ton of bricks. Maybe, just maybe, this new relationship with Jill would become permanent. As long as Alexis and her crazy family don't ruin things for a second time.

SIX

J ill sprang out of bed the moment her alarm went off. Today was a day off even for those on assignment from a Chicago news service. It was also a day off for Kentucky State cops, even though Nick had already put in for a full week of vacation. The sun was shining and the temperature was neither too hot nor too cold, all-in-all, a perfect day to visit a cousin who lived an hour away. But Jill had no intention of going alone. She searched her purse for her phone, then pressed the speed-dial button for Nick.

He picked up on the second ring. 'Good morning, sugar. Are you on your way to church?'

'Nope. Since we just attended Mr Scott's memorial service, I'm good for another week. Did you sleep well after all that barbeque?'

'Like a baby,' he said. 'How about you? Did Michael's snoring from the other room keep you awake?'

'Not with earplugs in. This girl got her beauty rest.' Jill poured her first cup of coffee. 'I was wondering what your plans were for today.'

'I hope to spend it with my best girl.'

'If she's busy, would you drive to Roseville with me?' Jill teased. 'There have been plenty of changes since you last stayed at Sweet Dreams B and B. I need to make sure those two women aren't pulling each other's hair out.'

'Which two?' Nick sounded appropriately concerned.

'All questions will be answered at breakfast – my treat. Pick me up in half an hour. We'll stop at Bob Evans and then head to Roseville.'

As usual, Nick pulled up to the Thurman House Hotel just as Jill walked out the door. Typical of Sundays, Bob Evans was crowded, so they ate at the counter – pancakes and sausage for him, strawberry French toast for her. Jill waited until they left the restaurant to fill Nick in. 'I haven't told you my news about Aunt Dot,' she said once on the road. 'I told Michael, but I wanted to tell you in person.'

Nick glanced over at her. 'Don't tell me she's found a new husband this soon after Roger's death.'

'Goodness, no, but thanks to me she now has someone to help run the B and B . . . my granny!'

'Your grandmother – the one who didn't speak to Dot for forty years because of a teenage argument?'

'That's the one!' Jill crowed with enthusiasm.

'The grandmother who broke her hip and has been living in a nursing home?'

'Yes, Nick. I only have one living granny.'

'How can a crippled, elderly woman help another elderly woman run a huge house like Sweet Dreams?'

Jill pulled down her sunglasses and glared. 'My grandmother is not crippled, buster. She fell and broke her hip, so my parents put her in a nursing home to rehabilitate. Her hip has fully healed and she gets around just fine. All she needs is someone to remind her to take her meds. Granny planned to move back home, but my parents sold the house out from under her. Let that be a lesson to you. Be careful who you give power of attorney.'

Nick stopped for a red light. 'Your parents sold the house without telling her?'

'Basically, yes. They decided it was too much for her to take care of, especially with the bedrooms upstairs. They told Granny she could move in with them if she didn't want to remain in assisted living. Well, my grandmother had no desire to live in the suburbs. Besides, my parents both work and are gone all day, so they wouldn't know if she took her noon pills or not.'

'Was she mad about her house being sold?' Nick accelerated as soon as the light turned green.

'Hot as a hornet, until I suggested she live with her cousin in Roseville. Remember, Granny and Dot had been best friends until that argument over a boy. Apparently the young man was Granny's boyfriend first. Then Dot stole him away because she thought they were just "friends".'

'Hard to imagine Dorothy Clark as a man-stealer.'

'That's because you think of her as the tea-sipping, scone-baking community volunteer she is now. Everyone was eighteen at some point. The young man in question should've made it clear he and Emma were an item . . . or whatever they called dating back then.'

Nick cackled like a crow. 'So men are the root of all evil?'

'I hope that's not true in your case.' Jill leaned back to watch the scenery. 'Anyway, when I approached Aunt Dot, she was all for it. My grandmother, Emma, has always been a wonderful cook. Dot loves taking care of the business end of Sweet Dreams, but the kitchen has never been her favorite place. A B and B must serve breakfast each morning to their guests. Emma excels at making breakfast memorable. They both enjoy teatime with scones at four and happy hour at six for those guests who imbibe.'

'It's still a lot for two old ladies to manage. That is one huge house.'

'Since we're on our way there, I caution you about throwing around the term "old lady". You might discover exactly what Emma and Dot are still capable of.'

'Duly noted, Miss Curtis.' Nick bit back a smile.

'To put your mind at ease, they pay a local woman to change the linens, clean the bathrooms, and do the laundry every day. Plus a service gives the place a thorough cleaning once a week. All Dot has to do is walk around with the feather duster and help Emma in the kitchen. Like I said, Emma has wonderful recipes that are easy and quick to make.'

'The B and B generates enough income to cover those kinds of expenses?' Nick asked.

'Right now it does, but buying a B and B is definitely not on my bucket list.'

'I can see it now . . . Jill and Nick's Home-Away-from-Home. Breakfast would be boxes of cereal and granola bars, juice in the fridge, coffee pods next to the Keurig machine. Guests must help themselves and then clean up afterwards, while their hosts sleep until nine.'

Jill might have balked at his poor estimation of her domestic abilities, but since he had put himself in the imaginary picture, she didn't. In fact, it all sounded rather wonderful. 'Could possibly work,' she murmured. 'The world will be a very different place by the time we retire.'

'Sounds like Granny and Dot Clark might be a match made in heaven, now that Roger is gone and Emma no longer has a home.'

'According to them so far so good, but with the new set-up they have time on their hands. I suggested they come up with a hobby.'

'How is *that* going?'

'You and I are about to find out. I asked you along for back-up, in case there's gunplay or fisticuffs.'

Nick barely cracked a smile. 'I locked my service weapon in the gun safe.'

'I was joking about gunplay. And if there are fisticuffs, I believe we can subdue two women in their seventies.'

Before they knew it, Nick turned off the freeway and started down the familiar road to Roseville. Jill loved the charming, turn-of-the-century village. That is, turn of the twentieth, not the current, century. Vibrant downtown shops and restaurants surrounded a shady town square, with a gazebo and bandstand for summer concerts and Christmas caroling. Jill could never have pictured herself living anywhere but Chicago until she came to Roseville.

'We're here,' Nick sang out twenty minutes later. 'Should I park in my usual spot in the back?'

Jill noticed plenty of cars in the driveway. 'No, park on the street. We don't want to inconvenience Dot's guests.'

She climbed the steps and stood for a moment on the wide porch of the Victorian mansion, unsure how to approach. 'Let's enter through the front door and not the kitchen. We'll pretend we're just another couple checking in.' Hooking her arm through Nick's elbow, Jill pushed open the screen and stepped into the foyer. On Sundays the front door was kept unlocked and ajar to welcome friends and would-be guests.

'Hello,' she called. 'Is anybody home?'

'We're in here,' someone answered. 'Although I doubt we're who you're looking for.' There was a smattering of laughter.

Jill and Nick cut through the parlor to the grand dining room and stopped short. Three couples sat at the table with dirty plates in front of them and empty coffee cups. 'Hi, folks, I'm Jill, Mrs Clark's cousin. Let me refill those cups for you.' She marched to the sideboard for the carafe.

'Thanks, Jill, but the pot's empty. We've just had a delicious breakfast. Now we're waiting for them to . . . finish,' said a silver-haired woman with a smile.

'Finish what?' Nick started stacking dirty plates. 'I'm Nick, not a relative, just Jill's boyfriend.'

'Our hostesses seem to be quarreling,' whispered a gentleman on the woman's left. 'But we're in no hurry.'

'Forgive me for saying so, but those two are rather entertaining.' This observation came from an apple-cheeked woman at the far end.

'No forgiveness necessary. The other lady is my grandmother.' Jill rolled her eyes. 'I'll straighten this out and fetch more coffee.' She picked up the carafe and marched through the swinging doors with Nick on her heels with the plates.

'Granny! Aunt Dot! What on earth is going on?'

'Jill?' both asked simultaneously.

'Yes, it's me. Why are you neglecting your guests?' Jill refilled the carafe from the giant coffeemaker as Nick filled the sink with dishwater.

As though awoken from a dream the women flew into action. Emma pulled a walnut coffee cake from the warming oven, while Dot grabbed the pot from Jill's hand.

'They could hear every word you two said,' Jill whispered under her breath.

Emma and Dot bustled into the dining room, red-faced and apologetic for their behavior. From the amount of laughter Jill and Nick heard with their ears pressed to the door, all was well with the three couples.

Jill bent down to pet Jack, a beagle she'd formed a strong attachment to during her recent stay. 'Let's take the dog for a long walk until the guests pack up and leave. Then I'll sit my relatives down for a good talking to.'

Nick snapped on Jack's leash. 'I wouldn't miss that conversation for anything in the world.'

The three of them covered the entire commercial area, along with the bulk of residential streets between downtown and the B and B. When they walked through the back door into the kitchen, the dishes were washed and put away and the room was spotless. Both women were sipping tea at the table.

'Wow,' said Jill, resting her hands on her hips. 'This is a different side than the one you showed your guests.'

Aunt Dot broke the ice first. 'We apologized to those lovely people and promised if they return, their rooms would be half price and there would be no repeat performance.'

Emma nodded. 'They insisted the rooms were beautiful, the food delicious, and they weren't the least bit put-off by our squabble.'

'What exactly was the squabble about?' Jill sat down at the table, knowing she was venturing onto thin ice.

'It was my fault.' Dot wrung her hands in her lap. 'If I see something needing to be done, I jump in and do it.'

'Young people call that being a control freak.' Emma crossed her arms over her apron.

Behind them Nick coughed to cover up his chuckle.

'Go on, Grandma. You've got the floor,' Jill prodded.

'Dot told me that breakfast would be my domain, just like teatime and how the house looks is her domain. When I cook, I'm not used to people sticking their big noses in.'

Aunt Dot pressed the sides of her nose with two fingers. 'My nose is normal size. Thank you very much.'

This time Jill couldn't help but laugh. 'That was it? No fighting over the mailman's attention?'

Emma hooted. 'Goodness, no. You can have him, Dot.'

Dot turned to her cousin. 'No, I insist. He's yours.'

Jill looked from one to the other. 'The solution is simple: Granny reigns in the kitchen at breakfast. Don't help with anything, Aunt Dot, unless Emma asks for help.'

Dot nodded her head solemnly. 'I promise, Em.'

'Then teatime, happy hour, and the house are Aunt Dot's territory. Other than keeping your room tidy, Granny, butt out unless asked to pitch in.'

'I agree. Sorry we argued, Dot,' Emma added.

'No, I'm the one with a short temper—'

Jill quickly cut her off. 'Moving on, ladies, I thought we discussed on the phone the subject of hobbies. Have you come up with anything?'

'We certainly have,' they both chimed.

'Emma has taken up knitting again,' Dot explained. 'Right now she's making a shawl for a special somebody for Christmas.'

'Blabbermouth,' Granny cried.

'Jill never would've known she was the special someone if you hadn't said that,' Dot calmly pointed out. 'And I volunteered to chair two committees at church – the monthly bake sale and our annual coat drive.'

'Plus, we came up with a clever evening project.' Emma beamed at her cousin. 'Together we're hosting the weekly Book-and-Bourbon Club. We've already had our first meeting. At each meeting we vote on a book to read during the following week. Then we'll gather Tuesday nights in Roger's study to discuss the book around the fireplace.'

'How does bourbon figure in?' Nick asked, settling his hands on Jill's shoulders.

'Oh, I almost forgot the best part. Most of the ladies in town have only tasted one brand, if they've tasted bourbon at all. And they know nothing about the distilleries in the area other than Founders Reserve and Black Creek. At each meeting, we'll taste a different Kentucky brand and learn about the company that produced it. At our first get-together, we picked out the book to read while sipping a bit of Roger's pride and joy, and chose the book *Little Women* by Louisa May Alcott.'

'What about you, Granny?' Jill asked. 'Are you ready to try a little bourbon?'

Emma bobbed her head. 'I am. I've already bought a bottle

of Founder's Reserve to sample at the next meeting, which is in two days.' She dropped her voice to a whisper. 'Dot told me the master distiller's son turned out to be a *murderer*. I did some research on the company to share with the group.'

Jill angled a pained expression over her shoulder at Nick. 'What about the teetotalers in the reading group?' she asked. 'Surely not everyone wants to sample whiskey.'

Dot grinned. 'There are at least two abstainers, so we'll always have tea and coffee, plus plenty of snacks and desserts for everyone.'

'Which reminds me . . .' Granny jumped to her feet. 'I baked an extra carrot cake this morning. It's on the dining room buffet. Why don't we have a slice with a cup of coffee?'

'I'll get plates and the coffee carafe.' Dot followed her cousin through the swinging doors.

'What could possibly go wrong with this *bright* idea?' Nick muttered under his breath.

'Now, now, Trooper. Let's not discourage them right off the bat. I can handle this.'

'What will you do,' Jill asked Dot when she returned, 'if one of your guests loves the week's selection too much and becomes tipsy?'

Dot had an answer ready. 'We have a plan for that. Although we'll discourage over-imbibing at meetings, anyone who gets tipsy will spend the night here.' She pointed at the ceiling.

'After all, this is an inn,' Emma added, placing large slices of cake in front of them.

'Most of the ladies walk here anyway.' Dot filled mugs with fresh coffee.

Jill swallowed her first mouthful of cake. 'Sounds like you've covered your bases.'

Nick wasn't quite so convinced. 'If someone refuses to stay overnight, make sure you send them home in a cab or an Uber.'

'Will do, Lieutenant.' Dot saluted as though in the military. 'You do know that these two are dating, right?' She said this to Emma. 'And Nick is a state cop?'

'Of course I knew they were an item. Jill is my granddaughter.' Emma giggled like a child.

'Feel free to talk about us all you like,' Jill suggested. 'We'll just enjoy our cake.'

'That sounds like a real *bright* idea, kids.' Both women broke into a round of laughter, while Jill and Nick ate with blushing faces. They hadn't been the only ones listening at the swinging doors.

It was late when Jill and Nick got back to Louisville from Roseville. And even later when she was finally able to fall asleep. After they'd had cake and coffee with her relatives, Jill had stripped the beds in the guest rooms, started the laundry, and remade the beds with clean linens. That way Dot's hired woman could get a head start on the cleaning that week.

While Jill was occupied, Nick had found a hedge trimmer in the garage and attacked the shrubbery, despite Dot's insistence that her gardening service would eventually get to it. After staying at Sweet Dreams B & B for two weeks, Nick felt indebted to Mrs Clark, who had fed him an enormous number of meals.

When Jill finally climbed into bed that night, she tossed and turned for an hour, thinking about Nick. Were they just 'dating' as Dot described? 'An item' in the words of her grandmother or 'boyfriend and girlfriend', as most people would describe? But for how much longer? This was the start of her second week in Louisville. She and Michael had another week, two at the most, before the boss insisted they return to Chicago. Jill needed a plan . . . or she needed another job in a hurry.

She awoke to her phone ringing next to her ear on the pillow. 'Hello? This is Jill Curtis.'

'Good morning, Jill. Alexis Scott. Would you like to finish that interview this morning?'

It took Jill less than five seconds to regain her faculties. 'Nothing would please me more. But are you sure you're ready? You just had your dad's service two days ago.'

'I cried all day yesterday. Today I need to get busy or I'll go stark, raving mad.'

'That makes sense.' Jill climbed out of bed. 'Shall I come to your office? I can be there within the hour.'

'I would prefer you came to my apartment, if you don't mind. In case we discuss matters other than the distillery, I want complete privacy. I'll have breakfast for us here. Oh, and I'm sorry about your run-in with my mom the other day. I'll make sure you get another chance.'

Jill wasn't sure how anyone could have privacy with a mother like Rose. Nevertheless, she readily agreed and jumped in the shower. Half an hour later, Jill found Michael sulking in the tiny kitchen of their suite.

'I suppose you're off without me again?' he asked.

'Unfortunately, yes. May I use the car? I want to finish my interview of the operations manager at Parker Estate and Alexis might have some off-topic questions for me. There won't be anything for you to videotape.'

Michael slugged down his coffee. 'I'd have thought you'd have asked her what you needed to by now.'

Jill stared at him. 'When would that have been? While I was paying my respects at the funeral home or perhaps during the memorial service? Today is Alexis's first day back to work since her father died.'

He blew out his breath. 'What am I supposed to do?'

'Start getting the narrative along with video at the next distillery. You know you really enjoyed interviewing Broadhust. Then maybe I won't have to visit that one.'

'I already took the tour once. It's the same story that we heard in Roseville – charred oak barrels, limestone water, corn mixed with malted barley, blah, blah, blah.'

Jill stamped her foot in frustration. 'It only sounds the same because you lack imagination. Ask the workers what makes their distillery different from their competitors and you'll hear plenty of fodder you can use. Stop being so dependent on me.'

'But I thought we were partners.' Michael gazed up with puppy-dog eyes.

'We are partners, but we're not joined at the hip.' Jill softened her tone. 'What would you do if I decide not to go back to Chicago?'

Michael jumped to his feet. 'What went on in Roseville? Did Nick propose?'

'Don't be ridiculous. We haven't been dating that long, but maybe I don't feel comfortable about leaving two old ladies alone in that big house.' Jill filled her travel mug and grabbed her purse. 'We'll talk more tonight, and don't worry, I'm not going anywhere until you and I finish the bourbon tours of Kentucky.' She held out her hand, palm up. 'I don't want to keep Alexis waiting. Keys, please?'

The moment he handed her the ring, Jill was out the door. She reached Parker Estate in record time and found the apartment door ajar like before. Bolting up the steps, Jill locked the door behind her to prevent uninvited interruptions.

'Wow. That was fast.' Alexis called from the kitchen. 'Let's work and eat at the table. I've got an egg and cheese casserole for us.'

This time Jill didn't ask who made breakfast. Instead she carried her travel mug to the table and picked up a fork. 'This looks delicious.'

'My parents' cook is wonderful. She can whip up anything in no time flat. While we eat, feel free to ask any questions you like. That will save time. Oh, and our public distillery tours will resume on Wednesday, if you'll still be in town.'

Jill swallowed a mouthful of the delicious casserole. 'I will be. I plan to stay as long as possible.'

'Because Nick is here?' Alexis concentrated on cutting her breakfast into small pieces.

'Yes, partly because of him. And partly because I don't want to leave you with so many questions about your dad.'

Alexis met her eye. 'I'm grateful for that. Now let's get your interview out of the way.'

Jill pulled out her notebook and verified the information she had learned online about the distillery. Then she asked a plethora of questions and finished up with the one she told Michael to ask. 'What makes the Parker Estate process different from your competitors?'

Alexis smiled with all the self-confidence that money can buy. 'We've had one hundred years to make sure we're nothing like our competitors.' She laughed joyously. 'We mix, ferment and distill in small batches – ten or less at a time and use a double finishing process – in oak barrels first, then the bourbon ages in port casks and the rye in rum barrels for a truly unique flavor. To my knowledge, no other distillery does that.'

'None that I know of,' Jill chimed, hoping to hide her limited knowledge.

'We also treat our customers with the upmost respect here, both the novice sampler and the aficionado. We offer evening cocktail classes for both bourbon and rye drinkers, and let customers fill bottles straight from the source if they so choose. Our goal is to turn every tour guest into a lifelong fan of our products.' Alexis concluded with another high-wattage smile.

Jill tucked away her notebook. 'I believe that's it. On Wednesday, my videographer and I will take the tour and complete our article on Parker Estate.'

Alexis pulled two purple cards from a kitchen drawer. 'Use these press passes for the tour. That will save you twenty bucks each. Don't forget to wear comfortable clothes since parts of the plant aren't air-conditioned, and no high heels or open-toed shoes. Oh, and I'm sorry you ran into my mother. Feel free to roam anywhere you want afterward, as I promised.'

'Thanks.' Jill slipped the passes into her purse. 'Have you given any more thought to potential enemies of your father, such as recently fired employees?'

Alexis's chin snapped up. 'In a company as large as ours, I'm sure there have been. But it's hard to imagine someone committing murder because they were fired.'

Jill stared at her, wide-eyed. 'Unfortunately, people have killed over far stupider reasons than that. Do you have access to employment records?'

'Of course, but they're not online. We'd have to go to my office.'

'Since we finished the interview, the rest of my day is yours. Michael is researching at another distillery.'

Alexis jumped up, kicked off her sneakers, and slipped on high heels. When she grabbed a flaming red blazer from the closet, her T-shirt and black yoga pants assumed a professional appearance. 'I'm ready. Let's take my car since it's faster.'

That goes without saying.

Jill buckled her seatbelt and they were soon waved into a special section of the employee lot, allowing easy access into the corporate headquarters. From the moment Jill stepped out of the BMW, she had a hard time keeping up with the executive, despite wearing far more sensible shoes. Alexis marched up one corridor and down the next, barely acknowledging the employees' friendly greetings. Once inside her office, Alexis shut the outer door to the hallway in a hurry.

'Good morning, Miss Scott. I didn't think you would be in until tomorrow.' The assistant offered a stack of cards and messages.

'Good morning, Roxie. For all intents and purposes, I'm not here. My friend and I are here on a personal matter.'

'You got it, Miss Scott.' The assistant dropped the stack on her desk and returned to her computer.

Behind the closed inner door, Alexis slumped behind her desk while Jill took the upholstered chair. 'Are you training for a marathon?' she asked.

'Sorry 'bout that. I learned the faster I walk the less likely I'd be interrupted with non-essential stuff. Otherwise it could take thirty minutes to get from the parking lot to my office.' Wasting no time, Alexis turned on her computer.

Jill used the moment to appreciate artwork on the walls. 'These are really good. Are they prints or *giclees*?'

'They're originals done by a friend of mine. No one makes *giclees* unless you're already famous.'

'Fame should only be a matter of time.' Jill walked over to a painting of a bridge over the Mississippi at dawn. 'The details and colors are incredible.'

Alexis smiled above her monitor. 'I will pass along your praise. Come look at this.'

Jill walked around the desk to study a computer spreadsheet of data in a very small font. 'What am I looking at?'

'Wait a sec and I'll create a sublist and enlarge the font.' She tapped a few keys and the screen bloomed with names, address, and pertinent information. 'This is a list of every employee who recently retired, quit or was fired during the last twelve months. Each had been given an exit packet. Look at that.' Alexis tapped the screen. 'If the employee had been dismissed, it lists the reason and the name of his or her immediate supervisor.'

Jill leaned over Alexis's shoulder. 'This is exactly what we need.'

'I hope you don't have a photographic memory. This is all confidential information.' Alexis lowered her brows.

'I can't remember a shopping list of three items,' Jill said, shaking her head. 'Don't worry. Everyone's privacy will be respected. Print that out, then Nick and I will have a place to start.'

With list in hand they headed to the door, but Alexis's assistant beat them to it. 'Sorry, Miss Scott,' she said. 'I didn't think your condition of "I'm not here" included the police.'

'It did not. Thank you, Roxie. Please come in Lieutenant Grimes. I've been expecting your call.' When the detective moved towards the chair she had just vacated, Jill took a position by the wall.

'I prefer to deliver this kind of news in person.' Grimes grasped the back of the chair but didn't sit. 'The M.E. received the toxicology report and has determined your father was poisoned. His death has been officially ruled a homicide. I will be personally handling the investigation.'

For several minutes, Alexis just stood there. 'Although this is what I expected, the news still comes as quite a shock.'

'That's understandable,' Grimes murmured. Then she turned her attention to Jill. 'May I ask what's in your hand, Miss Curtis?'

Jill gazed down at the paper. *How could the cop know this had anything to do with the murder?*

Alexis answered the question for her. 'Jill suggested I print out a list of employees who'd been recently fired, in case Dad had made some recent enemies.'

Grimes walked over and pulled the list from Jill's fingers. 'I could've sworn you told me you were a travel writer.'

'I am,' Jill said, 'but crime-solving is sort of my hobby.'

'Then may I suggest bird-watching? We don't like civilians interfering with police business.'

'We were only trying to help.' Alexis joined Jill's side.

'I'll go through this list of names to see if anything pops out, Miss Scott. I'll be in touch. Have a nice day, Miss Curtis.' The detective marched out of the office as though on a mission.

As soon as they were sure Grimes was gone, Alexis hit the print button on her computer. 'I never said I wouldn't make another copy.'

'Good idea, and could you text the list to Nick? He can get started while you drive me back to my car.' Jill punched in Nick's number. 'I'll bring him up to date, then he and I have some work to do.'

SEVEN

When Alexis parked next to Jill's car in the driveway, Jill spotted exactly what her rather blasé story about Parker Estate Distillery needed – a human interest angle.

'Who is that older man with a dog in your parents' garden?' Jill asked. 'I saw him with you at the funeral.'

'Hi, Grandpa,' Alexis shouted and waved out the window. The man waved back, while the dog gave a small yip. 'He's my grandfather and actually, the house is still his, not my parents'. Grandpa hasn't signed it over to Mom yet.'

'He's the Robert Parker who started the distillery?' Jill asked.

'It was started by his father, Robert Parker, Senior. But it was small and barely survived Prohibition.'

'I would love to interview him. Is that at all possible?'

Alexis slipped an arm around Jill's shoulder. 'For you, I'd make just about anything possible. I'm so grateful you believed in me about my dad.'

Jill flushed. 'But I haven't solved anything yet.'

'No, but if you hadn't stopped the cremation, Lieutenant Grimes wouldn't be tracking down a murderer right now.' Alexis used the key fob to lock her car. 'The thing is Grandpa is getting forgetful. They haven't nailed down whether it's dementia or not. All I know is his memory of the past remains top-notch, but he can't remember what he ate for lunch today.'

Jill pulled out her notebook. 'Maybe his lunch wasn't memorable. Anyway, it's the past that I'm interested in. Readers love to hear the history behind a family business. It gives them something to identify with, whether it's a chocolate bar or a snifter of bourbon. If you don't think answering questions might upset him, I'd love a few minutes of his time.'

'Are you kidding? Old people love rehashing the past. Grandpa will probably tie you up and never let you leave.' Alexis laughed and practically dragged Jill toward the back entrance of the mansion. 'We'll go inside through the kitchen – a sure way to avoid my mother. She doesn't cook and has no interest in seeing how it's done. But I will warn you, my mother is overprotective of her dad, for no reason I can see.'

Jill followed Alexis into the kitchen, through a well-stocked pantry, and down the hallway to a wing that apparently had been added after the mansion had been built. Jill barely drew a breath for fear of Mrs Scott, while Alexis provided family backstory along the way.

'We're entering a classic mother-in-law suite – living room, bedroom, small kitchen and bath,' she explained. 'Mom added this on for her parents when Grandpa was forced to step down as head of Parker Estate.'

'Who forced him?' Jill asked.

'Who do you think? My mother! She insisted Grandpa wasn't healthy enough to work and so my father took the helm. Shortly afterwards, my grandmother died.'

'How awful,' Jill said. 'Was it triggered by her husband's demotion?'

'Not really. Grandma had been struggling with cancer for a long time.'

'I'm sorry to hear that,' Jill murmured inadequately.

'Don't be. Grandma is out of pain, and Grandpa loves still living on the estate, but far removed from activities in the big house.' Alexis imbued the final words with emphasis. 'Grandpa cooks his own meals, putters in the garden, and watches what he wants on TV, as loud as he likes. He joins the family only when and if he chooses.' Alexis knocked twice, then opened the door to the suite. 'Grandpa?' she called. 'It's me, Lexi. I brought someone who wants to meet you.'

A white-haired, elderly man, the same man who was just in the garden, pushed himself up from the recliner. 'Who would want to meet me?' He muted the TV with the remote.

'I do, sir. I'm Jill Curtis, a journalist from Roseville, Kentucky.' *How easily her new hometown slipped from her mouth.* 'I'm writing a travel log about the bourbon distillery tours of Kentucky. And in Louisville, my prime focus is Parker Estate.' She bent down to pat the dog's head.

The man's wizened face blossomed into a smile. 'What a good

choice you have made, young lady. Sit, sit, both of you!' Robert Parker pointed at the chintz couch as he scratched the dog behind the ears. 'This is Buster, formerly known as Buster-the-Terror. But old age has settled him down quite a bit. How do you know my beautiful granddaughter?'

'I . . . met Alexis while researching distilleries. We became immediate friends.'

'How could you not?' Robert slapped his knees. 'Lexi, dear girl, make us some coffee and find us cookies in the cupboard.'

'Coming right up, Grandpa.' Alexis strode toward the tiny kitchen.

'Now, what did you want to know, Julie?'

'It's Jill, sir, and I'm interested in the early days of the Parker Estate Distillery. May I tape our interview while I ask a few questions?'

'Of course, you can. The statute of limitations ran out long ago for my daddy's crimes, even if he were still alive.' He hooted with laughter.

Jill switched on the recorder. 'I understand the Parker Estate brand was started by Robert Senior before the Great Depression.'

Grandpa's blue eyes twinkled with delight. 'Yes and no. There certainly wasn't any Parker *Estate* back then. My father owned a small distillery in a seedy part of downtown. When that part of Louisville burned to ground, Dad didn't have much to lose. He moved Parker Bourbon, as it was known then, to a secret location underneath a profitable dry goods store. The owner of the building took the rent in whiskey, and believe me he was well paid over the years.' He pulled on his white mustache. 'During Prohibition, Dad also ran a small speakeasy six nights a week in an abandoned building down the street. That's how the brand, as you call it, managed to survive.' Grandpa settled back in the recliner as nostalgia took him to another place, another time. 'I was just a baby, but from what I heard, Dad's speakeasy wasn't like the fancy dives you see in movies, with pretty gals in short dresses, high heels and diamond tiaras in their hair. Dad served our bourbon and draught beer at ten barstools and two tables. His joint was for working men who needed a bracer after a hard day on the docks or in the foundry or in some hellish factory. Those were hard times back then. The only women who entered came to drag her husband home by his ear.'

Jill sat mesmerized by the man in a herringbone cardigan and penny loafers as she visualized the speakeasy through his vivid description. 'I can just picture this place,' she enthused. 'Too bad we don't have a time machine.'

'If we did, I'd jump in it with you.' Alexis set a tray with three mugs and a plate of cookies on the coffee table.

'My dad called the joint Silky's, for no reason other than he liked the sound of it.' Grandpa reached for a mug, as did Jill.

'That's a great name.' Jill added milk from a small pitcher.

'Well, Silky's gave my dad the courage to continue making bourbon during America's darkest days – the Great Depression. When they finally rescinded Prohibition in 1933, Dad bought the buildings where Parker Estate is produced today. Real estate was real cheap back then, but Dad was still taking a chance. But as you can see, his vision and his courage paid off.' He bobbed his head toward the expanse of rolling fields beyond the window.

'Did he build this beautiful home?' she asked.

Alexis answered for him. 'Great-granddad bought all the land and a farmhouse. Corn and rye were grown here for the distillery, but unfortunately he didn't live long enough to see his dream completed.' She leaned over and kissed the top of Robert's head. 'Grandpa had this house built and gave the old house to his farm manager. He also improved the land and upgraded the distillery. He made Parker Estate into the profitable business it is today.'

Robert beamed at his granddaughter. 'I wanted to name you, Lexi, as my successor. But your mother insisted that your father be put in charge.'

'You know I wasn't ready yet.' Alexis planted a second kiss on his forehead.

'Stop fawning over me, girl. You're embarrassing me in front of your friend, Miss Custis.'

Jill let the minor name change pass. 'I'm intrigued by your story, sir. My readers will love this. I'm also a little envious of the relationship you two share. My grandmother just moved to Kentucky from Chicago. I want this kind of closeness with her.'

Grandpa took two cookies from the plate and ate one whole. 'It's easy enough if you make the time. That's how Lexi is different from my daughter. Rose is always in a hurry, always has something important to do.'

Jill waited for Alexis to defend her mother, but she didn't. 'Do you ever drop by the distillery to see how things are running?' she asked.

Sadness washed over the old man's face. 'I used to, until my son-in-law discouraged my impromptu visits. I couldn't help but make suggestions when I spotted something I didn't like.' Robert winked at Jill. 'You know how old people don't like change.'

Jill snorted. 'I'm only in my thirties, but I'm not big on change either.'

'I like you, Jean,' he said. 'You can come back any time, with or without my granddaughter.'

'Thank you, sir. I will if I have more questions.' She nibbled a cookie.

'Right now, we'd better let you rest.' Alexis stuck two cookies in her jacket pocket and then carried their mugs to the sink.

'Don't be shy. Fill your pockets.' Robert pointed at Jill. 'You never know when you'll get hungry.'

'Thank you, sir. It was lovely to meet you. You too, Buster.' Jill grabbed several cookies and followed Alexis out the door. 'Golly, Alexis,' Jill said once they were away from the house. 'I wanted to kiss his forehead too. What a sweet man.'

'He really is.' Alexis readily agreed. 'That's why I get so annoyed with my mother . . . or at least, that's one of the reasons. She has no patience with him, especially with Grandpa's increasing forgetfulness.'

'What a shame,' Jill said as they reached her car.

'That's life, I suppose.' Alexis glanced at her watch. 'I'd better let you get back to Michael and Nick, while I start writing thank-you cards for the people who sent flowers to the church.'

'I'm sure your mother will appreciate your help.' Jill climbed in her car and rolled down the window.

'My mother?' Alexis squawked. 'She would instruct her personal secretary to do it, but I feel they should come from a Parker Scott. Stay in touch, Jill, and call me after your tour of the distillery.'

On her way back to the hotel, Jill picked up a burger and fries from a drive-through. According to his text, Michael was still at the second distillery on their list, so she had time to transcribe the interview with Mr Parker into her laptop. The historical context that Grandpa Parker had provided was exactly what the article needed for the human angle to bourbon-making. Jill had just finished correcting her typos when her partner walked into their suite.

'Look who's home.' Michael slung his equipment bag onto a chair.

'This is *not* our home. And I hope you had a productive day, because I sure did. I interviewed Robert Parker, Alexis's grand-father, who built that gorgeous estate and made the distillery into what it is today. And I learned interesting tidbits about his father during Prohibition and the Great Depression.'

Michael pulled a Coke from the mini fridge. 'I thought alcohol production screeched to a halt during Prohibition.'

Jill stared at him over her laptop. 'Do you live under a rock when you're not at work? Haven't you seen any of the movies about bootleggers or Elliot Ness or Al Capone? Booze production and consumption didn't die during those thirteen years. It merely went underground.'

He slouched into a chair and drank half the contents of his Coke. 'Sorry, I hail from a long line of abstainers.'

'So do I, but I'm still aware of twentieth-century history.'

'Let me take a quick shower, then you can educate me over dinner. I've got a taste for garlicy pasta, so find us something appropriate.'

Jill reread her article about Parkers Estate, then found them an Italian restaurant a short walk from their hotel. She allowed herself one glass of Chianti while they shared antipasti and discussed how they had spent the day. Michael had done well with the narrative. He had asked the correct questions and received answers that might turn a ho-hum distillery article into something memorable.

'Well done, Mikey. If your video footage is half as good as your article, you're looking at a Pulitzer.' She lifted her wineglass in toast.

He scoffed at her extreme exaggeration. 'The video is fine, but I might need help polishing my prose. You've got a way with words.'

'It would be my pleasure to tweak the narrative.' Jill smiled at him. 'Now, as soon as we shoot video inside Parker Estate distillery on Wednesday, that segment will be finished too. They are resuming public tours. We'll have two distilleries under our belt.'

'I suggest we hit number three tomorrow, before we run short on time.' Michael refilled his wineglass from the bottle.

She hesitated before answering. 'Sure. Sounds like a plan.' Jill still didn't feel comfortable admitting she was helping Alexis solve her father's murder. 'Let's order our entrées, OK? I'm thinking eggplant parmesan.'

The two partners enjoyed a delicious meal while Jill filled Michael in on everything she'd learned from Alexis and her grandfather about the brand's early days. She also filled him in on the toxicology results they had learned from Detective Grimes.

'You're saying the master distiller, William Scott, had been injected with a poison? He was murdered?' he asked after swallowing a bite of lasagna.

'I am. Louisville homicide detectives have been officially assigned to the case.'

'Good,' he concluded. 'That means you're free to work with me like you should before Mr Fleming wonders what's taking us so long.'

Jill smiled as she dragged a piece of bread through the herbed olive oil. 'Absolutely, but I must admit I'm in no hurry to leave this town. I've grown rather fond of Louisville.'

'Or maybe, you've grown fond of one of its home-based investigators.'

'One or the other, Erickson.' Jill reached over to fork up some of his lasagna. The partners had shared each other's food since day one of working together.

On the walk back to their hotel, Jill's phone buzzed in her pocket. 'What's up, Mr Harris? Are you enjoying your vacation?'

'I'm a tad lonely. Where are you?' Nick asked.

'Waddling back to the hotel with Michael. We dined on Italian cuisine tonight. Care to eat my leftovers?' Jill meant the question as a joke.

'I would love them. I'll be at your hotel in fifteen minutes. Meet me on the roof. There's a lovely garden up there.'

'And how would you know that?' she asked.

'I'm a local and I subscribe to the newspaper. Come alone and bring the takeout box.' Nick promptly hung up.

Jill chuckled. 'Looks like I have a late-night rendezvous on the roof of the Thurman House Hotel.'

Michael laughed. 'Don't blow it, Curtis, with work chitchat. And please, brush your teeth first. You reek of onions and garlic.'

Taking her partner's advice, Jill brushed her teeth, sprayed on cologne, and reapplied lipstick. With the leftovers in an insulated cooler, she took the elevator to the floor labeled 'R' and approached the only other person appreciating the view of the city.

'Hey, Nick, how's it going?'

'It's going well, considering.' Nick motioned to two plastic chairs that had seen better days. 'Don't worry. I already cleaned the mildew off yours.'

'As a token of my appreciation here is some eggplant parmesan with garlic bread for your dining pleasure.' She placed the cooler by his feet.

'Thanks, but I thought you'd be back from Alexis's earlier than this.' Nick's expression remained unreadable.

'Sorry. I had planned to, but an opportunity came up for me to interview her grandfather, Robert Parker Jr. So I jumped on it. His name brand certainly has had an intriguing history.'

Nick sat down and leaned back in the rickety Adirondack chair. 'Yes, it certainly has, and I'm glad you got to interview Robert. But keep in mind I'm looking into these so-called suspects solely for your sake, Jill.'

His statement and tone of voice surprised her. 'I know that, and I'm grateful. After the interview, I'd planned to spend the rest of the day with you. But Michael reminded me I promised to have dinner with him.'

Nick reached over and patted her knee. 'You seem to be burning your candle at both ends.'

'I am, and I don't like it. But I don't quite know how to fix this.' Jill picked up his hand and kissed his fingers. 'Please don't give up on me.'

'It would take more than two days of avoiding me for that to happen.' He brought her hand to his lips. 'How about we spend tomorrow together? I'd like to take you to Lorraine to meet my mother. Then you could help decide if her memory is failing or not.'

Jill considered the memory loss in Robert Parker Jr, but talking about Alexis's grandfather wouldn't help with the dilemma regarding his mother. She also thought about her promise to accompany Michael to a distillery tomorrow. But that might seal her fate with Nick. Suddenly, every failed relationship of her life flashed through her mind, leaving her paralyzed with fear. Jill uttered the only logical words in such a circumstance, 'I would love to meet your mother.'

'Great.' Nick's smile expanded across his face. 'We'll leave first thing in the morning and grab breakfast along the way.'

'Super,' she said. 'Now, have you made any headway on the list Alexis sent you?'

'Actually, I have. How could I not with all this time on my hands?'

Jill swallowed the guilty taste in her mouth. 'Great, what have you found out?'

Nick withdrew the list he'd printed from Alexis's email. 'One of the recently fired employees stood out for me. Mr Otto Bach was fired two weeks ago and certainly wasn't happy about his dismissal. The man had to be dragged off the premises by security guards and a restraining order. William Scott, Alexis's dad, had filed a restraining order because Mr Bach issued several verbal threats against William and his family.'

'Wow,' Jill murmured. 'Otto Bach sounds like a loose cannon.'

'He does, indeed. What's more, Bach has a criminal record of poisoning the neighbor's dog. From what you told me, the medical examiner feels Mr Scott fell victim to some kind of toxin. Apparently an injection of the substance finished him off.'

'You are awesome, Harris.'

'This is what I do for a living, Jill. Wait, there's more.' He lifted her chin with one finger. 'While you were talking to Grandpa Parker, I contacted a friend of mine in the Louisville PD. He told me, off the record, that a search warrant has been issued for Mr Bach's house.'

'Holy cow,' she blurted out for a lack of something more profound.

'Keep in mind, off the record means you can't share this with Alexis.'

'I promise, I won't.' Jill drew an X across where she imagined her heart to be. 'I can't wait to hear what they find inside Bach's home.'

'Wait no more, pretty woman. Louisville's finest found plenty of poison and miscellaneous toxins in both the house and the garage. Apparently, Otto purchased them legally online, which is a very frightening thought. Bach also recently visited websites which detail a particular toxin's effect on the central nervous systems. The police arrested Bach and will hold him for twenty-four hours to see if any of the collected samples match whatever toxin killed Mr Scott once full results of the tox screen are in.'

Jill leaned over and planted a kiss on Nick's lips. 'You are unbelievable, Magic Man.'

'Like I said, share none of this with Alexis. The homicide detective in charge of the investigation will bring the family up to speed in due course. I'm hoping this break in the case will grant me a bit of your time, Miss Curtis. I *am* on vacation this week.'

'I believe it will, Trooper. How about tomorrow, starting at eight a.m.? Thank you, from the bottom of my heart.'

Nick leaned over and kissed her squarely on the lips. 'Perfect. I'll pick up breakfast sandwiches to eat along the way. In the meantime, let's get you back inside. I'll eat my leftovers when I get home. You're starting to shiver.'

Jill exited the elevator at her floor, opened the door with her keycard and announced in a loud voice, 'Erickson, are you still awake? We need to have a heart-to-heart chat.'

Her conversation with Michael went better than she hoped. At least the part about spending the day with Nick instead of working. Her partner understood this was her only chance to see if they had a future together. And since Michael hadn't had any more success with long-time relationships than she'd had, he cut her some slack. However, he still didn't like the fact she'd stuck her nose into Alexis's personal life.

'Haven't you learned anything at all?' Michael demanded. 'You got yourself kidnapped and nearly killed while trying to play Nancy Drew in Roseville. Let the police handle William Scott's murder.' With that Michael walked into his room and slammed the door. He would've been so pleased to know Nick agreed with him wholeheartedly.

Right then and there Jill made up her mind not to mention the words 'murder' or 'Alexis Scott' or 'poison' at all tomorrow. The day would belong exclusively to Nick and his mother.

When Nick screeched to a stop in front of Thurman House the next day, Jill was waiting under the awning at the entrance. 'Good morning, beautiful. Lovely weather we're having, no?'

'Rain won't dampen our little excursion to Lorraine. What's in the bag? I'm starving.'

He checked his side mirror before pulling into traffic. 'Fried egg sandwiches with bacon and cheese on croissants. Hash brown patties and coffee.'

'Sounds wonderful. Did you make them yourself?'

'Sure I did,' Nick teased. 'Don't believe what you read on the wrappers or the bag.'

Jill partially unwrapped one for him, then started nibbling on hers. For a few minutes they ate in silence. Once they left the busy Louisville streets behind, she packed up the trash and pivoted on the seat. 'According to Google, we have just under two hours. I want you to tell me *everything* about the Harris family – your parents, your sisters, every pet you've ever owned. Don't leave out a single juicy tidbit. And on the way home, I'll do the same for you. Before we fall head-over-heels in love, we'd better learn about the skeletons in the closet.'

Nick smiled, thinking how close to head-over-heals he already was. While nursing his cup of coffee, he considered exactly how much to tell. Would he mention how his father always had a difficult time keeping a job? That every time his mother had tucked away a bit of money for Christmas or an emergency household expense, Dad had decided he couldn't stand another day in the repair shop and quit? Would he mention that if their house hadn't been left to them by grandparents, they probably would have landed on the street? Should he tell Jill that his mother often used to drive to the food bank and Goodwill in the next town where she wouldn't be recognized? Or that she often went hungry to make sure her kids had enough to eat? Was this the picture he wanted to paint before Jill's first visit? In the end, Nick kept his narrative sweet and simple, suitable for all ages.

'Let's see,' he began. 'Dad worked as an auto mechanic, while

Mom stayed home raising three girls and one obnoxious son.'
That prompted a giggle from Jill. 'Money was usually tight, but
we always had clothes to wear and enough food to eat.' *No lie
there.* 'My older sisters all opted for vocational training and
married young. Today one is a hairstylist, one works in a local
bakery, and one sells cosmetics from home. All are married and
mothers.'

'You're the only one to graduate from a four-year college?'

'I am, but only because I had a football scholarship for two
years, and worked full-time during the other two.'

'You were ambitious.' Jill studied him over her cup of coffee.

'I was, but I also didn't need much sleep back then.'

'What position did you play?'

'I was a running back for the Louisville Cardinals, but after
two years they cut me from the team since I wasn't fast
enough.'

'And that's when you met Alexis?'

Nick glanced at her, not wishing the conversation to go in that
direction. 'I suppose so. But my greatest joy was when my family
showed up at away football games in high school. Grandpa raised
tobacco, so he wore a wide-brimmed straw hat and drove an old
pickup truck. Grandma wore these flowered housedresses straight
from *The Waltons.* They were a hoot from another era and I loved
them so much.'

'I've never seen a tobacco plant. How's it grown?' she asked.

Grateful for the benign topic, Nick launched into a description
of everything he knew about planting, harvesting, and selling the
formerly profitable crop. Next he told Jill everything he could
remember about his nephews' and nieces' accomplishments in
sports and academics. Not because he wanted to brag, but because
he didn't want to talk about Alexis. By the time Jill finished
asking questions, they had reached the sign *Welcome to Lorraine
– Friendliest town in Kentucky.*

'Let's drive by the high school,' she demanded. 'Then show
me where you went to church, got a pizza, or ate an ice cream
cone. I find small towns fascinating.'

Nick easily fulfilled the three requests by circling one city
block, then pulled into his mother's driveway. 'Here we are . . .
home sweet home.' Suddenly Nick noticed the peeling paint, one

shutter hanging lopsided, and several shingles missing from the roof.

'What an adorable Cape Cod,' Jill exclaimed, jumping from the car. 'I can't wait to meet your mom.'

Jill's fourth wish was soon granted when Julie Harris stepped onto the porch, wearing a sweater, slacks, and a touch of make-up. 'You must be Jill. Nick told me you were coming. Nice to meet you.' Julie stretched out both arms.

'The pleasure is mine.' Jill stepped into her embrace. 'Your rosebushes are gorgeous. Are they tons of work?'

'No, not really.' His mother offered pruning tips as they entered the living room and sat down where nothing was out of place. Even the stack of magazines was perfectly straight. Nick settled on the couch and tried to relax as the women chatted about gardens and flowers. At least for a little while.

'Nicky, why don't you get us something to drink?' Julie asked. 'I have soft drinks and a pitcher of iced tea.'

'Sure, Ma.' He sprang to his feet.

'I'll take tea, *Nicky*,' Jill called after him, chuckling.

He laughed too, since no matter how old you got, childhood monikers never seemed to die. But when he reached the kitchen his good mood faded. Taped to the refrigerator door was a paper with *Jill* printed in large block letters. His mother must have put it up after his phone call last night. Across the face of the cupboards were even more yellow Post-its than before with reminders such as: *Bring in the mail at lunchtime* and *Get news-paper from porch*. Nick felt a pang of sorrow deep in his gut. Opening the refrigerator, his breath caught in his throat. There were no cans of soda or pitcher of iced tea. He didn't see much food at all, even though his mom had insisted on cooking dinner for them that night. Inside the freezer Nick found only the single serving heat-and-eat purchased on their last shopping trip.

Nick filled three glasses with tap water and returned to the living room. 'Jill and I were just discussing we don't drink enough water. So that's what I brought us instead of tea.'

'Fine with me,' Julie said. 'Tell me how your work is going, son. Are you still writing plenty of tickets on I-65?'

'No, not anymore. Now I travel around the state helping local sheriffs and police chiefs investigate crime.'

His answer seemed to confuse her. 'What kind of crime?'

'All kinds – murder, arson, armed robbery, assault, especially if law enforcement thinks a serial criminal might be involved.'

'But you still write speeding tickets, don't you?' she asked.

'No, someone else brings the lead-foots to justice these days.'

Julie pondered this, then shook her head. 'So, what would you kids like for supper tonight – beef, chicken, fish?'

Nick had seen none of those in the fridge or freezer. 'On our way here, I decided to take my two best girls out to dinner. No arguments. I don't want you to fuss.'

'Absolutely.' Jill nodded in agreement. 'You pick the restaurant, Mrs Harris.'

His mother shrugged listlessly. 'All we have is a pizza shop and Asian takeout.'

'What about the Mexican restaurant next to the dry cleaner?' he asked, remembering their drive around downtown.

'I didn't know anything about that. It must be new.' Her brow furrowed.

'Let's check it out. Then you can report back to Inez Diaz. She's mom's next-door neighbor,' Nick explained to Jill.

'And she's the one who insists on those reminders in the kitchen.' Julie glanced at her watch. 'All right, son, if you insist. But if we're going out, I'll need time to change. Why don't you show Jill the photo albums of your days as a football star?' She pointed at the bookcase against the wall.

Nick waited until she left the room to roll his eyes. 'Why don't we just see what's on TV?' He reached for the remote.

But Jill had already sprung to her feet. 'Don't be silly. Let's look at pictures. Maybe we can find a few candid shots of Nick wearing a saggy diaper or with spaghetti sauce on his face.' Jill easily located the albums atop an assortment of cozy mysteries and light romance. Labels on the bindings indicated the year the photographs had been taken.

Jill plopped down on the couch and started paging through the most recent album first. Her reaction was immediate and exactly matched how he felt. 'Oh, no,' she murmured. 'This isn't good at all.'

Nick pulled the album from her fingers for a better look. Scattered throughout the album were small white labels, identifying the people in each photograph. Some labels made complete sense such as *Marcie, Carol, and Ruth from Bible study*. No one could remember the names of every casual acquaintance during a lifetime. But a few other labels chilled Nick's blood to ice water such as Reverend Davis, who'd been Mom's pastor for thirty years. And even more ominous, the photos of her children had been labeled: Sarah, Susan, Bobbie, and Nick.

Nick closed the album and returned it to the bookcase. When he sat back down, Jill enveloped him in a hug.

'Don't say anything,' she whispered. 'We don't want to spoil the evening. Maybe all this labeling is some kind of precaution.'

'Maybe so. Before I say anything to Mom I need to talk to her doctor and maybe a memory specialist. Then I'll talk to my sisters again.'

'I'm here to help if I can.'

'Thanks, Jill. That means a lot.' He hugged her back fiercely.

'OK, you two . . . can you stop hugging long enough to tell me which scarf looks more Latin?' Julie had changed into a black pants set and wrapped a ruby red scarf around her throat. She also waved a black scarf with red embroidery through the air.

Jill quickly disengaged herself. 'Oh, definitely the black one. With your outfit, the owner might hire you as a flamenco dancer.'

Julie grinned and tossed the red scarf on the table. 'In that case, kids, I'm ready to go.'

Dinner turned out to be an unqualified success. The threesome dined on chips and salsa, enchiladas, empanadas, black beans and rice, and a delicious, deep-fried pastry he couldn't pronounce. His mother enjoyed a margarita, while Nick and Jill opted for iced tea since they'd be driving back to Louisville. They brought home enough leftovers for both lunch and supper for his mom. On the way home, Nick stopped at a convenience store to buy bread, milk, lunch meat, and salad fixings. He didn't know why the grocery delivery hadn't started yet, but he would check with his sister.

'Thank you, Nicky,' Julie said inside her front door. 'I haven't had so much fun in a long time.' Spontaneously, she pulled Jill into another embrace. 'I love you already. Please come back often. I think we're going to get along just fine.'

Jill kissed his mother's cheek. 'I couldn't agree more. And Tres Lobos will be our regular hangout.'

Nick made sure his mother's house was locked up tight before joining Jill in the car. 'Well, what did you think?' he asked.

'I don't know, Nick. Either the neighbor, Mrs Diaz, scared her witless so your mom is taking precautions, or we are looking at early dementia. I have no clue.'

He sighed. 'I agree. Everyone gets forgetful as they age. How do we draw any kind of line?'

'Your old friend and my new friend, Alexis, said her grandfather suffers from some kind of dementia. Why has this become so commonplace?'

'Robert Parker?' he asked. 'What a shame. In my non-medical opinion, either our environment is to blame or people are simply living longer. Bodies might last longer with medical advances, but our brains might have a pre-determined shelf life.'

'My grandmother would say, "No one can outsmart God. He has the final say". And the longer I live, the more I agree with her.'

Nick was about to comment when Jill's phone rang.

'How odd,' she said, reading the caller-ID on her phone. 'It's Sheriff Jeff Adkins from Roseville. What on earth could he want with me?'

Unfortunately, Jill didn't put the call on speaker. Instead, she uttered a series of 'oh my' and 'dear me'. When she hung up, she swiveled towards him on the seat. 'Change of plans. Would you mind heading to Roseville? My grandmother and Aunt Dot have landed in a heap of trouble. I'll give you the gory details along the way.'

EIGHT

Jill slipped her phone into her purse, leaned her head back and closed her eyes.

'Uh, oh.' Nick took his eyes off the road to Roseville just for a moment. 'How can two old ladies get themselves into trouble during a book club meeting with their cronies?'

'Did you forget the part about bourbon along with the books?' Jill shook her head. 'Head to the sheriff's office. Aunt Dot and my grandmother have been arrested. You should still know the way since you worked there for two weeks.'

'*Arrested?* You're pulling my leg. Tonight was only their second official meeting.'

'Correct. They were supposed to snack on tiny sandwiches and sample bourbon crafted by Uncle Roger, while discussing the auspicious merits of *Little Women*.'

'And?' Nick prompted and increased his speed on the open road.

'Aunt Dot happened upon a thirty-year-old bottle of Black Creek Reserve in the library. Apparently, Uncle Roger had been saving it for a special occasion. Dot got the bright idea of selling shots of the stuff to raise money for the local food pantry. She and Grandma put up posters all over town, asking people to come to Sweet Dreams B and B from six to eight o'clock to help a good cause. The ladies had planned to talk about the book after the general public left.'

'That was such a bad idea.'

Jill nodded. 'Aunt Dot set up folding tables and chairs on the porch. Grandma baked lots of cookies to nibble and made plenty of coffee and tea. She also sold little bags of cookies for five dollars each.'

'I'm afraid to ask how much they were charging for a drink.'

Jill swiveled to face him. 'Fifty dollars, sweet man. Those two entrepreneurs were charging people fifty bucks for a shot of Roger's good stuff. And plenty of people were willing to pay that much. Word got around through some kind of bourbon grapevine. By six thirty the porch was mobbed. One guy told Dot that her price was too low for thirty-year-old whiskey, that she could easily get a couple hundred. He paid a hundred for his shot, since it was for charity.'

Nick clenched down on his back molars. 'Surely Dorothy Clark knew that liquor licenses are closely monitored in Kentucky.'

'Dot thought that since the money was going to charity, there wouldn't be a problem.'

'Who blew the whistle on them?' Nick asked.

'First Gordy Clark, the operations manager at Black Creek,

showed up to insist Aunt Dot stop selling booze from her front porch. But Dot was down to the last few shots so she paid no attention to him. Then one of her neighbors, either a teetotaler or someone who didn't like boisterous crowds, called the sheriff. He threw my kinfolk in the clink.'

'Take heart,' Nick said, keeping his focus on the road. 'If you look hard enough you can find a criminal element in the best of families.'

Jill pulled her sunglasses down with one finger. 'Are you having fun, Magic Man? This isn't funny. If the story makes the Louisville and Lexington newspapers, it could hurt Aunt Dot's business.'

'Or it might draw bourbon aficionados from around the world.'

'Please take this seriously.' Jill's voice cracked. 'I'm worried the ladies will have to spend the night in jail.'

Nick reached over to pat her arm. 'Sheriff Adkins would never keep them overnight. He probably just wants to restore law and order in Roseville. You know, there never was much trouble until Granny Vanderpool blew into town.'

Jill punched his arm playfully but couldn't keep from smiling.

For the next ten miles neither said a word until a phone call interrupted their quiet introspection. 'Nick Harris,' he answered when he didn't recognize the number. 'Hey, Detective. Thanks for the callback.'

Jill listened to Nick murmur a series of banalities like: 'Is that right?' and 'That's a surprise'. Unfortunately, he didn't put the caller on speaker. When Nick finally hung up, he stared mutely at the road.

'Well?' Jill demanded. 'What was the big surprise?'

'That was my friend on the Louisville police force. I asked him to keep me posted on the William Scott case. In all likelihood, Otto Bach, the disgruntled employee recently fired at Parker Estate, isn't our killer.'

'The guy who poisoned his neighbor's dog?' she asked, incredulous. 'Didn't the cops find an array of poisons in his house?'

'Yes, but none of them matched what killed the master distiller. The lab finished the tox screen and identified it as a rare toxin that mimics symptoms of a heart attack. It's very difficult to detect in the blood, but a high concentration was found in

Mr Scott's liver. This was no weedkiller or garden variety insecticide. So far the police haven't found evidence that Bach ever purchased the toxin.'

Jill crossed her arms over her chest. 'What explanation did the lunatic have as to why he has so many dangerous poisons?'

'Bach told the detective he wanted to start a pest control company with his brother. The brother, who's probably also a wacko, confirmed the plan.'

Jill smiled. 'It's funny to hear a cop use the term "wacko".'

'I only use the word when I'm not working. Today, I'm on a date with my best girl.'

'Which day does your worst girl get?'

'She can have any day she wants.' Nick winked in her direction, which resulted in a second punch to his arm.

When they reached the charming downtown area of Roseville, all was quiet with order restored at Sweet Dreams B & B. At the sheriff's department, Jeff Adkins waved them into his office the moment they walked through the door. 'Ah, Lieutenant Harris and Miss Curtis, a pleasure to see you both,' he drawled. 'Have a seat.'

'The pleasure is ours, sir.' Nick settled comfortably in a chair.

'Hi, Sheriff,' Jill greeted, too nervous to sit. 'I hope my relatives haven't caused too much trouble.'

A grin turned Adkins' face into a roadmap of wrinkles. 'I've had more cantankerous inmates than Mrs Vanderpool and Mrs Clark. But I must say both are accustomed to rationalization to get their way. They couldn't quite understand that good intentions and a worthy cause don't circumvent the law.'

'Where are they now?' Jill gripped the back of a chair.

'I considered putting them in a cell, but at the last minute I opted for an interview room. With only two plastic chairs, half a table and one-way glass, the room's austerity might convince them that selling booze without a permit is a crime.'

'If you'd thrown them in with hardened criminals, they would only learn more tricks,' Nick said, as though not taking the matter seriously.

Adkins laced his fingers together. 'I talked to an ATF agent who's willing to let them go with a warning. I'm just waiting for a call-back from the county prosecutor to make sure she's OK with me not filing charges. I don't want that neighbor complaining we gave special treatment to a bourbon master's widow.'

'No jail time, not even a fine?' Jill asked. 'Thanks, Sheriff Adkins.'

Adkins rubbed his stubbly chin. 'You two must reinforce this is not to happen again.'

'You can be sure of that.' Nick pushed to his feet. 'Can we take them home? I'm sure they're worried about the B and B in their absence.'

'A couple of book-clubbers promised to clean up and then lock up. I'd bet they're both ready to hit the sack. By the way, your grandmother purchased the last shot, Miss Curtis. Mrs Vanderpool pledged fifty dollars from her next pension check to the county food bank.'

Jill dropped her chin to her chest. 'My granny doesn't even drink. We might need EMTs to revive her.'

Sheriff Adkins led them down the hall to interview room two and swept open the door. Aunt Dot appeared to be praying while Granny was fast asleep, head on the table. A light snore rumbled from her open mouth with each breath.

'Jill, Nick, oh my goodness!' Dot closed her prayer book, her eyes filling with tears. 'I'd hoped and prayed Jeff wouldn't call you. I am so ashamed.'

'No need to be embarrassed.' Jill wrapped an arm around Dot's shoulder. 'Just promise me you'll never do anything like this again.' She felt like a parent scolding a naughty teenager after a missed curfew. 'What you two did was illegal.'

'Please don't blame Emma. This was my fault. I talked her into it.'

'Wake up, Granny.' Jill gently shook her grandmother's shoulder. 'Time to go home.'

Emma popped upright and gazed around the room. 'Are we still in the slammer? I hope no one stole the cookie sale money. I raised eighteen dollars before the cops busted the place.'

Jill felt her cheeks redden. 'Granny, where did you learn such talk?'

'In the nursing home. We never missed an episode of *NCIS*,

FBI, or *Blue Bloods*.' Emma smiled, but continued to hold her head with both hands.

'Sheriff, will you release these two on their own recognizance, pending the prosecutor's decision?' Nick asked. 'I'll take personal responsibility.'

Adkins pretended to ponder the question. 'All right, Trooper, but if they open another bottle and start peddling shots, all three of you will spend the night in the county jail.'

'The bar is closed.' Emma sliced the air with her hand. 'I won't jeopardize my granddaughter's future with this handsome man. After all, he's got a good job.'

While Jill cringed with embarrassment, Aunt Dot rose to her feet and placed her hand over her heart. 'You have my word, Sheriff. No more selling bourbon from Sweet Dreams and no more fundraising except on church property, since they have a non-profit license.'

'All right, you two may go. Drive safely, Trooper. And good luck, Miss Curtis.'

Good luck, indeed, she thought.

The club members who'd stayed behind to clean up the B & B thanked her and Nick for bailing out their fearless leader when they got back the previous evening. Jill didn't correct them that posting bail hadn't been necessary. It was better everyone involved realized the serious nature of their behavior.

On the way home her grandmother and Aunt Dot had been meek and contrite. After their friends left, they invited her and Nick to spend the night in a guest room, but looked relieved when they declined. Since she and Nick both had plenty to do in Louisville, they left without as much as a cup of coffee with the elderly lawbreakers. When Jill finally reached her hotel room, she fell asleep the moment her head hit the pillow.

Early the next morning the human alarm clock pounded on her door. 'Get up, Curtis,' Michael demanded. 'Let's get in line for the first newly resumed tour of Parker Distillery. With Mr Scott's death, there'll be plenty of interest from both locals and tourists.'

Knowing better than to argue, Jill dragged herself from the bedsheets and headed to the shower without bothering with caffeine. She'd have time for coffee along the way.

Michael had been right about the tourists. A crowd had already formed at the distillery's main entrance when they arrived, so they joined the second tour group. After they flashed their purple VIP passes, the guide explained exactly where Michael was allowed to shoot footage, but they could wander anywhere.

Good to be a VIP, Jill thought, pulling out her spiral notebook. But she took few notes during the tour since Alexis Scott had given her plenty of background information. Instead, Jill jotted a few unusual details that readers always enjoyed, then waited patiently while Michael took more video than he needed. The man never cared how much he cut as long as he ended up with flawless footage for the segment.

Just like at the previous distilleries, the final tour stop was a gift shop where those over twenty-one could sample or purchase bourbon. Jill bought an amusing coffee mug but declined the samples. Ten thirty in the morning was a tad early for strong spirits. She headed to the parking lot to wait for her perfectionist partner.

Michael walked from the distillery sporting a big smile. 'When you see your new best friend, Miss Scott, give her my compliments. The production department runs like a top.' He stowed his equipment in the trunk.

'I'll be sure to tell her. Where to now, Erickson?'

Michael stared at her as though she'd lost her mind. 'Back to the hotel, silly girl. I want to edit the video while it's fresh in my mind.'

Jill rolled her eyes. 'Would you mind taking Uber so I can use the car? Since my additions to the story won't take long, I want to take full advantage of this purple pass.' She held it up. 'I plan to wander around and question the employees.'

Michael shrugged. 'Sounds good. Then are you coming back to the hotel or do you have other stops?'

'Not sure, but you have plenty to keep you busy until I get back.'

'What about dinner tonight?' he asked, not giving up easily. 'Or do you have plans with Nick?'

'No plans so far. Nick's dealing with a family drama. But if he calls, we'll all have dinner together.'

Michael brought up the Uber app on his phone. 'Nick might as well know who he's up against, competition-wise.'

Jill laughed at his joke, since they were as romantically well suited as oil and water. When his ride pulled to the curb, she waved goodbye and headed to the employee entrance. After she flashed her laminated purple pass and ID the security guard waved her in.

'Come on in, Miss Curtis.' He tipped his hat as he handed back her driver's license. 'Miss Scott mentioned you'd be dropping by.'

Jill didn't know where to go first. She wandered aimlessly until she located a central lobby and chose the door marked 'Sales and Marketing' as her first destination. Inside everyone was so busy after the hiatus, nobody even noticed her. Of course, she didn't let that stand in her way.

'Excuse me,' Jill said to a well-dressed employee. 'I'm a journalist, here with Alexis Scott's permission. I'm writing a travel feature on the corporate dynamics of Parkers Estate Distillery.' She handed her a business card.

The woman blinked not once, but twice. 'This is the *sales* department, Miss . . . Curtis.' She read from the card. 'Unless you wish to order full cases of bourbon, I have nothing to say that would be helpful to a travel article.' The woman couldn't get away fast enough.

Undeterred, Jill chose a younger and less fashionable employee this time, who was on the phone in a small cubicle. 'Excuse me, miss,' Jill said when the woman hung up. 'I'm a journalist, hoping you could answer a few questions.' She produced a magnanimous smile.

The woman glanced around, bewildered. 'How did you get in here? This office isn't on the tour or usually accessible to the public.'

'Oops, I almost forgot.' Jill pulled the purple pass from her purse. 'Alexis Scott is a personal friend and gave me permission.'

'In that case, my name is Rayna,' she said, her expression warming considerably. 'What do you want to know?'

'I'm Jill. Mind if I sit?' Perching on the edge of a chair, she pulled out her notebook. 'What was the impact of Mr Scott's death on the employees? For instance, was the master distiller distant and reserved, so his passing didn't affect people on a personal level? Or was Mr Scott friendly and open to everyone, no matter their job in the company?'

Rayna nodded enthusiastically. 'Definitely the latter. William Scott was one of the nicest men I've ever met. He never failed to notice when I wore something new to work.'

'So he commented on your outfit, not the quality of your work?'

Rayna's face screwed up. 'Well, yeah. Mr Scott wasn't concerned with my job around here. After all, he was the *master distiller*, not one of my supervisors.'

Jill feigned confusion and pushed harder. 'Do you think Mr Scott just noticed you? For instance, would he have noticed if a male employee wore a new suit to work?'

Rayna giggled like a child. 'What planet are you from, girl? Mr Scott noticed all the women who worked here, not just me. But it wasn't anything inappropriate. The boss just knew that women liked compliments – to be noticed – while men usually couldn't care less.' Suddenly, Rayna's expression sobered. 'Make sure you don't make that sound sleazy in your article.' She pointed at Jill's notes.

Feigning shock, Jill closed the notebook. 'Absolutely not. Like I said, Alexis is a personal friend of mine. I'm not looking to cast aspersion on the dead, especially since Mr and Mrs Scott probably had a perfect marriage.'

Just for a split second, Rayna's expression revealed the truth. 'I wouldn't go quite that far. But I know that Mr Scott never flirted with me or any women his daughter's age.' She swiveled back to her computer. 'Now I gotta get back to work. Good luck with your article.'

Jill left the woman feeling blindsided. *Did she just imply William Scott hit on women close to his own age?* This wasn't what she'd been looking for in human interest stories. Knowing how close Alexis had been with her dad, part of Jill wanted to head for the exit and forget about pursuing more information. Then her journalist side began to rationalize: *Just because I find something out doesn't mean I have to use it in my article.*

Jill left the sales department and headed down the long hallway to production, where employees dressed more casually than those in the office. Assuming she shouldn't approach workers on the line, Jill followed signs to the employee breakroom. A potential interviewee – a fortyish blonde with a great figure – stood at the vending machine, deciding on which candy bar to buy. Jill immediately dug a buck from her purse and waited her turn.

'Which one to pick?' she mused, inserting her dollar bill.

'They're all fresh,' said the blonde. 'The guy refills the machine twice a week.' She unwrapped her purchase and bit into something nutty.

'That looks yummy. You helped make up my mind.' Jill pushed the button for the same candy.

'Glad to help.' The blonde took another bite while assessing Jill's appearance. 'Are you new here?'

Jill dropped the bar in her purse and stretched out a hand. 'I'm Jill Curtis, a journalist from Chicago. I'm writing an article on the late master distiller and the distillery in general.'

The woman shook hands reluctantly. 'Is that right? Do any bosses know you're snooping around in here?'

'Alexis Scott does. She's one of the bosses, right?' Jill flashed her purple pass.

'Alexis is the biggest and baddest, now that Bill is dead.' She took another bite of candy.

Jill unwrapped her bar to buy herself time. 'You called Mr Scott "Bill". Was he on a first name basis with everyone?'

She shrugged. 'He was with me. Bill was an all-around nice guy. You won't find one person in this plant with anything nasty to say about him.'

'I know the women liked Mr Scott, but what about the men? Was he friendly with male employees too?'

The corners of her lips turned down. 'Sure, with lots of them. Look, I don't know why Miss Scott gave you permission to poke around, but I don't like what you're implying. You should stop asking questions that are none of your business.' She tossed her wrapper towards the trashcan, missed, and stomped off.

Their conversation had drawn attention. Now a few people whispered among themselves. One pulled out a phone and appeared to be sending a text while another glared at Jill menacingly. Since no one looked receptive to an interview, Jill left the employee lounge and followed the arrows toward the rickhouse. However, she didn't even get close to where barrels of bourbon were aged to perfection.

'Hold up there, Miss Curtis,' a voice called behind her.

Jill turned to see the security guard who'd met her at the door. The man was no longer smiling. 'People have complained you're bothering workers on the line.'

'I haven't gone anywhere near the line.'

'And you're asking inappropriate questions about Mr Scott.' He rubbed the back of his neck. 'I'll take that pass and I'd like you to leave, young lady.'

'But Alexis said I could—'

'I'm sure Miss Scott didn't authorize questions about her father's relationships with other women.' The guard hissed the words through gritted teeth and pulled out his phone. 'Should we ask her directly?'

'That won't be necessary. I'll go quietly.' Like a chastised dog, Jill trailed him down the hall, into the elevator, and out the same door she'd come in. Inside her car, she pondered the guard's choice of words: instead of 'how well the master distiller got along with female employees,' he'd used the term 'her father's relationships with other women'. Had the guard implied that Mr Scott was involved with someone other than his wife?

Jill wasn't interested in gossip for her article and she had no desire to embarrass Alexis. But if William had a roving eye, did that put Mama Dearest into the category of murder suspect? Jill's suspicions about Rose deepened. With her magical purple pass rescinded, she decided to go straight to the source and set her GPS for Parker Estate. With any luck, Rose Parker Scott would be willing to chat.

The uniformed maid who answered the door confirmed that Mrs Scott was home but not receiving guests today.

'Could you ask if she might make an exception for a friend of her daughter's? I promise not to stay long.'

'I'm sorry, ma'am, but when Miss Rose takes a book to the solarium she doesn't like to be disturbed.' The door began to swing shut.

'Oh, please?' she whined. 'I won't be in town much longer.'

'Leave your business card, if you have one. Then come back

later in the week.' Without waiting for Jill to dig out a card, the maid shut the door in her face.

It took Jill a moment to remember what a solarium was, then she bolted around the house to the garden. The dome-shaped all-glass addition was easy enough to find . . . and easy enough to spot the sole occupant inside. Rose was fast asleep on an upholstered chaise with a novel and cup of tea beside her. Jill strode to the door and knocked before her courage evaporated.

'Hello, Mrs Scott?' She tapped gently on the glass. 'It me, Jill. Your daughter's friend.'

The befuddled woman bolted upright, then stared through the wavy glass as though trying to place her. When she did, Rose padded to the door, glowering. 'Why are you knocking here? I'm sure Alexis made it clear she doesn't live in the main house.'

'Yes, ma'am, she did.' Jill clasped her hands in front of her. 'But it's you I wish to talk to.'

The glower morphed to confusion. 'What on earth for? By now you must have plenty for your distillery article. My father said you even paid him a visit.'

Jill racked her brain for something that would open the door. 'Yes, Mr Parker provided excellent historical background. But my lady readers would love to know how a beautiful, couture-dressed woman could deal with corn, mash, and barrel-charring, yet always look chic.'

Flattery, no matter how insincere, usually worked. The door swung wide. 'I can give you five minutes, then I need to rest. Tonight is a fundraiser for the local battered women's shelter.' Returning to the chaise, Rose pointed at the other chair.

'That's a great cause.' Jill sat and braced her notebook against her knee.

'I'm not sure what you want to hear. I'm seldom at our headquarters or inside the plant. I might like bourbon, but I don't like the smell of distilling alcohol.' Rose's nose wrinkled.

'That surprises me. One of the girls in marketing said they enjoyed seeing you and Mr Scott working side by side. They hoped for that kind of relationship when they married.'

One thin eyebrow arched. 'Are you trying to pull my chain? No one in marketing would have said that. That particular department was William's favorite hunting ground.'

'Hunting for what?' Jill asked.

'Certainly not rabbits or squirrels, you little ninny.' Mama Scott's smile was downright gleeful. 'For his next female conquest.'

'You mean you knew your husband . . .'

'Played around on me? Yes, but I was free to do the same. And in my younger days, I took advantage of our *open* relationship.'

Shock and incredulity bloomed across Jill's face, rendering her momentarily speechless.

'Haven't you ever heard of the free-love generation?' Rose asked with a sneer.

'Yes, but I thought that was confined to hippies out in California.'

'What a prude you are, Jill. But now I see why my daughter likes you. You two have so much in common.' Strolling to the sideboard, Rose refilled her cup of tea. 'I'm afraid that's all the time I have for stupid questions. You may show yourself out.'

Jill, however, remained where she was. 'Why on earth did you marry William? You're the one who will inherit this gorgeous estate and the distillery.'

Already stretched out on the chaise once more, Rose lifted her head and glared. 'I owe you no explanation. And if you print any of this, you and your newspaper will be sued. However, I will answer so you don't remain stupid your entire life.' She pressed a button to bring the chair upright. 'I thought Bill knew more about business than he did. And with his good looks, I knew he would give me a beautiful child, which he did. Bill had always been discreet; he didn't spend my money foolishly, and he accompanied me everywhere I wanted to go. That man looked fabulous in a tuxedo. So all in all, he wasn't a bad husband and I might even miss him.' Rose sneered like the evil queen in a storybook. 'Close the door behind you, Miss Curtis, and forget how to find my private sanctuary.'

Jill couldn't wait to get out of there and take a shower. Instead of walking, she ran to her car. Rose was right – Jill would never write or speak about this to anyone. Not because she feared a lawsuit, but because she hoped Alexis never learned the tawdry details of her parents' marriage. If Alexis even suspected, she'd probably remain single her entire life.

Before leaving the estate, Jill texted her partner that she was on her way back and sent a second text to Nick, indicating she was free for dinner and that Michael would be joining them. Nick immediately replied that he didn't mind a crowd of thirty as long as they were together.

So very sweet. Keep that up and there might be a goodnight kiss in the offing. As Jill turned onto the county road from the Parker driveway, she spotted something in her rear-view mirror she didn't like – a black, full-sized SUV parked on the berm. If she wasn't mistaken, it was the same black SUV she'd noticed next to Michael's car at the distillery. Was she being tailed? And if so, by whom?

As the distance between her vehicle and the SUV grew in her rear-view mirror, Jill released the breath she'd been holding and tried to relax. Suddenly, the SUV spun around one-hundred-and-eighty degrees and accelerated to breakneck speed. It took little time for the vehicle to catch up with hers. Jill wasn't imagining anything. She was being followed.

NINE

Jill drove above the speed limit all the way to the hotel, hoping to lose her tail in traffic or even better, attract the attention of the police. She would happily explain why she was speeding to the officer. No such luck on either count. By the time she left the car with the valet, the same black Escalade was idling on the ramp to the garage. Part of her wanted to run inside, jump in the elevator with other people, and lock herself in the bathroom of their suite. But another part of her seethed with anger. How dare this guy – assuming the occupant was male – stalk her to a five-star hotel like the Thurman House in broad daylight with impunity?

Jill waited under the canopy until her brave side won out. Then she stomped over to the Escalade's darkly tinted driver's window and rapped on the glass. 'Excuse me,' she said. 'I'd like a word with you.'

A moment later the window lowered. Inside sat a thirty-ish man wearing sunglasses even though glare was no longer a problem at this time of the day. 'May I help you, miss?' he asked with a deeper accent than most residents of Louisville.

'Yes, you can help me.' Jill crossed her arms. 'I'd like to know why you were parked outside Parker Estate and why you followed me downtown. What is your problem?'

'Yeah, I'll tell you *my problem.* As a close friend of Miss Scott's, I'm concerned for her safety and that of her family.' He glared down his nose with haughty indignation. 'Why is a tabloid journalist from Chicago showing up everywhere Alexis goes and dropping in on the family unannounced? Can't you respect a family's need to grieve in private?'

Jill pressed a hand to her chest. 'I am not a tabloid journalist. I write respected travel features for syndicated papers and internet sites. I am no threat to Alexis or her family. I'm simply trying to . . .' She stopped herself before uttering the word 'murder'. The cause of death hadn't hit the papers yet, and the more time the police had to investigate the better. 'I'm trying to be supportive of Alexis. We were friends in college. What did you say your name was?'

'My name is Ross Lacey.' A muscle tightened in his neck as he pushed up his sleeve to check his watch. 'And I'm late for an appointment. I hope you're telling me the truth, Jill Curtis, because things don't go well for people who lie to me.' He threw the SUV into gear and backed down the ramp into traffic, triggering a barrage of horn blasts on the street.

As Jill walked into the hotel, she realized two things: Ross Lacey had just threatened her. And two, she had never mentioned her name. Jill wasn't sure which bothered her more. On the way to her room she also realized it was time to tell her partner exactly why she spent so much time with Alexis Scott.

'I knew it,' Michael shouted, jumping to his feet. 'You're starting to think every death is suspicious and murderers lurk behind each tree and hedgerow.'

Jill sucked in a breath to muster patience. 'No, not every tree. Some trees are too skinny. And I'm not the only one who finds

Mr Scott's passing suspicious. Detective Grimes of the Louisville homicide department thinks so too.'

'You probably talked her into the notion,' Michael muttered, shaking his finger at her.

'No way. That cop doesn't even like me. It was the M.E.'s report that made Detective Grimes a believer. Mr Scott died due to an ingested toxin.'

Michael's brows knit together. 'What kind of toxin?'

'Results from the tox screen revealed a rare poison, which mimics a myocardial infraction, had killed him.'

'Aren't you pleased as a pig in a corn crib?' He guzzled half a can of Coke.

Although the analogy sounded strange coming from a city boy, Jill let it pass. 'I'm certainly not pleased that Mr Scott was murdered, but since Alexis asked for my help, I couldn't say no. Look how many doors she opened for us.'

Michael scrubbed his face with his palms. 'You're not a cop. You graduated with an English degree and a minor in journalism.'

'I know that, and I'm nowhere near as involved with this investigation as I was in Roseville. The homicide department has the situation under control.'

'Does Nick know what you're up to?'

'He does.' Michael's expression remained skeptical, so Jill continued, 'You can ask him tonight. He's having dinner with us and it's your turn to pick the restaurant.'

'Don't think I won't,' Michael snapped, already Googling restaurants in the area. 'I can't believe Nick would let you stick your nose in another murder.'

'Nobody *lets* me do anything, buster. I march to my own drummer.'

He smirked. 'We'll see how much marching you do with Nick around.'

Jill stuck out her tongue on the way to her bedroom. She only had an hour before Nick picked them up, so she put it to good use.

Alexis picked up on the first ring. 'Hi, Jill, did everything go OK during the tour? I apologize for your earlier run-in with our security guard. Was Michael able to get the video he needed?'

'Yeah, everything went fine. Michael sends his gratitude and said your distillery runs like a well-oiled top.'

'Thanks, I've hired some good people. They make my job easy.'

'I doubt that. They just make your job look easy.' Jill let a few silent moments pass. 'I didn't call about the tour. I wanted to ask you about someone.'

'My mother, the annihilator?' Alexis asked, laughing. 'She told me you were sneaking through the bushes, spying in windows. Then you barged in when she was resting in the solarium. Those are her words, not mine. How on earth did you get on Mom's bad side?'

'I don't know, but I wasn't exactly sneaking around. The maid told me where she was and I figured out where the solarium might be. I did knock before I entered.'

'I know you did, but why is she so mad?'

'I have no idea, but your mother isn't who I wanted to ask you about.'

There was a momentary hesitation. 'Then who?'

'Ross Lacey.'

'How on earth did you meet him?'

'He was parked at the end of your driveway when I left your mother. I'd noticed the same SUV in the distillery lot after the tour. At first, I thought I was imagining things, but a car followed me back to the Thurman House Hotel. That's when I confronted the driver.'

'Oh, no, you didn't,' Alexis moaned.

'Why? Is this Lacey guy dangerous?' Jill glanced over her shoulder to make sure she'd shut the bedroom door.

'I hope not. I really don't know. What did Lacey say? Why was he following you?'

'He said he was worried a sleazy tabloid reporter was bothering the Scott family during their time of grief. He wanted to scare me away. Amusing, no?'

Apparently not amusing, because Alexis didn't laugh. 'Stay away from Ross. Who knows what he's capable of? I thought he was out of my life forever until I saw him at Dad's memorial service.'

'If you were close friends, he probably just wanted to pay his respects,' Jill suggested.

'Ross hated my father, and the feeling was mutual. He accused my dad of trying to break us up.'

'You two were in a relationship?'

'Only in Ross's mind. He and I dated a few times and then he started getting possessive. He wanted to know where I went after work and didn't like me meeting my friends. He even criticized some of my outfits that according to him were too suggestive for the office. After three or four dates the guy thought he owned me.' Alexis clucked her tongue.

'A control freak,' Jill concluded.

'Definitely. Lacey left a sympathy card with the funeral director which I read the next day. Inside was a hundred-dollar bill toward the charity of my choice, along with the message: *I will always love you, Ross*. We never uttered those kinds of words to each other. We never got close to that.'

'How did you meet him?'

'Parker Estate held a charity fundraiser for the Red Cross and sold tickets at one hundred dollars each. We donated the beverages while local restaurants donated the food. It was a huge success. Ross approached me that night and struck up a conversation. We seemed to get along well. So when he asked me out, I said "yes".'

'One hundred bucks a ticket . . . what does Lacey do for a living? I noticed he drives an expensive car.'

'He told me he was a day-trader in stocks and bonds. But much of what he said turned out to be lies.'

'Such as?' Jill asked, unsure where this was going.

'He said his mom was an opera singer and that his dad wrote stage plays. But I found no evidence of their association with the arts. They live on a small farm near Bowling Green.'

'Did Lacey ever get physical or violent with you? He came off as a bit threatening to me.'

'Oh, Jill, I'm sorry you got dragged into this,' Alexis murmured. 'Ross never got physical with me, but he did have a nasty run-in with my dad.'

A frisson of fear ran up Jill's spine. 'Mind telling me what happened?'

'After I broke it off with him, Ross began parking outside the distillery so he'd see me when I left the office. I ignored him for the first week and drove past his car. When he was still there on the Monday, I made the mistake of mentioning it to my family.' Alexis released a loud sigh. 'The next day Dad and a few security guards were waiting for Ross when he took up his vigil across the street. Dad told Lacey he would file a restraining order if he didn't go away. Ross became irate and started cursing my father. So Dad got mad and said he'd pegged Lacey for a lowlife right from the start and said he would never be good enough for me.'

Jill shuddered. 'What happened next?'

'Ross tried to exit the car, but the guards held the door shut. Ross screamed foul words that Dad wouldn't repeat. Dad said if he ignored the restraining order, his security team would "take care of him". I know that sounds horrible, but it was just an empty threat. My father would never hurt a fly.'

'I believe you, but I'm worried Lacey might not be the type to take threats lightly.'

'You don't think . . .' Alexis let the rest of the sentence hang in the air.

'Who knows? Someone killed your father and we shouldn't rule out anyone, especially since Lacey has difficulty discerning reality. In my opinion, saying "I will always love you" is a tad creepy after you made the situation very clear to him.'

'I swear I did. I tried to let him down easy, but he started crying. Ross claimed he moved to Louisville to be close to me. I said that was a mistake and we had no future together. Then I hung up.'

'Did you follow through with the restraining order?'

'Yes, and apparently it did the trick. Or at least my father's intimidation worked. Ross didn't show up the next Monday and hasn't been back since. I never saw him again until the memorial service, but I must admit I haven't been looking that hard. At least in the church he stayed far away from me.'

'I think we need to tell Detective Grimes about this nutcase.'

'OK, if you think we should. I'm sorry I didn't tell you about Ross when you asked about enemies. I wasn't thinking in terms of my potential enemies. I was embarrassed how things turned out with Lacey. I should have broken it off sooner.'

'Hey, don't beat yourself up. Nobody is handed a playbook or roadmap when they start dating. We all make mistakes. Let's just make sure Lacey isn't guilty of something much worse than being gum stuck to your shoe.'

'Should I call Detective Grimes?'

Jill reconsidered this. 'So far he hasn't violated the restraining order. Right now following *me* around Louisville isn't against the law. Tonight I'm having dinner with Nick. If it's OK with you, I'd like to run this by him.'

'Of course it is. I trust both of you with my life.'

'Hopefully it won't come down to that.' Jill forced a chuckle. 'Since it might be late when I get back to my room, I'll call you in the morning. Lock your door tonight, Alexis. This might be a good time to adopt a big dog from the animal shelter, one you can train to keep the creeps at bay.'

Jill hung up just as a text buzzed from Nick. *Come downstairs where I have a surprise waiting. Bring your partner, but no surprise for him.*

She only needed five minutes to change her clothes and brush her teeth. Then she and Michael fought their way through a crowded lobby to the entrance. Nick was parked in the exact spot Ross Lacey had occupied earlier. Her surprise turned out to be the largest bouquet of red roses she'd ever seen. And for no reason at all.

Jill decided to wait with her update about Lacey until after their delicious entrées in the Italian restaurant. *Leave it to Michael to choose pasta, rich sauces, and bread dipped in olive oil.* During dinner Jill and Nick told Michael about yesterday's trip to Roseville. Since twenty-four hours had passed, they were able to imbue the story with more humor than they'd felt at the time.

'Are you telling me Sheriff Adkins arrested your grandmother and Mrs Clark?' Michael's eyes bugged from his face. 'But I thought Adkins and his wife were lifelong friends of Dot and Roger Clark.'

'They were, but a sheriff must uphold the law no matter how fond he is of the criminal.' Nick delivered this maxim with a perfectly straight face.

'Criminal?' Michael scoffed. 'The last time I saw Granny Vanderpool she was eating lime Jello in a nursing home while *Wheel of Fortune* blared on the TV.'

Jill swallowed her last bite of lasagna. 'Now she's helped her cousin turn Sweet Dreams into a hot spot, where people who love good bourbon love to hang out.' She laughed at the memory.

'I hope they plan to walk the straight-and-narrow from now on.' Nick pushed away his plate and folded his napkin. 'How did the tour go? Did either of you learn anything interesting?' His gaze rotated from one to the other.

Michael took a swallow of red wine. 'I learned that Jill has been investigating a murder, just like in Roseville, instead of finishing our travel feature in a timely fashion.'

'This is nothing like Roseville,' she said, frowning at Michael. 'I'm merely poking around for leads for Detective Grimes to follow. After all, their current suspect was ruled out by toxicology.' Jill turned to Michael. 'A recently fired employee had been found with dozens of poisons in his home, but Nick learned last night that none were a match for what killed William Scott. So the police have to let him go.'

'Jill dragged you into this, too?' Michael asked Nick. 'I thought you were on vacation.'

Nick refilled his wineglass from the bottle. 'I am on vacation, but since Alexis is an old friend and Jill is a new friend, I'm serving as an advisor.'

'Why am I not surprised?' Michael's gaze shifted from one to the other. 'Life just spins in circles in the Keystone state.'

Jill suddenly felt the need to stick up for Kentucky. 'Oh, like only *normal* people live in Chicago?'

Her comment triggered plenty of laughs at the table.

'Before this conversation deteriorates into fisticuffs, did you discover anything new, Miss Curtis?' Nick asked.

'I did.' Jill leaned back as the waiter delivered dessert. 'After our tour of Parker Distillery, I poked around inside their main office and in the employee lounge. I learned some interesting details about the master distiller.' Jill waited for a reaction, but both men remained focused on their tiramisu. 'Mr Scott had an eye for the girls, as my mama used to say, and was definitely friendlier with the female employees than the males.'

'In this day and age?' Michael peered up from his dessert. 'I'm shocked. That behavior is so twentieth century.'

'Be that as it may, I went to the Parker Estate to discuss this with Mrs Scott.'

Nick dropped his fork on his plate. 'Without proof that these rumors and innuendos are true? Not only can you be sued, but you will certainly lose Alexis's trust.'

Jill hadn't expected that particular response from Nick. 'I didn't accuse Mr Scott of anything. I merely dropped a few innuendos of my own and Rose laughed in my face. She described their marriage as *open* and said she enjoyed the same privileges as her husband.'

'I don't understand why you're meddling in their personal business.' Ice crystals could have formed on Nick's words. 'I know you wouldn't smear William Scott in your article, so why are you stirring up trouble?'

Jill blinked. 'I wanted to learn if Rose had a motive for murder – her husband's bad behavior. If I found out my husband had been unfaithful, I might be tempted to kill him. But if Alexis doesn't know the truth about their marriage, she won't find out from me.'

Nick studied her from across the table. 'Now that you've interviewed Rose, do you consider her a suspect?'

Goosebumps rose on Jill's neck. 'I haven't ruled her out, but I bumped into a more viable suspect as I was leaving the estate.'

That caught everyone's attention. Jill had no choice but to launch into a full report of the drama with Ross Lacey. When she was done, she didn't know which man was madder.

'Good grief, Jill,' Michael moaned. 'Leave murder investigation to the pros and stick to the tourists!'

'Are you saying this Lacey threatened you?' Nick's complexion darkened to the color of port wine.

'In a manner of speaking, yes. He wants me to stop bothering Alexis and her family. Lacey said they are close friends, but according to Alexis, that's not true.' Jill then relayed the details of her before-dinner conversation.

'Do something, Nick,' Michael demanded, scowling at Jill. 'Before this lunatic gets herself killed.' He shook his finger at her.

'Does Alexis still have a restraining order against Lacey?' Nick asked, ignoring Michael.

'Yes, but so far he's never violated it. Even at Mr Scott's memorial service, he kept far enough away from her.'

'If Lacey really is a sociopath, he might have reason to kill William Scott. But right now, he hasn't broken any laws. The threat against you will boil down to his word against yours.' Nick rubbed his chin, a sure sign an idea was in the works. 'If you and Alexis are willing, you could draw Lacey into the space restriction of the TRO.'

'But isn't that entrapment?' asked Michael, jumping into the discussion.

'No, it's not, because Jill and Alexis aren't law enforcement.' Nick answered without taking his eyes off Jill. 'There is risk involved, but I'm afraid if we don't try something, you'll do something even riskier.'

'I'm in.' Jill rubbed her palms together. 'What's the plan, boss?'

'Simmer down, while I work out the details with Detective Grimes. If Lacey is involved with the murder, Grimes needs to be the arresting officer. Finish your dessert, Jill, and I'll take you back to the hotel. Then I need to make a few phone calls.'

Jill took one bite and pushed away the plate. 'I can't eat anymore. Get out your credit card, Mikey, while I flag down the waiter. This dinner is on us. Nick, why don't you bring your car around to the front? I can't wait to get this show on the road.'

After dinner with Nick and Michael, Jill barely slept a wink. It took Nick little time to dig up plenty of dirt on Alexis's ex-boyfriend, thanks to the state police databanks. These days Ross Lacey might pay his bills by buying and selling stocks and junk bonds from home, but that hadn't always been the case. Lacey had been fired from three different brokerage firms before going out on his own. With two arrests for assault, both in the workplace, Lacey apparently was a hothead. He also had two prior restraining orders filed against him by women co-workers. Since Lacey had no convictions and never spent a single night in jail, the complaints against him must have been settled out of court. As a security broker in Kentucky, Lacey had to list his place of business on his license, which in his case was his residence. He did not live in a good part of town, despite his flashy car and expensive watch. Armed with this information, Jill planned to turn the tables on the sociopath and hopefully, Ross Lacey's luck was about to run out.

'I should come with you,' Michael said as he helped Jill pack his camera and video equipment in the car. 'You might know how to set things up, but you don't know the first thing about taking long-range photos.'

Jill rolled her eyes. 'It only has to *appear* like I'm taking sleazy, tabloid shots. Lacey won't know if I photograph the gas station next door or the back of his head. Besides, Nick and Detective Grimes will be listening in on every word I say.' She climbed in behind the wheel and patted where she'd been wired for sound. 'If I end up in danger, Nick and Detective Grimes will rush to my rescue.'

'You get to have all the fun, Curtis,' Michael muttered, backing away from the car.

'So *that's* what this is about?' Jill bit the inside of her cheek. 'If you do the preliminary research on our fourth and final distillery, I'll make sure you have fun before we leave Louisville.' With a wave of her hand, she headed to Phoenix Hill, a neighborhood which had seen its heyday sometime around the Second World War, but never recovered after the last recession.

Nick called along the way and fell in behind her long before they reached Ross Lacey's house. Jill checked to make sure her microphone was working by whispering sweet nothings to Nick to see if he heard. He not only caught every one of them, but responded with a few tender endearments of his own.

'Will Detective Grimes meet us there?' Jill asked three blocks from Lacey's house.

'No. She's a homicide detective, not a beat cop. She can't join our stakeout when all he's suspected of is stalking. But if you can get Lacey to follow you to Alexis's apartment, that's a different story. I can arrest him for violating the court order and take him down to headquarters. Then Detective Grimes can question him about the murder and request a search warrant for his residence.'

'Sounds like a plan.' Jill pulled up to the curb two houses down from Lacey's.

'Are you worried because it's just me watching your back?' he asked.

'Do I sound worried, Magic Man? You rushed to my rescue

in the mountains, so I don't think a city street in broad daylight will be a problem.'

Truthfully, Jill was worried, and it had nothing to do with Nick's proficiency as a cop. She had looked into Lacey's eyes and seen two black pools of hatred and discontent. As strong and talented as Nick was, protecting someone against pure evil wasn't easy. But since she was the one who dragged Nick into this, Jill parked the car and pulled the tripod and camera with a long-range lens from the trunk. It took her only a few minutes to position herself across the street and secure the camera onto the tripod.

Lacey lived in a two-story row house connected to eight other units. These days, real estate agents called the structures townhouses. But the Willow Terraces had been built more than seventy years ago and hadn't been refurbished since. Normally Jill never would judge a person by where they lived. She'd grown up in a neighborhood of tiny bungalows packed so close together you could hear if a neighbor's microwave dinged. But the home of Ross Lacey didn't match his Rolex or the Escalade he'd followed her in. Most likely, he had never brought Alexis home for a nightcap when they'd been dating.

The man was a façade, a phony who'd woven a pretentious web in hopes of snaring a wealthy wife. Alexis had gone out on a few dates with him, but she wasn't into alpha males with big egos. Breaking up with Lacey had probably unleashed in him a type of nastiness that Alexis – or Jill – weren't familiar with. She would keep that in mind as she aimed her camera at his living-room window.

'You OK, sweet thing?'

Nick's question through her earpiece almost knocked her over.

'Sure,' she said, regaining her composure. 'For a minute I forgot you were down the street.'

'Lacey's car is parked next to the trash bins in the alley, so we know he's home. While you watch his house, I'm watching you. So just try to relax.'

'Don't worry about me,' she muttered toward her shirt pocket. 'This sleazy tabloid journalist has nerves of steel.'

For the next fifteen minutes Jill took pictures of the cracks in the foundation, the dead shrubbery, and the broken window three doors down, just for something to do. The resident had replaced the missing pane with cardboard and judging by the deterioration, not recently. On the steps of Ross's neighbor lay a bent and rusted tricycle. The condition of the kid's toy broke Jill's heart. When she finally stepped back from the tripod for a sip of water, the front door of number five burst open and Ross Lacey stomped down the steps.

'What do you think you're doing?' he shouted as he approached.

'What does it look like, Mr Lacey?' Jill spoke calmly despite the fact her stomach had tied itself into a knot. 'I'm taking still shots and video of where you live.' She switched off the camera and slipped the SIM card into her pocket.

'What the heck for? All I'm doing is working.' Lacey looked every bit as confused as angry.

Jill folded the tripod and leaned it against her shoulder. 'That's what I assumed. But since you accused me of being a tabloid journalist, I thought I could make a few bucks with these pictures.' She carried Michael's equipment back to the car.

'Who would pay you for pictures of these apartments?' He hooked a thumb over his shoulder, laughing as though she was quite foolish.

With the camera stowed in the trunk, Jill climbed in the car and started the ignition, lowering the window to finish their conversation. 'Normally, no one would care enough to pay a dime for pictures of a rundown row house with peeling paint and dead shrubs. Honestly, you should report your landlord to the housing authority. But I talked to Alexis yesterday after our encounter. She remembers you fondly and regrets how things ended, especially how her father had bullied you.' Jill locked gazes with him to lend credibility to her words.

'That's bull,' he snapped.

'I couldn't believe it either, but sometimes there's no explaining human attraction. Alexis said you two enjoyed some good times together. That's why I needed the pictures.' Jill flashed a smile. 'With the expensive suit and nice car, you painted a picture of being a successful stockbroker. But once Alexis sees where you live, she'll think twice about picking up where you left off.' Jill trounced down on the accelerator to put distance between them before daring to look in the mirror.

Ross Lacey stood in the street, shaking his fist and shouting obscenities. The only phrase she heard was: 'You're a dead woman, Jill Curtis,' before he ran toward his house. Hopefully it was all she, Nick, and Detective Grimes needed.

'You catch that, Magic Man?' she asked, keeping her eyes on the road.

'I only heard what you said, Jill, and you did a great job of insulting the man. If he's as hot-tempered as the police report indicates, he won't let those pictures get close to Alexis. What did Lacey say?'

'He called me every nasty word in the book and then said I was a "dead woman".'

Nick blew out his breath. 'I'm a few car lengths behind because I don't want to scare Lacey off. But I won't let you out of my sight. I just called Detective Grimes and she'll meet us there. Officers are already in place at Parker Estate. Follow the instructions we discussed to the letter.' Then he went quiet. 'Are you sure you can do this, Jill? It's not too late to back out.'

'Don't be ridiculous. I can do this.' Jill sounded far more confident than she felt as she wove her way through Louisville's backstreets. She saw no sign of Ross Lacey . . . or Nick Harris, for that matter. Then again, she kept her focus on parked cars and drivers changing lanes without bothering to signal. It wasn't until she reached the country road leading to Parker Estate that a black SUV appeared in her rear-view mirror. And the Cadillac was gaining on her at a ridiculously high rate of speed.

As Nick had promised, the gate to the estate stood open with no security guard in the booth. Nothing and no one would impede Lacey from violating the restraining order against him. Jill turned into the driveway faster than any sane woman as her pursuer closed the gap between them.

Heedless of his expensive vehicle, Lacey banged the bumper of her car with his front end, causing her right wheels to veer off the pavement. 'Pull over,' he shouted out his window. 'We need to talk.'

Jill struggled to regain control as she sped up the tree-lined lane. Just as the driveway widened into two lanes near the mansion, Lacey pulled up beside her. 'Stop, Jill, and talk to me. I'll make it worth your while to hand over those photos.'

'No, thanks,' she shouted as they passed the house and braked hard to negotiate a corner. Will all his attention on Jill, Lacey didn't notice Nick gaining ground on him or that the driveway curved around to the left. Lacey drove his SUV off the pavement into the damp grass, giving Jill just enough time to jump out of the car and sprint for the stairs to Alexis's apartment. Along the way she prayed the madman wasn't carrying a gun.

When she was midway up the steps, the apartment door opened and Alexis stepped onto the landing. 'Hi, Jill,' she said, sounding calm, cool and collected. 'I wasn't expecting you today.' Then Alexis's pale blue eyes landed on Ross Lacey who'd just reached the bottom of the staircase. 'Ross, what are you doing here? I'm getting all sorts of company today.' She flashed a friendly smile.

'Alexis, you've been duped by this corrupt journalist.' Ross pointed at Jill, halfway up the steps, so there would be no confusion. 'If you invite me in, I can explain everything.'

During the several moments Alexis pondered the offer, a uniformed officer pushed Alexis back into the apartment and aimed his weapon at Ross. 'I've got a better invitation for you, Mr Lacey. You're under arrest for violating a restraining order.' The cop hurried down the steps, passing Jill along the way just as Nick and two more officers stepped out from behind Alexis's car.

In no time at all, Lacey was cuffed, read his rights, and led to a squad car.

'She tricked me!' he shouted over his shoulder. 'That reporter tricked me into violating the order.'

Feeling braver with Nick's presence, Jill shouted back, 'I did nothing of the sort. It's not my fault you didn't want Alexis seeing a few pictures.'

'Looks like I missed all the fun,' said Detective Grimes, joining Nick and Jill. 'Your little plan seems to have worked.'

'How do you want to handle this, Detective?' Nick asked.

'While Lacey's in custody for violating the court order we'll get a search warrant for his apartment. If his DNA and finger-prints match the evidence we have, or if we find any connection to William Scott's murder in his apartment, he'll be charged.'

'And if not?' asked Alexis, joining the cluster.

'He'll have to be released, but a judge might grant you a

permanent RO aganist the guy. Keep in mind that you and Miss
Curtis might have just made a permanent enemy.'

That little detail had already occurred to Jill.

TEN

After yesterday's non-stop action with Ross Lacey, Jill
readily agreed to tour their last distillery the next day.
As Michael pointed out for the umpteenth time, that's
what they were being paid to do, not lead psychopaths on high-
speed chases through Louisville. Over drinks the previous evening
at the Thurman House, Jill had filled Michael in on the details
of the high-speed chase, including the unfortunate damage to his
car. Their favorite bartender gave up all pretense of clandestine
eavesdropping and hovered in front of them. Ray completely
ignored his other customers until Jill wrapped up her story with
Lacey's arrest.

'You should be more careful, Miss Jill,' Ray interjected,
always ready to offer his opinion. 'Men like Lacey are unpre-
dictable. He could give up on your unnamed friend and start
stalking you.'

'And she will remain unnamed, Ray, but thanks for your
concern.' Jill winked playfully, while Michael fumed about her
recklessness.

But today her partner was smiling and their fourth and final
distillery turned out to be a touristy mock-up on the edge of the
town. The real Jim Beam distillery that made one of Kentucky's
premier bourbons was two hours away, but this replica gave
visitors a good place to start their tour. The facility was spotless
and the tour guide knowledgeable. Since there was no chance of
stumbling across proprietary secrets, Michael was given carte
blanche to shoot video anywhere on the property. The actual
distillery sat twenty-seven miles away in Clermont, Kentucky.

When they finished the tour, she and Michael split a sandwich
and an order of fries in the visitor center's restaurant. 'What do
you say?' he asked in between bites. 'Should we drive to the

main distillery? According to their website, it's one of the largest in the state and that's saying a lot.'

Jill dragged a fry through catsup. 'Sure, why not? Let's ask Nick to join us since he's still on vacation.'

'I'll refill our iced tea for the road.' Michael jumped to his feet.

But by the time he returned, their plans for the rest of the day had changed. 'I just spoke to Alexis on the phone.' She wiped her mouth with a napkin. 'In yesterday's excitement, she forgot to extend an invitation to a party at the distillery tonight.'

Michael grabbed the last French fry. 'What kind of party?'

'She's about to announce the new master distiller at Parker Estate. And although who it will be isn't much of a surprise, Rose wants to make this a big deal.'

'Am I invited too?' He lifted an eyebrow.

'Of course, you are! You're my partner.'

'What about Nick?' Michael grabbed the last fry.

'Funny you should ask. Alexis said she already called Nick and invited him. He plans to come but said he'll be late.' Jill tried unsuccessfully not to sound uneasy about Nick and Alexis's renewed friendship.

'Is that right? Did she deliver an engraved invitation to *your* boyfriend by uniformed courier?' His laugh sounded downright malicious.

'Don't be immature, Mikey.' Pushing to her feet, Jill stacked their dirty plates on the tray.

'Just voicing what you were thinking.'

As they walked to the car, Jill tried to think of something clever to say and came up empty.

'So are we driving to the main distillery tomorrow? We should be able to see it all in one day.'

'I'm afraid not. Alexis wants me to attend the reading of her father's will in the morning. She could use some moral support.'

'Once again I'm shoved to the back burner,' he said.

But Jill had more important things on her mind than Michael's disappointment. She had to figure out what to wear to the reception – the age-old conundrum faced by all women. According to Alexis, the business-casual event would be outdoors in the courtyard between the three main buildings. Guests could also wander through the distillery's public areas.

After much deliberation Jill settled on black pants, a cream-colored silk blouse, and black heels, along with a tapestry jacket in case it turned chilly. While waiting for Michael to get ready, she thought about calling Nick. After all, wasn't he still her boyfriend? But she didn't want to appear immature, the deadly sin she had just accused Michael of.

'Ahh, you're finally ready.' Jill tapped the app on her phone, summoning Uber to their location.

'I am. What's the hurry?' In his tan Dockers and navy blazer, Michael wore the only dressy clothes he had brought to Kentucky. 'You look nice, by the way.'

'Thanks, so do you.' Jill slipped her phone in her bag. 'I want to find a good table for people-watching. Who knows what guilty faces we might see?'

Michael shook his head. 'Why do you think there'll be tables? This isn't an ethnic wedding at the VFW hall. We'll probably just mill around all evening, grazing on tidbits that leave you hungry.'

Jill grinned all the way down in the elevator. But on the drive to Parker Distillery, she thought about Nick and stopped smiling. What was so important today that he couldn't call or send a text? And why did he tell Alexis he'd be late to the party and not her? Now that Ross Lacey was in custody, he should have his evening free and clear.

Unfortunately, Jill's curiosity won over her female pride and she sent him a short text: *What's up? Is everything OK?* She held her breath until his reply popped up on her phone: *I'm fine. Will explain later.*

So much for satisfying her curiosity.

Jill shook thoughts of Nick away as the Uber arrived at the destination. She and Michael entered a flagstone courtyard so exquisitely decorated it put all other work parties to shame. No guide had shown them this hidden oasis during the tour. High-top tables covered with starched linens and small votive candles were scattered under the shade of huge magnolia trees. Strings of white lights crisscrossed overhead, providing ambiance besides plenty of illumination. Tuxedo-clad waiters circulated among the guests with trays of champagne and snifters of bourbon – Parker Estate, of course. A bar had been set up at one end of the courtyard for those wishing for something different.

'Wow, when I get married I want this kind of reception,' Michael said under his breath. 'Classy, but my friends can still wear jeans.'

'Me, too,' Jill agreed. 'It must be good to be Alexis.'

Michael lifted two flutes of champagne from a waiter's tray and handed her one. 'Do I hear a note of jealousy in your voice?'

Jill took a swallow. 'I'm feeling more than a note. More like an entire concerto.'

'What does Alexis have that you don't besides money, prestige, and a cool car? You've got a way better sense of humor.' He drank his glass in two swallows. 'Will you be OK by yourself for a while?'

'Of course, I'll rely on my great sense of humor.' Jill leaned one shoulder against a light pole.

'Great. There's a group of women by the bar I bet are single.' Michael set his empty flute on a table and sauntered across the courtyard, trying to appear sophisticated.

Jill grinned and rolled her eyes. Her partner had to be the least subtle man she'd ever met, yet she could never tell him that. Feeling self-conscious at the table alone, she wandered indoors where a buffet of canapes had been set up. Everything looked artfully prepared and festively presented, but as Michael had predicted, nothing would fill an empty stomach. Nevertheless, Jill fixed a plate of grilled shrimp, oysters on the half shell, and a few raw veggies. On the way back to her wallflower position by the light pole, Alexis intercepted her.

'There you are! I was hoping you'd be here on time. Mama is getting ready to announce the new master distiller. Far be it from Rose to let people unwind with a drink and something to eat before they're forced to greet their new boss.' Alexis hissed her words under her breath.

'Well, I made a plate and these shrimp are delicious.' Jill licked cocktail sauce from her fingertip.

'I can't wait to eat. Hey, where's your partner?'

'Over by the bar.' Jill aimed a carrot stick across the courtyard.

'At least he looks like he's having fun.' Alexis stole a shrimp off Jill's plate and gobbled it in record time.

'If you're hungry, get some food before your employees devour it all.'

'I would love to, but my mother would have a fit. According to her, the host doesn't eat until the guests are finished.' Her words dripped scorn that had been brewing a long time.

'Rose was born in the wrong century. Why don't I fix you a plate, then you could hide in a closet to eat?'

'A smashing idea, my friend, but that will have to wait. My mother has stepped up to the podium.' Alexis pulled two flutes from a waiter's tray and tried to hand her one.

Jill shook her head. 'Not for me, I just finished a glass.'

'Good grief, girl. The caterers are barely putting a mouthful in these flutes. I'll make sure you get back to your hotel safely.'

'All right, fine. But don't worry about me. Michael and I took Uber here.' Jill accepted the glass as they walked into the courtyard.

'OK, this is what we'll do.' Alexis helped herself to another shrimp from Jill's meager supply. 'As soon as my mother names the new master distiller, you load two plates up with food and head down the hallway marked *Corporate Offices*. I'll look for you once my speech is done.'

'Sounds like a plan.' Just for a moment Jill wondered if anyone ever told Alexis 'no' or to 'back off.' But that was probably just the green-eyed-monster rearing its ugly head again.

'Good evening, everyone.' Rose Scott's well-polished drawl boomed from the loudspeaker. 'Thanks so much for joining us tonight as we name my beloved husband's successor as the new master distiller.' Rose waited for the smattering of applause to die down. 'William loved working at Parker Estate. There wasn't a single day that he complained to me or our daughter, Alexis, about having to go to work.' While the audience chuckled, Rose motioned for Alexis to join her at the podium.

'Oh boy, here we go.' Alexis handed Jill her flute. 'Don't forget to find me later with a plate of grub. I love those little meatballs in cocktail sauce.' Then with a practiced hand, Alexis smoothed an unseen wrinkle from her silk dress and joined her mother at the microphone.

Since Jill could only carry so many things, she finished the last sip in Alexis's glass and placed both glasses on the table. She cast a longing gaze around the courtyard for Nick to no avail.

'To those of you in production,' continued Rose, 'my announcement will not come as a surprise. After interviewing several candidates from both inside and outside the company, the board of directors has chosen . . . Anthony Rossi to be our new master distiller. For those of you not in production, Anthony has been with us for eleven years and served as my husband's chief assistant for the last five. Please join me in welcoming Anthony Rossi as Parker Estate's new master distiller.'

As Rose and Alexis clapped politely the crowd broke into uproarious applause. Rossi either had plenty of fans at work or his friends and family had crashed the party. Jill finished her canapes as Anthony thanked everyone but the governor of Kentucky and then went on to pledge his undying loyalty to the brand. *Yada, yada.* His speech made Jill glad she worked in journalism where advancement was impossible, so schmoozing was usually unnecessary. During Rossi's entire monologue, Rose smiled like a pageant winner, while Alexis appeared to be biting the inside of her cheek.

When Rossi finally finished, Jill headed indoors to where the food had been replenished on several tables. A long queue soon formed behind her as Jill piled tiny meatballs and shrimp dipped in cocktail sauce on two plates, then glanced around the courtyard. Although she spotted Michael with a gorgeous redhead under the magnolias and Rose chatting with her husband's replacement, Jill didn't see her friend. Not one to give up easily, she waited until the guard's back was turned and slipped through the door marked 'employees only'. Once Alexis had had enough of her mother and work socializing, she would appreciate the food and a few minutes alone.

Jill wandered down a long hallway of offices, including public relations, community outreach, and human resources. Then she spotted an interesting brass plate labeled Historical Archives. *What would it hurt to browse for a few minutes until Alexis turned up?* Books lined two walls of the room, while the other two displayed blown-up photographs of downtown during a bygone era. Unfortunately, the room Jill wanted to peruse wasn't empty. A small man sat in a leather chair at the desk, a bottle of bourbon and snifter in front of him.

'Excuse me, Mr Parker,' she said, recognizing him from her visit to the estate. 'I hope I didn't disturb you. I'm just waiting for Alexis.'

Robert Parker peered up through thick spectacles. 'Good to see you again, Jane! Please, join me. Is one of those plates for me? How did you know I was hungry?'

'It is indeed, sir.' Jill ignored the incorrect name and placed the heaped plate of food in front of him. After all, she could always get more later.

'I love meatballs.' Parker speared a meatball with a toothpick and popped it in his mouth. 'My granddaughter's not here, but I would love to buy you a drink!' Chortling at his joke, he took a second glass from his drawer, filled it with an inch of amber liquid, and pushed it across the desk.

'No, thank you. I've already drunk my quota of champagne.'

His eyes widened in horror. 'You came to a distillery to drink champagne? This ain't Paris, France, young lady. This is Kentucky!'

'I know, but . . .'

Grandpa Parker cut her rationalization short. 'No buts! I was the master distiller when this bourbon was bottled. Aficionados would stand in line for hours for a taste of this. I'll consider it an insult if you refuse to at least try it.'

'In that case, I would love some.' Jill picked up the glass and took a small sip. 'Absolutely delicious.' She had to admit it was far smoother than any bourbon she'd tasted thus far.

'So tell me, Jane, do you have enough information for your travel article yet? That is what you're writing, isn't it? My daughter thinks you're up to no good. She also thinks my memory is going bad.'

Jill sipped a bit more. 'Yes, my article is finished. Tonight I'm here as a guest of your granddaughter's.'

'In that case, I hope you have a good time. Just don't let Rose see you back here.' Parker studied her intently for a moment. 'For some reason you rub my daughter the wrong way. Maybe it's because you're cute as a button.' He lifted his glass as though in toast.

'That's very kind.' Although Jill had never seen a particularly cute button, she clicked his snifter with hers and finished the drink, as not to ruffle his feathers.

'One more for the road?' Robert lifted the decanter. 'Although I trust you won't get behind the wheel of a car.'

'No, thank you. I'm already feeling the effects of that one.' Jill steadied herself with the edge of the desk. 'I should keep looking for Alexis.'

Robert ate another meatball and smiled. 'I would try the mixing room. That was Alexis's favorite hideout as a little girl. Down the hallway to the end, then go through the double doors.'

Jill tried to focus on the elderly man. 'Thanks, Mr Parker. It was nice seeing you again.'

'Likewise, Miss Curtis.'

Oddly, this time the former master distiller got her name right. But Jill had more important things to worry about. Like staying upright when she really needed a nap. Focusing on the double doors ahead of her, Jill put one foot in front of the other. She never should have drunk that bourbon, especially not on top of champagne. Right then and there she pledged never to touch hard spirits again, no matter whose feelings were at stake. Hopefully she would find her friend on the other side of the doors. Alexis would know where the closest restroom was since she felt very dizzy.

Pushing open the doors, Jill stepped into the mixing room just as her knees buckled and the floor rose up to meet her. For an unknown amount of time she remained flat on her back on the cold concrete floor with the other plate of canapes down the front of her pants. When Jill's eyelids finally fluttered open, she saw Rose Scott and the new master distiller staring at her. Neither was smiling.

'Who are you?' Anthony Rossi asked.

'This is the nosy reporter who has insinuated herself into my daughter's life.' Rose huffed in supreme indignation.

'My name is Jill Curtis,' she whispered with great effort. 'Could you help me up, please?'

Rossi placed a hand under each armpit and hoisted her

ingloriously to her feet. 'There are some people who should never drink, young lady. And you are one of them.' The new boss scolded Jill like a child. 'Don't you dare return to the reception in this condition. I'll have security send you home in a taxi.'

Rose laid a manicured hand on Rossi's arm. 'Perhaps we should find out what she's doing here first. This woman was already warned about venturing into prohibited areas. Maybe she's being paid by a competitor to spy or plant dangerous materials in our distillery.'

The new boss's expression changed from disappointed parent to nasty prison guard. 'I don't know what you had planned, Miss Curtis, but you're trespassing on private property. If I catch you inside Parker Estate Distillery again, I'll have you arrested, whether you're a friend of Miss Scott or not. Do you understand?' Rossi shook Jill like a ragdoll, increasing her nausea exponentially.

'I understand, but I think . . .'

That was all the thinking she had time for as the champagne, shrimp, meatballs and aged bourbon suddenly bubbled to the surface and across the tile floor.

'Oh, good grief!' Rose muttered, jumping back a step.

Jill might have collapsed in a heap if Rossi hadn't held her upright. 'I've got you, young lady. Bend over and get it all out. You'll feel better tomorrow.'

Just then the double doors banged open. 'What's going on in here?' asked a familiar male voice.

'What has happened to Jill?' screeched a familiar female voice.

'Nothing,' Rose insisted. 'Your *new* friend had too much to drink and went snooping around the distillery. This is the end result.' Rose pointed at the mess on the floor with contempt.

Nick caught Jill up in his arms. 'Are you all right?' he asked tenderly.

'I think I'd like to go home now,' Jill moaned, never so embarrassed in her entire life.

'Can you walk or shall I carry you?' Nick swept an arm under her knees.

'No, no. I can walk.' Hanging onto Nick's arm, Jill moved slowly toward the door then stopped. 'I apologize, Mr Rossi, for the mess, and congrats on your promotion.'

Jill didn't try to say anything else. She was too busy focusing on not being sick . . . and the fact that Alexis and Nick had walked into the mixing room together.

Jill remembered very little after climbing into Nick's car. At some point she fell asleep, which, needless to say, was a blessing. When she awoke she was on a couch under a blanket in unfamiliar surroundings. 'Where am I?' she asked, rising up on elbows.

After a few moments Nick emerged from the bathroom with wet hair and a towel around his neck. 'You're in my apartment.'

'What day is it?' Jill pressed her temples as snippets of recent events returned.

Nick glanced at his watch. 'Still Friday, but not for much longer.'

'Good grief. Michael is probably worried what happened to me!'

Nick sat on an ottoman near the couch and took her hand. 'While I drove you home from the party, Alexis looked for your partner. She assured Michael you were safe and well taken care of. He'll take an Uber back to the hotel.'

Jill drew her arm back. 'About that, what's with you and Alexis showing up together? Where were you all day? What's going on?'

Nick laughed as though she'd said something amusing. 'Nothing's going on, sweet girl. My heart belongs solely to you.' He thumped his chest with his fist. 'Alexis spotted me when I arrived at the reception. She said she couldn't find you in the crowd, but was about to search the distillery. She asked if I wanted to join her and of course, I agreed.' Nick grabbed her hand again and kissed the back of her fingers.

'So, no funny stuff behind my back?' Jill leaned against a pile of pillows.

'None whatsoever. Alexis was worried about you. She wanted you away from her mother's claws as soon as possible. So I brought you here to my humble abode.' Nick flourished his hand around the room. 'Now, if you feel like talking, I'd love to hear why you passed out on the distillery floor.'

With the ball decidedly in her court, Jill chose her words carefully. 'I have no idea. Alexis said she was starved, so I fixed us both plates of food.'

'Why couldn't she fix her own?' Nick asked, confused.

'Her mother said she wasn't allowed to eat until *after* the party.'

'That sounds like Rose. Go on.'

Jill ran a hand through her tangled hair. 'I fixed the plates of food but I didn't see Alexis in the courtyard after the speeches. So I knew she was hiding from the whole ordeal.'

'What ordeal? It was just a party.'

'I don't know, Nick, I'm just trying to remember everything that happened.'

'Sorry. Go on.'

'I went through the door marked "employees only", but instead of finding Alexis down the hallway, I found her grandfather. Robert Parker is a sweet old man who said he was hungry, so I gave him a plate of food.' Jill paused, but when Nick's expression didn't change, she continued. 'Mr Parker asked me to have a drink with him. Since I'd already had two champagnes I declined, but he insisted.'

'That's how you ended up drunk?'

Jill sucked in a breath. 'I'm sure that's how it looked, but I don't think I was drunk. I think I might have been drugged. I saw Rose Parker lurking around my champagne glass.'

Nick released her hand. 'Do you know how ridiculous this sounds? You almost never drink, yet you had two glasses of champagne and a high-proof bourbon. That amount would get a regular drinker drunk. That plus not eating much was what made you sick in the mixing room.'

Jill dropped her chin to her chest. 'Oh, dear, I'd hoped that was part of the bad nightmare I had on your couch.'

'It really happened, but at least Rose Parker didn't make you clean the mess up yourself.' Nick grinned. 'She was madder than I've ever seen her.'

'Mr Rossi said he would have me arrested if I set foot in the distillery again.'

Nick sat next to her on the couch and wrapped both arms around her. 'Let's not worry about that. Your travel article is done and the Louisville police are investigating the homicide. If you still wish to see Alexis I suggest a coffee shop or restaurant.'

'Speaking of Alexis . . . was she horribly mad at me for ruining the reception?'

'You didn't ruin anything. The reception was in the courtyard, not the mixing room. Alexis was very worried about you. You passed out cold, Jill. You could have cracked your skull when you fell.'

'Not to worry. Hard as rock.' Jill tapped her head with her knuckles.

Nick pulled an afghan from the back of the couch. 'OK, Miss Rock-Head, time to lie down and go back to sleep. Alexis still wants you at the attorney's office tomorrow for the reading of the will, if you're feeling up to it. She left you the lawyer's business card with his address. Alexis said sparks could fly if her mother doesn't get everything she's entitled to.'

Jill stretched out her legs. 'Do you think it's wise, considering how Mrs Scott feels about me?'

'That's entirely up to you.' Nick pulled the afghan up to her chin.

'Will you be there?'

'Definitely not. Mama Rose doesn't like me either.'

Jill bolted upright, causing a sharp pain between her eyes. 'You never told me where you went today. You were going to explain but I stole your thunder.'

Nick pushed her back down. 'I drove to Lorraine because my sister was having problems with Mom, but it's nothing that can't wait until tomorrow. Go to sleep. Morning will be here before you know it.'

'OK, Nick. And thanks. You and Alexis saved me and I won't forget it.'

Whether Jill would remember or not was anyone's guess, since she was sound asleep in under a minute.

ELEVEN

Jill studied the business card left by Alexis while waiting for her taxi to arrive. Since the official reading of William Scott's will was scheduled for a Saturday, she called a cab in case Michael wanted to use his car to get estimates on the damage. Jill was dropped off directly in front of the law firm of Bradley, Cooper and Day on the same street as the distillery. After riding the elevator to the top floor, she opened the conference room door to two warm smiles, owned by Alexis and Grandpa Parker, and two sour frowns, belonging to Rose Scott and the distinguished man sitting at the head of the table.

'Excuse me, miss. I am Kenneth Bradley, senior partner of this law firm. This is a private reading for those expressly named in the estate.'

'Excuse me, Mr Bradley,' interrupted Alexis, jumping to her feet. 'I invited Miss Curtis here for emotional support. Come sit by me, Jill.' Alexis patted the chair next to hers.

'Oh, for goodness' sake, Alexis,' Rose muttered. 'After the stunt your *friend* pulled at Rossi's reception, we should've had her arrested.' The woman's nostrils flared like an angry bull's.

'Hiya, Jane,' Grandpa Parker said merrily. 'I heard you ate a bad oyster or two yesterday. How ya feeling today?'

Jill waited until she was seated to reply. 'I'm fine, sir. Thank you for asking.'

This time Rose turned her withering glare on her father. 'Since I doubt you will be named in the will, Dad, I insist that you remain quiet. We don't need you encouraging the nosy travel writer.'

'That pretty gal is a writer?' Robert pointed a finger at Jill, looking confused. 'I thought she worked for the catering staff. She delivered my meatball dinner last night.'

Kenneth Bradley cleared his throat. 'If we could get started, I'd like to identify everyone in the room for the audio recording being made by my assistant.' He bobbed his head at the young woman across the room.

'You're taping this?' asked Grandpa Parker. 'Your daddy never monkeyed around with such nonsense and he practiced law for years.'

'Dad, please,' Rose pleaded. 'If you can't sit quietly I'll have security remove you until we're finished.'

'You'll do no such thing.' Alexis hurried around the table and wrapped an arm around her grandfather's shoulder. 'Please go on, Mr Bradley.'

After a second clearing of his throat, Bradley continued. 'We are assembled on the twentieth day of June for the reading of the Last Will and Testament of William Douglas Scott, born and raised in Shephardstown, Kentucky and a resident of Louisville for the past thirty years. I am Kenneth Bradley, Esq., senior partner of Bradley, Cooper and Day, and executor of the estate. With me are Mrs Rose Parker Scott, widow of the deceased; Alexis Scott, daughter and sole child of the deceased; James Thomas Scott, of Shephardstown, Kentucky, brother of the deceased; Father Timothy Webster, parish priest for the family; Miss Jill Curtis, personal friend of Miss Alexis Scott; Mrs Mabel Hawkins, the family's long-time housekeeper; Wilson Clark, personal chauffer of the deceased; and Miss Trixie Scaggs, my legal assistant.' The lawyer glanced around the room, making sure he hadn't missed anyone. 'If there are no additions or corrections, I shall commence with the reading. As required by law in the Commonwealth of Kentucky, I will read the document in its entirety.'

'Get on with it already, Bradley,' mumbled the man identified as James Scott. 'You ain't getting paid by the hour this time.'

'Don't worry, Jimmy,' Rose sneered. 'The blackjack tables stay open twenty-four-seven on the riverboats. They'll wait until you get re-bankrolled.'

Jimmy Scott tipped his cap to his sister-in-law. 'I've missed you too, Rosie. Maybe we could hit the tables together, just like old times.'

Jill glanced over at Alexis who was still with her grandfather. They both seemed to be trying not to laugh. What kind of rich family was this? Infidelity between spouses? Open hostility among in-laws? What's next? Gunplay if the settlement doesn't go as planned? Suddenly Jill's own family, including jailbird Granny Emma, seemed downright normal.

Apparently tired of clearing his throat, Bradley tugged down his cuffs then read the entire document from top to bottom. Unfortunately for everyone in the room, which was growing stuffier by the minute, there was plenty of legalese before the actual disposition of William Scott's assets and earthly possessions. Finally he got down to what everyone other than Jill was waiting for.

'To St Patrick's Episcopal Church of Louisville I bequeath the sum of ten thousand dollars to be entrusted to Father Thomas Webster and spent at his discretion within the parish.

'To Mrs Mabel Hawkins, I leave the sum of five thousand dollars along with my collection of watercolor paintings of the Mississippi River that hangs in my study. Mabel always admired those paintings.'

Upon hearing the bequest to the housekeeper, Mrs Scott turned very pale, leading Jill to assume either Rose really liked the artwork or more likely, they were worth a lot of money.

'To Mr Wilson Clark, I leave the sum of five thousand dollars along with my diamond stud cufflinks and my Land Rover. I know Wilson has been looking for a reliable car for his grandson, Willie, to get him back and forth to school.'

This time Rose couldn't keep silent about a bequest. 'A forty-thousand-dollar SUV for an eighteen-year-old kid? He couldn't afford the upkeep.'

'Shush, daughter!' demanded Grandpa Parker. 'I thought there was to be no talking during the meeting.'

Rose crossed her arms, seething. 'I beg your pardon, Mr Bradley.'

The lawyer nodded before continuing. 'To Mr James T. Scott, my sole sibling, I leave the sum of fifty thousand dollars, along with my Rolex watch, and any or all of my clothing and personal effects he wishes. Maybe you could wear some of my sport shirts on the golf course.'

As a ripple of chuckles could be heard around the table, Jill focused on Rose in anticipation of another outburst. But this time the widow only rolled her eyes.

'To my beloved wife of thirty-five years, Rose Parker Scott, I leave my four-hundred-and-one-thousand-dollar retirement account, my half of our jointly owned investments, including the condo on Sanibel Island, and the remainder of my art collection in our home.'

'What about his shares of Parker Estate stock?' Rose swiveled toward her father. 'I know you sold William some shares over the years because you refused to stop pouring money into that farm.'

'Not some of them, daughter, all of them.'

'*All?*' Rose sputtered.

Mr Bradley pushed his glasses up his nose. 'If I might continue, ma'am, there is one additional bequest.'

'Only one more?' Grandpa asked. 'But what about Jane, Lexi's friend? Shouldn't she get something? She's here, isn't she?'

'Dad, please!' Rose was close to exploding. 'Her name is Jill, for heaven's sake, and she's not one of William's heirs. She's here because Alexis likes her for some odd reason.'

Jill couldn't remain silent another moment. 'Look, I'm sorry about the mess last night, but I believe someone drugged me.'

'If there were any drugs involved, young lady, you took them yourself. You seem to have self-control issues.' Rose arched her neck like a goose.

'I do not! I seldom drink and I've never taken drugs other than aspirin. I am tired of you besmirching my reputation.' Jill wiped away beads of sweat from her upper lip.

Grandpa clapped his hands as though watching a sporting event. 'Atta girl, Julie. Stick up for yourself.'

'Everyone, please settle down,' Bradley shouted above the din. 'And let me finish.' He waited until the room grew quiet, then he read the final bequest.

'And to my beloved firstborn legitimate child, Alexis Nicole Scott, I leave the proceeds of my one-million-dollar annuity and my fifty percent share of Parker Estate Distillery. Those, along with the shares she already owns from profit sharing, will give Alexis the voting majority. Alexis will become CEO of the corporation and appoint a new director of operations at her discretion.'

Rose wobbled as she scrambled to her feet, as though her stilettos could no longer support her body weight. 'William gave you his shares and made you CEO, not me?' If her demeanor could be trusted, this news came as a surprise to the widow.

Alexis shook her head, her eyes moist with tears. 'I had no

idea what Daddy had planned. But he knew you didn't like hanging out inside the distillery.'

'I've been in the distillery plenty! I was practically brought up in the stinky place. But usually your father sent me on some fool errand to get me out of his hair.'

'Sounds like Billy picked the right person for the job.' James Scott's comment was met with plenty of smiles and a few laughs.

Rose slapped her palms flat on the table. 'How dare you come around with your hand out after not seeing William in years?'

James jumped to his feet and began launching epitaphs across the room like pellets from a shotgun. While the in-laws verbally attacked one another and the lawyer tried to quiet the crowd down, no one noticed the door open or the two well-dressed men walk in. Except for Jill.

'Who are you?' Jill asked the younger of the two men.

Her softly spoken question attracted plenty of attention. Rose, James, and everyone else stopped jabbering and stared at the late arrivals.

'Excuse me, gentleman,' said Ken Bradley. 'You have wandered into the wrong office. Trixie will help you on your way.'

The legal assistant dutifully jumped to her feet and approached the men.

But the younger of the two held up his hand. 'That won't be necessary, Trixie. We were looking for the reading of William Scott's will and from what we've overheard at the door I believe we're in the right place.'

'How dare you, sir!' Bradley demanded, outraged. 'These are closed proceedings. I'll have security remove you from the premises immediately.' He pulled a cell phone from his briefcase.

'Please, Mr Bradley,' Alexis said. 'Let's see what the gentlemen want.'

'Thank you, Miss Scott.' The young man bowed slightly. 'I should have started with identification of myself and the gentleman on my right. I am Kevin Scott of Bardstown, Kentucky and this is my attorney, Justin Delacroix of Delacroix and Broussard Attorneys at Law.' Kevin pulled a driver's license from his wallet to show those closest to the door, namely Jimmy Scott and Mabel Hawkins. Mrs Hawkins showed no interest whatsoever, but Jimmy Scott became almost gleeful. 'Yep, that's what the license says.'

Everyone at the conference table looked bewildered, except for Mama Rose. Her face flushed so bright red, Jill thought steam might burst from her ears.

'Have these men removed, Ken. In fact, call the police and have them arrested for trespassing.'

Alexis rose to her feet with supreme dignity. 'No, Mother, as one of my father's principle heirs, I insist that we hear Mr Scott out.'

After her pronouncement Alexis returned to her chair next to Jill, who slipped a reassuring arm around her shoulder. After all, hadn't she been invited expressly for emotional support?

'Alexis,' Rose pleaded, moisture glistening in her eyes. 'Please trust my judgement this one time. This man is a fraud, a scammer who lies to fill his pockets with money.'

'So I gather you've met Mr Scott before?' Alexis asked in a voice Jill had never heard before – low, precise, controlled, devoid of emotion. 'That gives you an unfair advantage, one you've had your whole life. Let's all sit down. I am no longer a child and I want to hear what Kevin has to say. Then if anyone calls security, it will be me.'

Jill tightened her arm around Alexis's shoulder. 'I don't know who you are,' she whispered, 'but I want to be you when I grow up.'

Alexis didn't reply, but one corner of her mouth pulled up into a half-smile.

Then the other attorney, Mr Delacroix, spoke with a faint Louisiana accent. 'Without prejudice or animosity, Mr Scott refutes the assertion that Alexis Nicole Scott was the firstborn child of William Douglas Scott.' As all eyes turned in his direction, he pulled a sheaf of papers from an inside pocket. 'These papers are a mere courtesy of our intention to contest the will as read by Mr Bradley. We shall offer evidence in probate court of the birth certificate of Kevin Scott.' Delacroix handed the papers to Mrs Hawkins who dutifully passed them down to Bradley. 'You will see that Kevin Scott is eighteen months older than Miss Alexis. And by the wording "to my legitimate firstborn child I bequeath" we feel we have legal precedent. Also, I have proof that William Scott and my client, Kevin, have been in contact, albeit sporadic, since his birth. We will also present as evidence a recent email indicating William Scott's intention to amend his will to include his son.'

'Holy Toledo,' exclaimed Grandpa. 'That man you married, Rosie, was a sly little devil.' He punctuated his description with a cackle of laughter.

'Shut up or I'll have you committed to an asylum.'

Rose's threat prompted plenty of conversation at the table, but Jill remained focused on Alexis and her new . . . half-brother. Alexis looked downright shell-shocked, while Kevin, on the other hand, didn't appear particularly joyful at the chance for long-awaited justice. Instead, he gazed on his half-sister with an expression of pity.

After several uncomfortable moments, Kevin cleared his throat and spoke in a clear voice. 'Whether the probate court recognizes my claim as a legitimate heir of William Scott I'm willing to let the judge decide. But I can assure you my father wished me to be part of his world. Although his position in the company was due to his marriage to Rose Parker Scott, my father worked his entire career at Parker Estate Distillery and wanted me to be part of that legacy.' He bobbed his head respectfully in Grandpa's direction. 'And he wanted me to know his family, namely Alexis.'

'Over my dead body,' Mama Rose muttered.

'I don't know what to say.' Alexis grasped the edge of the table, looking weak and very young.

'Sit down, girlfriend.' Jill tugged on her arm until she complied.

'You don't need to say anything, Alexis,' Kevin continued. 'I just want you to know I harbor no animosity.'

'You're correct, young man,' said Attorney Bradley, finally pulling himself together. 'Alexis has nothing to say. This ridiculous claim has a snowball's chance of holding up in court.'

With that Delacroix and Kevin Scott turned and walked out the door.

'Do I still get my paintings of the Mississippi?' Mrs Hawkins asked, recognizing the significance of the interruption.

'What about the Land Rover for my grandson to take him back and forth to school?' Mr Clark was equally as exasperated as the housekeeper.

'Let's not overreact, folks. All bequests must await the judge's approval. Mr Scott's appearance is nothing but smoke and mirrors, an unfortunate turn of events.'

Without warning, Alexis jumped up and ran from the office with Jill on her heels. 'Wait,' she called as Kevin and Delacroix stepped into the elevator.

A quick reaction by one of the men stopped the door from closing. Kevin stepped back into the hallway to face his half-sister.

'Why now?' Alexis rested her hands on her hips. 'For all those years growing up I would have loved a brother or a sister, but you wait until we're grown and our father is dead?'

'We don't know if this guy is telling the truth or not,' Jill said in Alexis's ear, none too softly.

'Who are you, miss?' Kevin's pale blue gaze landed on Jill.

'I'm Jill Curtis, her friend.'

'I don't blame you for protecting her, but I assure you a blood test will prove I'm telling the truth.' He refocused on Alexis. 'I didn't know who my father was until recently. When my mother suffered a health scare, she had to face her own mortality. She contacted my father and asked him to publicly acknowledge me. He kept stalling, insisting the time wasn't right. But at least he started writing me letters on a regular basis. I can produce those letters in court if necessary.'

'You wish to have my share of my father's estate?' Alexis asked in a strangled voice.

Kevin's features seemed to soften. 'Not particularly your share. Whether or not I end up inheriting anything, we'll let the courts decide. But my father wanted me to learn the business and become part of his world, part of his life. I hope you can accept the fact I'm not crawling back under a rock.' With that, Kevin stepped back and the elevator door closed in Alexis's and Jill's face.

Nick pressed the redial button for the twentieth time. If Jill didn't pick up this time or answer his texts he would put an APB out on her car.

'Hello. That you, Magic Man?' Jill asked sweetly.

'Yes, it's me. Where have you been? And why didn't you answer my texts?'

'I told you that today was the reading of Mr Scott's will. Wait until you—'

But Nick had no time to wait. 'How long does it take to read who gets what in an estate? It's after two o'clock.'

'Alexis took me to lunch after the meeting with her lawyer. With that kind of mind-boggling news, she needed to calm down without her mother nearby. Nothing settles a person like a—'

Nick interrupted a second time. 'Why couldn't you at least text me? After the condition you were in last night, I was worried.'

Jill let a few silent moments spin out. 'What do you think happened – Alexis and I went for a four-martini lunch and I passed out face-down in my Caesar salad?'

'Of course not.'

'I told you, Nick. Someone drugged me last night.'

'And who would've done that?'

'It could have been anyone at the party – Mama Rose, the new master distiller, Mr Rossi, even . . . and I can't believe I'm saying this . . . Alexis. But why on earth would she do something like that?'

'Didn't you get your last drink from Grandpa Parker?

'Why would that nice old guy want me dead? I've only talked to him once or twice. I doubt someone who suffers from memory loss could be a calculating murderer. Grandpa was probably the intended victim.'

Nick knew he'd better tread carefully. 'I'm sorry, Jill. I just had news of my own to share. Tell me what happened at the lawyer's office.'

'Oh, no, by all means, you go first,' she insisted, still sounding annoyed.

He tossed his overnight bag in the trunk and took a deep breath. 'I got a call from Detective Grimes. When the police executed a search warrant at Ross Lacey's, they found pictures of Alexis plastered all over one bedroom wall. Lacey has been charged with violating the restraining order and stalking. Unfortunately the techs found nothing that connected him to William Scott's murder, not inside his townhouse or his car. And Lacey has an alibi for around the time Mr Scott died. So as soon as he posts bail he will be released.'

Jill sighed. 'That's not good. I was sure we had our man . . . I mean, Detective Grimes had her man.'

'Exactly, that's why I wanted to alert you and Alexis. Both of you need to watch your back. Ross Lacey will soon be free as a bird until his stalking trial.'

'Alexis just dropped me off at the hotel. Michael is using the car. Why don't you pick me up and we tell Alexis together?'

'I can't. That's the other half of my news. The sheriff of Nelson County, where I grew up, called. He has my mother at the station and asked me to come take her home. I threw some clothes in a bag and I'm on my way there now.'

'Oh, dear, has your mother been arrested? This is starting to sound way too familiar.'

Nick snorted. 'I don't think so, but Sheriff Wilkins didn't want to go into details on the phone.'

'Have you tried calling her?'

'Since Mom refuses to carry a cell phone, I haven't spoken to her in a few days.'

'Have you talked to your sisters?'

'Not yet. I'd rather get to Lorraine and gauge the situation then give them a call later.' Wiping sweat from his neck, Nick climbed behind the wheel to get out of the sun. 'Now, tell me your news. What happened at the lawyer's office to upset Alexis?'

'Gosh, where do I start? Everything was going along as expected – Mr Scott remembered his brother, his housekeeper, the chauffer, and his parish priest with generous bequests. But when he got to his wife and daughter, the bigger chunk went to Alexis not Rose.'

'What's the big deal? Alexis could always write a check to Mommy Dearest to even the pot.'

'No-ooo.' Jill dragged out the word. 'Because a man named Kevin Scott walked in with his lawyer and claimed he's Mr Scott's son by another woman. This so-called son alleges he was born first and therefore entitled to Alexis's half by the specific wording in the will. Somehow this Bardstown attorney must have obtained a copy of the document.'

Nick whistled through his teeth. 'What a bombshell. No wonder Alexis needed to vent. Is she afraid of losing her legacy?'

'She sounded more upset by the existence of an unknown half-brother. I guess she really wanted a sibling while growing up.'

'I can vouch for that. Whenever I complained about one of my sisters in college, Alexis said she'd gladly take her off my hands.'

'You don't suppose this half-brother bumped off dear old dad? He insists that Mr Scott pledged to take care of him. Maybe he got tired of waiting around for Dad to do the right thing.'

Nick tightened his grip on the steering wheel. 'Hold on there, Jill. Probate court will determine the legality of the will and the homicide department will track down Scott's killer. You need to keep your pretty little nose out of this.' Realizing how patronizing that sounded, Nick braced himself for an argument.

'You're right,' Jill said sweetly. 'Would you like me to go to Lorraine with you? I could be your emotional support for a change.'

'Thanks, but I'll make this trip alone. You stay close to the hotel. If you go to Parker Estate for any reason, take Michael with you.'

'OK, Nick. Give your mom a hug from me and stay in touch. I won't turn my phone off.'

'Please be careful. Don't underestimate Ross Lacey.' Nick hung up with a bad feeling in his gut. He hated the idea of leaving town with a stalker about to be released in society – one who had already threatened Jill – along with some mysterious sibling of Alexis's who had suddenly crawled from the woodwork. Could this brother possibly have anything to do with William Scott's murder? As much as Nick wanted to stay in Louisville and check into this Kevin Scott, his mother needed him more. Since his three sisters had families of their own, besides living out of town, Nick needed to step up as head of the family. Or he'd never be able to look himself in the mirror again.

Nick trounced down on the accelerator and reached Lorraine in record time, grateful that none of his peers had radar along his route. He would have a hard time rationalizing why he had driven fifteen miles above the speed limit. Taking the steps into the sheriff's department two at a time, Nick flashed his identification before reaching the front counter. 'Nick Harris of the Kentucky State Police to see Sheriff Wilkins.'

'Lieutenant Harris, come on back.' Wilkins's bald head appeared in the doorway. 'Let's talk in my office for a moment. Then I'll take you to her.'

Ignoring the curious looks from several deputies, Nick circled the front counter, entered Wilkin's office and closed the door behind him. He didn't sit down. 'How is my mother?' he asked.

'Fine, fine. Have a seat, Lieutenant. One of my female deputies seems to have calmed her down. I believe they're having chamomile tea at the moment.' Wilkins perched on the corner of his desk. 'But I must tell you we're not equipped to handle civilians experiencing any type of breakdown. Normally, we would have EMTs transport them to the nearest hospital. We kept Mrs Harris here as a professional courtesy to you.' He met and held Nick's gaze.

Nick exhaled breath he hadn't realized he was holding. 'I understand, sir, and I appreciate it. Could you explain what happened?'

'As you requested, Hickory Street was placed on regular patrol. An officer drove by your mother's house once each shift.' Hawkins tugged on his earlobe, a gesture Nick's dad also had been fond of. 'Last night around midnight, Deputy Davis spotted your front door standing open during her drive-by. She immediately radioed dispatch and requested backup. Davis canvassed the home's exterior until another officer arrived a few minutes later, then both deputies checked the interior of the home thoroughly. No sign of your mother. After they supplied her description to everyone on duty, Mrs Harris was spotted fifteen minutes later on the sidewalk two miles away.'

'*Two miles?*' Nick asked, incredulous. His mother had never been fond of exercise.

'Yes, sir. The deputy asked if she would like a ride home and she said, "No, I prefer to walk, thank you. It's a lovely evening." Unfortunately, Mrs Harris was headed away from her house and it was starting to drizzle.'

This time when the sheriff looked him in the eye, it felt like someone had kicked him in the gut. Each disappointment Nick had ever caused his parents came roaring back, filling him with guilt and shame.

'When the second deputy left his patrol car and approached

Mrs Harris on foot, your mother became agitated and took off running through the backyards. Deputy Davis caught up to her when a chain link fence boxed her in. Your mom seems more at ease with female cops than males. Davis was able to coax her into the patrol car and bring her to the station.'

'The officers didn't take her home?' Nick asked.

'I advised them against it since I didn't feel comfortable leaving her alone.'

'Thank you, Sheriff. I'm afraid my sisters and I have underestimated the severity of Mom's forgetfulness.' Nick raked a hand through his hair.

'That's easy enough to do when it's your own family member. No one likes to confront their parents' decline. Deputy Davis has been with your mother ever since.'

'Davis spent the night here?'

'She did. We set up two cots in our small conference room and supplied blankets, snacks and bottled water. Mrs Harris demanded to know why she was being arrested. Remaining with her was the only way Davis could convince her she wasn't under arrest.' Wilkins chuckled. 'When your mom has a lucid moment, she can be quite spunky.'

'That is the truth.' Nick rose to his feet. 'May I take her home now? I appreciate the professional courtesy and you have my word, she won't be left alone again. My family and I have some tough decisions to make.'

'I certainly don't envy you. I'll take you to her.' Wilkins led him down the hall, then opened the door on where his mother and Deputy Davis were having tea at a long table. Two plates with toast crusts and the remnants of an omelet indicated a recent meal.

Both women glanced up. 'There you are, Nicky,' Julie chimed. 'They said you were on the way. Took your sweet ole time, didn't you? Do you know Deputy Davis? Shannon is a lovely woman. Too bad you already have a girlfriend. What was her name – Jenny?'

'Hi, Ma. How ya doin'?' Nick, never so relieved to see anyone in his life, wrapped his arms around her neck. 'How do you do, Deputy Davis? I'm very grateful and I apologize for any inconvenience my family caused.'

'What inconvenience?' Julie asked. 'We've been having fun,

discussing the stupid shows on TV. She prefers PBS documentaries just like I do.'

Shannon Davis stretched out her hand. 'You're welcome, Lieutenant Harris. Your mother was a pleasure to spend time with.'

Nick shook her hand heartily, then slipped an arm around his mother's waist. 'Are you ready to go home?'

'I've been ready for hours.' Julie practically dragged him toward the door.

After thanking the sheriff and deputy again, Nick guided his mother to the car and buckled her in. 'Should we stop at the grocery store on the way home? Can you think of anything you need?'

'I don't need any groceries, but let's swing by the Dairy Queen for a hot dog and a milkshake.'

'Didn't you just finish breakfast?'

'No, that was hours ago. I'll pay, Nicky, if money is the issue.' She smirked at him.

'No, money is not the issue. If Dairy Queen is open, you may order whatever you like. I haven't had one of their cheeseburgers in a long time.'

His mother not only ate her chili dog and drank a milkshake, but she finished an order of fries too, which made Nick wonder how regular her meals had been. But an inspection of her refrigerator would have to wait, because the moment he pulled into the drive Mrs Diaz marched from her house carrying a pot.

'Yoo-hoo, Julie. It's me, Inez. I've been worried about you.' The neighbor hurried toward the passenger side of the car.

'I know who you are, you ninny. We've lived next to each other for thirty years.' Julie buttoned her cardigan up to her throat. 'What were you worried about?'

Inez peered from Julie to Nick. 'You didn't come home last night. And I saw the police enter your house.'

'You're confusing real life with those shows you watch. I stayed over at a friend's house. What do you have there?' Julie pointed at the foil-covered Dutch oven.

'Chicken and rice. Reheat for thirty minutes at three hundred.'

Nick rounded the car and accepted the pot from the neighbor. 'Thanks, Mrs Diaz. That was very nice of you.'

'Yes, very nice, but unnecessary,' Julie hollered on her way in. 'I can cook every bit as good as you, Inez Diaz.' She let the screen door slam behind her.

'Sorry, Mrs Diaz. Mom's not been herself lately.'

'I know, Nicky. The other night when I came to the back fence to chat Julie didn't recognize me. She asked if I was housesitting for the Diazes. Carlos told me to mind my own business, but I thought you should know.'

'I'm glad you told me. I've let this situation go on too long.' Nick backed away from her. 'Thanks again for the casserole.'

'You're welcome. Don't worry about the pot.'

Nick had no trouble finding room for the chicken and rice. The refrigerator was empty except for condiments. In the living room his mother was already engrossed in a television show. 'What happened to the grocery deliveries arranged from the IGA?' he asked.

She barely glanced up. 'I sent those deliveries back. If I can't pick out my own fruits and vegetables I don't want them.'

'Then what on earth have you been eating?' Nick struggled to keep his voice even.

'I eat just fine. You worry too much, Nicky. You should be more like your sisters.'

Nick pulled the ottoman up to the sofa. 'Tell me what you mean by that.'

Julie waited for a commercial to answer. 'Your sisters aren't the least bit worried. I haven't heard from any of my daughters in weeks.'

'Well, you just relax and enjoy your show.' Nick draped a quilt around her shoulders, then went through the house slowly, methodically. Most of her Post-it notes were gone and the house was in a state of disarray. Trash overflowed the can. Dishes and glassware were in the wrong cupboards. Clothes lay in heaps on the floor of her closet as though she couldn't find a particular garment. It took Nick several hours to put things back where they belonged, then he cleaned the house from top to bottom.

About the time he started getting hungry and remembered Inez's casserole, he found his mother sound asleep on the couch. Nick tucked a pillow beneath her head, the quilt up to her chin, and found a second blanket for the recliner where he would sleep tonight. Tomorrow he would arrange twenty-four-hour care for his mother until space in a permanent facility could be arranged. But first, the time had come for a heart-to-heart conversation with his sisters, one at a time or all at once. And he knew none of them were going to like it.

TWELVE

Jill woke up out of sorts, despite it being a bright and sunny morning. The perfect Sunday stretched out before her, yet she had no one to spend it with. Michael declined her offer of walking to church with breakfast to follow, preferring the concierge's advice to try the game of golf with a free pass to a country club and a rented set of clubs. Her partner had always preferred sports on TV to anything that might make a person sweat, so his impromptu decision came as a surprise. Next, Jill suggested to Alexis they spend the day at the Louisville Zoo. Maybe an afternoon in the company of elephants, giraffes, and orangutans might distract her friend from her current woes. But Jill's second brilliant idea was also declined. Attorney Ken Bradley was taking Alexis and her mother to brunch, followed by an intense strategy session on how to deal with the new heir.

Jill no longer envied Alexis and it had nothing to do with the potential loss of great wealth. Alexis truly hadn't known either of her parents. Both had kept secrets from each other and from her. Now her father's secret had returned to haunt the family.

On her walk back from church Jill called Nick, hoping he was on his way home from Lorraine. But if this was baseball and Jill was up to bat, she just struck out.

'Sorry, sweet thing,' Nick drawled. 'I'll be in Lorraine all day. If I'm lucky, I'll be home tomorrow morning.'

Jill swallowed her disappointment like a bitter pill. 'Was your mother arrested or taken to the hospital?'

'No, but the sheriff kept her overnight at the station for her own safety and as a courtesy to me. One of the deputies spent the night on a second cot so she could keep an eye on her.' Nick released a weary sigh. 'Mom's fine now, but she gets so confused it's not safe to leave her alone, especially at night.'

'Can't one of your sisters stay with her?' Jill hoped that didn't sound as selfish to his ears as it did to hers.

'All of my sisters are on their way here. Then we'll sit down and decide a short-term solution and a long-term plan for Mom.'

'Things are that bad?' Jill felt a lump form in her throat.

'On Friday Mom couldn't sleep so she went for a walk. At midnight. She was already two miles from her house when a deputy caught up with her.'

'Oh, no. That's awful.'

'When I took her home from the station the house was a mess with almost no food in the fridge. She had cancelled the grocery deliveries I had set up.'

'What can I do? Should I rent a car and drive to Lorraine? I can entertain your mother while the four of you hash out a plan.'

'Thanks, but no. The neighbor invited her over for a hot dog and marshmallow roast over their firepit. Mom never could turn down a hot dog or a S'more.' Nick's laughter sounded forced. 'Besides, with my three sisters here, who may or may not be bringing kids, this place will soon be very crowded.'

And maybe contentious? Jill felt sorry for Nick yet understood his desire to keep one more variable – her – out of the mix. 'I'll cross my fingers for a positive outcome,' she said.

'Thanks, you keep the home fires burning in Louisville. I'll be back before you have a chance to miss me.' After a few tender endearments, Nick hung up.

And Jill was left feeling lost and alone, which struck her as ridiculous. She had been single for a long time but almost never felt lonely. She had plenty of friends, at least back in Chicago, a great partner who usually was happy to spend time with her, plus a grandmother and aunt who lived less than an hour away. So what had changed?

She had changed. She was in love and she was missing Nick with a ferocity that scared her.

*   *   *

For ten minutes of pure bliss Jill stood in the shower, letting the hot water soothe and loosen her tight muscles. After the three people she held near-and-dear abandoned her, she'd spent Sunday afternoon inside the hotel's workout room, punishing herself on treadmills, stationery bikes and rowing machines. Someday she would remember 'getting back in shape' takes longer than one afternoon. In the meantime, she never wanted to have to leave the thirty pulsating water jets.

'Good grief, Curtis! Did you die in there?' Michael's voice intruded on Jill's serenity. 'Get a move on. It's a two-hour drive to Clermont, the last distillery for our Louisville article.'

'You better go without me. I think I got hit by a truck.'

'You caused that pain yourself,' said the man who now fancied himself Tiger Woods after his first thirty-six holes of golf. 'Just take two aspirin and get dressed. I poured you a bowl of frosted flakes.'

'All by yourself? There must've been directions on the box.'

Jill turned off the faucets, wrapped a towel around her head, then dug out two pain relievers from her purse. By the time she finished dressing and applying make-up, the hot water and pills had worked their magic. She felt almost human when she emerged from the bathroom and heard her phone buzzing on the charger.

Jill turned her back on Michael's scowl when she spotted caller-ID. 'Hello, Alexis. How are you on this lovely morning?'

'I'm fine, but I have another favor to ask. Are you busy right now?'

Feeling Michael's stare boring holes in her back, Jill walked out onto the balcony. 'Michael wants to drive to Jim Beam to finish our distillery article.'

'Could that possibly wait another day? One of the security guards at the distillery just called. Apparently, my new half-brother is wandering around the plant, asking questions.'

'How did he get inside? I'm sure you didn't issue him a pass.' Jill glanced back at Michael, who was drumming his fingers impatiently.

'I certainly did not,' Alexis said. 'Apparently he showed his ID, flashed some kind of letter from his lawyer, and the security guard gave him a pass. Could you meet me at my office? Considering Kevin might end up a major shareholder at Parker Estate, I don't want to make a scene in front of employees. I thought we could keep an eye on him on the monitors. I have a bad feeling about this.'

'And you want me, not Mr Bradley or your mother?'

'Goodness, I don't want either of them here. My mother would turn this into a three-ring circus, while Bradley would probably make sure the police or the media shows up. Any kind of publicity is good for his law firm. What do you say, Jill? I'll owe you one or maybe two dozen favors.'

'You owe me nothing. I'll be there in ten minutes.' Jill walked into the suite, ready to face the music.

However, Michael took the news he would be driving to Clermont alone fairly well. He even promised to take plenty of notes on the tour for her to spin into a story. All she had to promise was dinner on her, along with the price of a bottle of Jim Beam's Select and a set of snifters with their logo. Even though this might cost half a week's salary, Jill agreed. It was too late to call Alexis back and she was in no position to negotiate.

'Could you drop me off at Parker Distillery on your way out of town?' she asked, pouring her frosted flakes into a to-go cup.

'Sure, as long as this trip to see Alexis doesn't involve dead bodies or any kind of violence.' Michael picked up his keys and wallet.

'You worry too much.' Jill grabbed her purse and followed him out the door. 'Alexis only wants to keep an eye on her half-brother. We'll be in the safety of her office the entire time.'

At the entrance to the corporate headquarters a guard waved her in and offered to escort her to Miss Scott's office, but Jill declined since she remembered the way.

Alexis bounded from her chair the moment Jill arrived. 'I'm so glad you're here,' she said, pulling another chair to her desk. 'Grab yourself a coffee and watch the security monitors with me. Right now, my new relative is walking through every room on the tour, reading each signboard and studying every display. Kevin is apparently determined to learn bourbon production in one day.'

Jill carried over a cup of coffee and for several minutes they watched the half-brother study pie charts of grain percentages in each type of distilled bourbon. 'Maybe he hopes to become a master distiller after one self-guided tour.'

'I have no idea what he's planning, but I told security not to intervene. For now, we'll just keep an eye on Big Brother to make sure he doesn't sabotage the equipment.' Alexis sipped coffee without taking her eyes off the screen.

Jill scooted her chair in closer. 'Maybe he just wants to learn the business.'

'Maybe, but a phone call would have been nice. Instead he just wormed his way into the building.'

Suddenly Kevin moved out of camera range. 'Where's he going now?' Jill tapped the screen as though a mechanical malfunction caused him to disappear.

Alexis jumped up. 'I'm not sure, but there are no cameras in the mixing room since certain processes are proprietary. Let's see where that sneaky trespasser shows up next.'

But after they checked each live-feed monitor twice, Kevin Scott still hadn't shown up anywhere. Alexis slipped off her high heels and pulled a pair of sneakers from her desk drawer. 'Ready to track down a varmint?'

'You bet I am. I've got pepper spray in my purse and Detective Grimes on speed dial in case things turn ugly.' Jill headed to the door but stopped when Alexis uttered an expletive.

'I found him. A camera picked him up in the hallway by marketing and publicity.'

Jill rushed back to the monitor. 'Who's he talking to? Isn't that the new master distiller, Mr Rossi?'

'It sure is. What is that nutcase talking to him about? He's had exactly one tour of the plant. I wish we could hear what they're saying.' Alexis bent over to tie her sneakers.

As Jill continued to watch the grainy video, Anthony Rossi suddenly staggered, reached out for Kevin's arm, and crumpled to the floor. Not unlike Jill's own inglorious collapse three days ago. 'Oh, no, look!' she cried, pointing at the screen.

Alexis refocused in time to see Rossi sprawled across the tiles with Kevin looming over him. 'What has that crazy person done? I must get down there. Call an ambulance, Jill.' Alexis bolted out the door.

Jill dialed 9-1-1 and gave the dispatcher specific directions. She took the stairs instead of waiting for the elevator and caught up to Alexis just as she reached the surreal scene. Kevin Scott had his ear pressed to Rossi's chest.

'What on earth have you done?' Alexis shouted, dropping to her knees. 'Get away from Mr Rossi! What are you doing?'

'He's not breathing, Alexis,' Kevin said calmly. 'I haven't done anything to him, but Rossi isn't breathing. Somebody call nine-one-one.'

'I already did. The cops and an ambulance are on their way.' Jill pulled out her pepper spray and aimed it his face. 'I believe Alexis told you to back off, buster.'

Kevin peered up at her. 'It's Miss Curtis, right? I need to start CPR or the man will die. You can spray me if you like, but I mean no harm to Mr Rossi . . . or Alexis.' Without waiting for her reply, Kevin locked his hands one over the other and began to press on Rossi's chest at rapid, regular intervals. *Promise me this trip won't involve any dead bodies or violence.* Michael's cryptic words floated through Jill's brain just as a security guard burst through the door with his gun drawn.

'Are you all right, Miss Scott?' The aim of his weapon vacillated between Jill and the would-be heir.

'Could you not point that at me?' Jill asked, hearing the sound of sirens in the distance.

'Holster your weapon, Randy,' Alexis ordered in a strangled voice. 'Please make sure the paramedics and police find their way here.'

'No, wait.' Kevin stopped his ministrations on the inert master distiller. 'Instead, Randy, go to my car in the employee lot. It's a white Chrysler 300 in the first row. You'll find Narcan in the glovebox. Bring it here at once, along with a defibrillator if the distillery has one.' Kevin tossed the guard a set of keys and resumed CPR on Rossi.

'*What?*' Alexis screeched. 'Isn't Narcan used for opioid overdoses?'

'It is. And I'm sure that's what we're witnessing here.'

'What should I do, Miss Scott?' Randy shifted his weight from one hip to the other.

'Get the Narcan or this man's death will be on you,' Kevin roared.

'Go to his car, Randy,' Alexis shouted, her eyes filling with tears. 'Just in case we need it.' Alexis picked up Rossi's hand as soon as the security guard had bolted through the double doors.

With a gun no longer pointed at her, Jill put away her pepper spray and dropped to her knees. 'How can I help?' she asked, looking from one to the other.

Kevin was first to answer. 'Watch what I'm doing in case I need you to take over. Sometimes my hands cramp up due to neurological problems. If we can't revive him, we'll need to maintain compressions until the paramedics arrive.'

Jill tried to locate a pulse in Rossi's neck to no avail as she memorized the procedure of CPR.

'I don't know how Rossi could possibly overdose.' Alexis spoke in an almost-childlike voice.

'Why is that?' Kevin stayed focused on what he was doing. 'Addiction can affect every age and every walk of life.'

'I know that, but Rossi worked for my . . . our father for a long time. It was no secret that he'd suffered breathing problems his whole life. He takes so many meds and herbal supplements for asthma he won't even pop an aspirin for a headache. He knows how drugs can adversely interact.'

Kevin met her gaze. 'I believe you, but I'm also familiar with the signs of opioid overdose.' He patted both of Rossi's jacket pockets, extracted a nasal inhaler, and handed it to Alexis. 'Make sure the police bag that as evidence. If Rossi didn't take opioids willingly, maybe someone tampered with this.'

Jill made a mental note. If Kevin Scott's fingerprints weren't already on the inhaler, they certainly were now. There was plenty of time when the two men were off-camera. 'What will happen to Mr Rossi if you administer the antidote and he's not OD'ing?' she asked.

Kevin didn't answer right away. 'I don't think it'll have any effect at all.'

'You don't *think* but you're not sure?' Alexis asked as Randy burst through the door with the nasal spray in hand.

'Not for certain, no, but the guy's not breathing, right?' Kevin looked at Jill for confirmation.

Jill checked for the third time. 'I still can't find a pulse.'

'Give that to me and check on that ambulance,' Kevin said to the guard, who promptly did as instructed. Then Kevin looked to Alexis to make up her mind.

'All right, go ahead.' She sat back on her heels.

As three people held their breath, Kevin unwrapped the

package, pulled out the inhaler and depressed the plunger up one of Rossi's nostrils, delivering a full dose.

Jill silently counted to sixty. 'Nothing's happening,' she whispered, whereupon Alexis started to cry.

'Give it another minute or two. The stuff doesn't work instantly.' Kevin resumed the chest compressions.

Before Jill reached sixty a second time, Rossi suddenly bolted upright and began to cough.

'Take it easy, sir,' Kevin cautioned, supporting him with an arm around his back. 'Paramedics are almost here.'

'What the heck happened?' Rossi asked. 'One moment we were talking, the next moment the world went dark.'

'The hospital will have to run tests, but I think someone might have tampered with your inhaler.'

'My inhaler?' Rossi immediately felt his shirt pocket. 'I used it right before I ran into you and now it's gone.'

Kevin stilled his flailing arm. 'Alexis has it. She'll give the inhaler to the police so they can have it analyzed. They're on their way.'

Eager to do something useful, Jill scrambled to her feet. 'I'll try to see what happened to that ambulance.' Just as she reached the main lobby, several paramedics burst through the front doors with a gurney, followed by two police officers and the ever-helpful Randy.

'Did it work?' he asked.

'It did. You did well,' Jill said to the security guard as they led the first responders back to Rossi. For the next few minutes, she watched medical professionals at their finest, while the police took statements from both Alexis and Kevin Scott. Since Jill had witnessed exactly the same as Alexis, she remained in the background. Once the paramedics had loaded a conscious and alert master distiller into the ambulance, Alexis climbed in beside him for the trip to the hospital.

Jill and Kevin Scott stood on the sidewalk, watching the ambulance pull away, sirens blaring, while office workers behind them whispered and speculated what had happened. 'Looks like you were right, Mr Scott,' Jill said after a moment.

'I got lucky, Miss Curtis.' The would-be heir pulled out a cigarette and lit up.

'This is a non-smoking facility,' she admonished, sounding like her grandmother.

'I'll keep that in mind should I get the honor of working here.' Kevin inhaled deeply before giving her a long perusal. 'You're my sister's best friend.'

It was more of a statement than a question. 'I doubt I'm her best friend, but I might be her newest,' Jill clarified.

He exhaled a plume of smoke. 'Even after a brief amount of time, I could tell that Alexis trusts your judgement. So I hope you and I can also be friends.'

'Let's get one thing straight – I'm not jumping ship.' Jill arched one eyebrow. 'You might have a legitimate beef against the late Mr Scott, but Alexis doesn't deserve to be denied her inheritance.'

'I agree. That sideshow was my lawyer's idea, meant to throw off that viper Rose Parker. I wish to take nothing away from Alexis.' He took another drag on the cigarette.

Jill stared up at him, confused. 'You do realize that Rose Parker's grandfather started the distillery and her father built it up? Your dad, if he is your dad, William Scott, married into the business.'

Kevin snorted with contempt. 'That's what the PR department wants you to believe. Yeah, it was old man Parker's distillery, all right. But Grandpa poured all the profits into creating that mansion stuck in the middle of nowhere. It had been a working farm when his father was alive that grew the best corn, barley and rye in the county. But Grandma Parker didn't like being a farmer's wife so she leased out the productive acres and got rid of the chickens and cows. Then Grandma Parker insisted on tripling the size of the house. Parker Farms soon became Parker Estate.'

Jill stared at him. 'Who told you all this?'

'My father, who else? What Grandma Parker didn't spend on expensive furnishing to impress the garden club, she spent on entertaining, trips to Europe and turning her daughter into a debutante. That's how Rose Parker got to be the snob she is today. The money should've gone into capital improvements at the distillery, but by the time Rose married my father, the company was bleeding red ink. William not only saved the distillery, he made the brand into what bourbon lovers enjoy today. He had also been buying shares from Grandpa Parker for years. That old man couldn't live within his means. Those shares were not a gift.'

Jill blinked several times. 'You should explain everything to Alexis, not a travel writer from Illinois.'

This time Kevin's chuckle sounded genuine. 'You're exactly right, but for some reason, you're much easier to talk to. My little sister intimidates me.' He stubbed out his cigarette on a lamp pole and slipped the butt back into the pack. 'It was nice meeting you, Miss Curtis.' He started walking in the direction of the employee lot.

'Wait!' Jill called and quickly caught up to him. 'Since we're so comfortable talking to each other . . . how did you know Rossi was overdosing on opioids?'

Kevin looked down his Romanesque nose while considering. 'For several years, my mother was married to a man with a son from a previous relationship. The son was nice enough, but unfortunately Justin developed a drug problem. It started with pain relievers after a football injury. When the doctor cut him off those, he turned to street drugs that often were laced with cheap fentanyl.'

When Keven remained silent, Jill filled in the blanks. 'This stepbrother OD'ed?'

'Several times paramedics or the cops brought him back to life with Narcan. So my mother bought one to keep at home and I started carrying one in my car. One day Justin decided to call his girlfriend instead of me or nine-one-one.'

'What about those dry-out clinics like Betty Ford?'

Kevin produced a patient smile. 'We tried to get him into rehab, but private clinics are expensive and the state-funded rehabs have long waiting lists. He was on the list when he died.'

'I know you did everything you could,' Jill said, even though she didn't *know* anything.

'Thanks. You're a nice person, Jill.' Kevin stepped off the curb and kept on walking.

'Likewise. See ya around.' At least, she hoped he was a nice person.

Since Alexis was at the hospital with Rossi, Jill had no choice but to call Uber for a ride to the hotel. It wasn't until she had got out of the cab that Nick called to let her know he was back in town.

'What's up, pretty girl?' Nick drawled.

'Why didn't you call me half an hour ago?'

'I guess I could have, but what's the big deal?'

'I just paid eleven dollars for an Uber ride.' Jill released a long-suffering sigh.

'Let me make it up to you with a nice dinner.' Nick purred like a cat.

'Sounds marvelous, but Michael will be joining us. He's on his way back from Clermont and this meal will be on me. I have plenty to tell you, but let's wait until we're together so I don't have to chew my food twice.'

'*What?* I'm not following your analogy.'

'You'll understand everything later. Tell me what happened at the family pow-wow. I'm glad you didn't have to stay in Lorraine another night.'

'That's because my sisters had already decided what to do with Mom on the phone along the way.'

'Uh, oh. Sounds like they left little brother out of the loop.'

'Yes, but I'm not unhappy with their decision. This stop-gap might make Mom's transition easier.'

'Not unhappy isn't the same as happy, Magic Man.'

'Nothing we do will be perfect. They decided Mom will move in with my oldest sister's family. Sarah's kids are older and more independent. Sarah plans to hire a caregiver for the eight hours while she and her husband work and the kids are in school. We'll split the cost four ways. In the meantime, we'll also research possible nursing homes for when the situation becomes unmanageable at Sarah and Bob's.'

'How did your mom take the news?' Jill asked, afraid to hear the answer.

'She loved the idea, because she enjoys being with her grandkids.'

'What about your mother's house?'

'Right now, my sisters are packing up the food I had delivered and all her clothes. Then they'll lock the place up. We'll deal with a permanent solution down the road.'

'You're a good son, Nick.'

'Only time will tell. Why don't I pick you and Michael up at seven? The three of us will enjoy the best dinner of our lives that will be on me. No arguments.'

True to his word, Nick picked them up on time and drove them to his favorite restaurant – a seafood joint specializing in oysters. It wouldn't have been Jill's first choice, but since they also served blackened fish, all was well. Since nothing out of the ordinary happened during Michael's tour of Jim Beam's distillery, Jill monopolized most of the conversation with Alexis's mysterious half-brother sneaking into the distillery in an attempt to learn everything about bourbon in a few hours.

'Are you saying this Kevin Scott broke into the place?' asked Nick.

'Why didn't the guards throw the guy out?' Michael demanded.

Jill waved them off. 'Because he sweet-talked his way in. By the time Alexis and I caught up with him, the new master distiller was on the floor and no longer breathing.'

From that point on Jill had her hands full finishing the recap about an opioid overdose and Kevin Scott's experience with an addicted stepbrother. By the time she reached the part about William Scott saving the distillery after Grandpa Parker practically bankrupted it, Michael had lost interest and focused instead on the dessert menu. But Nick definitely had not.

'Do you think Alexis is aware of the real story?' Jill asked him.

'Probably not all of it. I remember whenever Mrs Scott belittled her husband in front of me, Alexis always defended him.' Nick drank the last of his beer. 'Are you planning to tell her, considering Kevin's plans to cut Alexis out of her inheritance?'

Jill thought for a moment. 'Despite what he said at the meeting, I don't think that's really what Kevin wants.'

Although her answer appeared to confuse Nick, he let the matter drop. For which Jill felt grateful, since she had no idea why she wanted to believe the best about a man she'd only known ten minutes.

THIRTEEN

Jill spent most of the morning going over the notes Michael took at Jim Beam Stillhouse. He had done a good job and asked plenty of questions during the tour. After lunch she put all her anecdotes, interviews and research into a cauldron, waved her magic wand, then six hours and one headache later she had a brilliant, cohesive article on the Louisville bourbon tours, worthy of Michael's outstanding photography. But as thrilled as she was to have the Louisville segment finished, she was far less thrilled about returning to Chicago.

Jill had spent her entire life up north where she seemed to have fallen in a rut. No matter how good her travel articles were, she was no closer to becoming an investigative reporter than five years ago. Plus, how could she leave Aunt Dot now that her grandmother had moved in with her in Roseville? In addition to that, she didn't want to leave Nick. Yet she loved working for the news service. So she'd better come up with some kind of idea before the boss sent her and Michael to cover haunted lighthouses in New England.

The moment she ripped open a bag of salt-and-vinegar chips, Nick called. 'What's up, Jilly? Are you on your way back from Jim Beam?'

'Nope, Michael got everything we needed yesterday, so unless you're inviting me on a romantic getaway, Clermont is off the table.'

His husky, deep drawl never failed to lift her spirits. 'I wouldn't rule that out for the future, but in the meantime, how 'bout dinner at my place?'

'Who's cooking?' Jill stapled the bag of chips shut.

'Me, who else? I heard about the multiple visits from the fire department whenever you turn on a stove.'

'Michael lies or at least he exaggerates. Two visits shouldn't constitute the term "multiple". What time should I come over?'

'I'll pick you up in half an hour. Wear something slinky.' Nick laughed and hung up before she could argue.

And it was just as well, because Sheriff Jeff Adkins crushed their plans for a romantic dinner. When Nick knocked on her door thirty minutes later, Jill was still in jeans and wearing a frown.

'Good evening, Miss Curtis. You're looking especially pretty tonight, although I wouldn't describe a Loyola shirt as slinky.' He handed her a bouquet of flowers.

'Sorry, Nick. Dinner's off. I need to drive to Roseville.'

'Says who? I'm simmering gumbo in the crockpot.'

'Thanks for these.' Walking into the kitchen, Jill stuck the flowers into a pitcher of water. 'Says Jeff Adkins.'

'No. Way.' Nick leaned one shoulder against the doorjamb. 'Don't tell me he arrested your aunt and grandmother . . . again.'

Jill rolled her eyes. 'Not just Aunt Dot and Granny this time, but the entire Tuesday night book club.'

He glanced at his watch. 'It's barely eight o'clock. How could a bunch of ladies get into trouble this early?'

'It doesn't take long at their age.' She plopped down on the sofa. 'Apparently, no one liked the book they read. So one of them came up with the brilliant idea to take a taxi to a bourbon club.'

'I've been to Roseville. They have no clubs.'

'No, but two different restaurants serve flights of bourbon. The club secretary, Mrs Penny Whittaker, did some research.'

Nick scrubbed his hands over his face. 'Please don't tell me one of the members drove drunk.'

'No, they took taxis downtown and had planned to call for rides home. However, the sheriff provided their next means of transportation, right to the station.' Preparing to leave, Jill collected her phone, purse and keys. 'Apparently, the ladies were seated at high-top tables, enjoying tasters of bourbon, when one of the ladies slipped off her stool and landed on the floor. She wasn't hurt but she attracted quite a bit of attention, which the manager didn't like. The woman told the manager it was because of her vertigo, but the manager didn't buy it. He told them to finish their drinks and go home. But instead the club went to another bar where they ordered two more flights of bourbon.'

Nick tried to suppress a grin. 'Sorry, Jill, but the mental picture of this is priceless.'

'I'm glad you think so, lawman. At the second unfortunate establishment, two ladies got into an argument about politics. Of course, this attracted attention. Then when the woman jumped up to use the restroom, she stumbled into an entire display of merchandise and broke plenty of glassware.'

Nick straightened to his impressive height. 'Good grief. Was this woman injured?'

'Apparently not, since she couldn't stop laughing. Which made the manager furious and he called the police. Sheriff Adkins arrived and arrested the entire group. Drunk and disorderly. How is this going to look in the local paper?' Jill found her keys under a stack of restaurant menus. 'Go home and relax, Nick, and enjoy your gumbo. Soon you'll be back to work and your vacation hasn't exactly been memorable.'

He plucked the keys from her fingers. 'I wouldn't miss this drama for anything in the world. I hope you plan to give Granny and Aunt Dot a good lecture.'

'You bet I am. I have the entire drive to Roseville to choose the perfect words.'

As it turned out, Jill had no time to plan what she'd say to her relatives. Instead she and Nick talked about growing up, life during high school and college, and their dreams for what they wanted in life.

Then out of the clear blue sky, Nick asked, 'Are you still going back to Chicago?'

Jill's palms began to sweat. 'Unfortunately, that's where my job is.'

'Have you looked for journalism positions in Louisville?'

His directness unnerved her. 'I wanted to, but I've been too busy.'

Nick focused on the road. 'With the article, yes, but also on Alexis's problems. It's time you told me where your head is and specifically, what it is you want.'

She swiped her palms down her jeans as the entire world tilted on its axis. 'Let's see . . . I'm not keen on moving back to my apartment in the city. I would prefer to stay in the Louisville area because it's close to Roseville. My relatives can't seem to be left alone for very long. Although it's no Chicago, there might be opportunities for journalists here or I can always freelance.'

'And us, Jill? Where exactly do I stand in your plans?'

Every now and then a woman must take a chance and go out on a limb, even if it breaks off. And this was Jill's now-and-then. 'Even if I have to move back to Sweet Dreams, I'm not going back to Chicago. I want you, Nicky. I want us. I've been waiting for you to suggest we move in together. Now is that clear enough for you?'

Nick smiled. 'Since I'm an old-fashioned guy, I was thinking about a more permanent arrangement.'

'What does that mean?' Jill pivoted to face him on the seat. 'Are you proposing to me?'

'I am.' Nick slowed his speed as they entered Roseville's city limits.

'Who does that anymore, without running a background check and having a trial run of several years?'

'What makes you think I haven't researched your past? I am a lawman.' He pulled to a complete stop before turning right on red. 'I did like those braids in the seventh grade, by the way. Did you discover some Native American ancestry?'

Jill made a face. 'Unfortunately, no, I just thought they looked cool. Let's not change the subject. Are you proposing or not?'

Nick waited to answer until he turned off the ignition at the Spencer County Sheriff's Office. 'I am, Jill Curtis. I'm in love with you. What do you say? Will you marry me?'

'Maybe, as long as we have a *long* engagement. After all, we've only known each other for five weeks. I need time for my own background check. You weren't always a lawman. Who knows what skeletons are buried in Lorraine?'

'Fair enough. Now let's post bail for your kinfolk. After all, I've got a vested interest in their future.'

Jill climbed out of the car. 'Please don't say a word about our engagement. I want nothing to distract those two criminals from the seriousness of their actions.'

'My lips are sealed.'

Sheriff Adkins walked out of his office the moment they entered the station. 'Looks like members of the book club are becoming regular guests.' He tucked his thumbs into his belt.

'This will be the last time, Sheriff. My grandmother is officially grounded and without her partner in crime, Mrs Clark should settle down too.'

'Has bail been set yet for the ladies?' Nick asked.

He exhaled a sigh. 'Since I released the other perpetrators on their own recognizance to their families, I'll release Mrs Clark and Mrs Vanderpool in the same fashion, providing changes are made to the book club. Otherwise my wife won't speak to me for a week. Dot Clark is her friend and she's mad that I arrested her. I suggest alcohol-free discussions from now on.'

Jill placed her hand over her heart. 'I will insist upon it, Sheriff, and provide Tuesday night enforcement if necessary.'

The sheriff paused on their way to the basement. 'In all

fairness it wasn't either Mrs Clark or your grandmother who argued with the bar manager or caused the damage. In fact, my deputy reported that Mrs Vanderpool attempted to pay for the broken glass.'

'Good to know, but that doesn't get either of them off the hook,' Jill said as they rounded the corner to the cell block.

'They're in the first cell. I will leave you to it.' Sheriff Adkins tipped his hat to her and shook Nick's hand.

Rolling up her sleeves, Jill approached the cell. Inside, two elderly, silver-haired ladies sat side-by-side on a cot. Their heads were bowed as if in prayer, deep meditation, or sound asleep. 'I see your friends have abandoned you,' Jill said, lifting her chin. 'What do you have to say for yourselves?'

Pale and exhausted, Granny looked up first. 'They didn't really abandon us. Their rides got here first, but thanks for coming.'

'Oh, Jill,' Dot wailed. 'I'm so ashamed. I knew it was a bad idea to go downtown, but Emma and I were outvoted. The member in charge of bringing the pint of bourbon forgot to get it, so she insisted on buying a round at Harry's.'

Jill leaned towards them. 'That's your excuse? You couldn't just discuss the book over coffee or tea like normal grandmothers?'

'We are the bourbon-and-books club,' Emma pointed out. 'Not the tea and crumpets.'

'You *were* the bourbon-and-books club, granny. There will be no more alcohol at the meetings.'

'Agreed.' Aunt Dot wrung her hands in her lap. 'But I'm not sure there will be much club left. We listened while several husbands showed up to take their wives home.' Dot shivered as though a cold breeze blew through the basement. 'Penny's husband told the sheriff that a night in the slammer might do her some good, so he refused to pick her up.'

Granny cupped her hand around her mouth and whispered conspiratorially. 'Penny called her daughter since Adkins hadn't confiscated either her cell phone or her belt.'

Nick coughed to cover his laugh, but Jill maintained a stern expression. 'Believe me, I had the same idea as Penny's husband.'

Dot pushed stiffly to her feet, then helped up Emma. 'We're both very grateful. If you and Lieutenant Harris drive us home, we promise to cause no more trouble.' Dot held up her hand as though testifying and elbowed Emma until she did the same.

'Do *you* promise, Granny?' Jill asked, crossing her arms.

'I promise.' Emma's eyes filled with tears. 'The last thing I want is to be sent back to that nursing home. I love it here in Kentucky with Dot.'

Jill reached between the bars for her grandmother's hand. 'No matter what you do, Granny, nobody will ever send you back to Chicago.'

'We can always slap ankle monitors on them,' Nick said, slipping his arm around Jill's waist.

'Would you please get the sheriff?' she asked over her shoulder. 'I believe these ladies are ready to apologize for wasting taxpayers' money.' Jill turned back to Dot and Granny. 'You will also apologize to both bar managers and pay for the damages.'

'Penny Whittaker already promised to do that tomorrow morning,' Granny said. 'But Dot and I can take the managers candy and cookies when we apologize. Sweets usually soften people up.'

Aunt Dot stepped forward. 'I owe you an apology too, Jill. You not only pulled me through a difficult period at the B & B, you helped solve my husband's murder. I'm very sorry, and I plan to make this up to you.'

'You're both forgiven. Now let's get you home and in bed.'

'You should have held out for one of Dot's apple pies,' Nick whispered loud enough to be heard.

After Sheriff Adkins unlocked the cell, Dot Clark stretched up and kissed Nick on the cheek. 'Baking a few apple pies would be my pleasure, Lieutenant Harris.'

Jill and Nick dropped off the repeat offenders and munched burgers and fries on the way back to Louisville. His well-cooked gumbo would have to wait for another night. Considering she had just agreed to marry him, they should have quite a few future evenings together.

Nick stared at the Weather Channel, sipping coffee for a long time that morning. Yet he wouldn't have been able to recount Louisville's forecast if his life were at stake. He couldn't stop thinking about Jill and his impromptu proposal. And the fact she hadn't exactly said 'yes'. Was he making a mistake by trying to rush things? Maybe they should just see where they were at in six months.

Now in the harsh morning light, after a good night's sleep, and without her family's antics stressing her out, was Jill regretting her answer altogether? There was only one way to find out, but so far Nick hadn't mustered the courage to call her. When his phone rang a few minutes later he reached for it, grateful that Jill had taken the timing out of his hands.

'Good morning, sweet thing. I trust you slept well.'

'Like a baby, Lieutenant Harris. This is Lisa Grimes of Louisville Homicide.'

Nick felt a flush of embarrassment crawl up his neck. 'Sorry, Detective. I was expecting a call from my girlfriend.'

'No problem. Other than that, am I interrupting anything?'

'No, what can I help you with?' Nick began to pace his apartment.

'We've been checking into Ross Lacey's alibi for the night William Scott died. Lacey said he'd spent the evening bar-hopping with an old friend from high school. When we finally tracked the guy down, he hadn't seen Lacey in months. Since this friend works as a long-distance truck driver Lacey probably thought his alibi was safe.'

'So our stalker is also a liar.' Nick poured coffee into a travel mug. 'I'd like to go with you, Detective, when you question him.'

'I thought you might, hence the phone call. Unless you'd rather wait for your girlfriend to call.' Grimes actually giggled on the other end.

'That's the miracle of mobile phones. Wherever a person goes they're still available twenty-four-seven. Where should I meet you?'

'Come down to the main precinct. Homicide is on the third floor. I'm having Lacey brought here for questioning. With any luck you two should arrive around the same time.'

As Grimes predicted, two uniformed officers were delivering Lacey just as Nick walked up. 'Come in, Lieutenant.' Grimes waved him into the conference room. 'We're happy to welcome the state police as consultants today.'

Lacey looked like he hadn't slept in days. He also didn't look happy to be there. 'Why am I here? This is Homicide and you've got nothing to connect me to any murder.' He growled more like a dog than a licensed stockbroker.

'You're here, Mr Lacey, because I don't like being lied to. We found Paul Woodley, the friend you supposedly bar-hopped with the night William Scott died. He said he hadn't seen you in years.'

Lacey shrugged. 'Yeah, so what? I was home watching TV alone that night. You would have interpreted that as a guilty plea. I know how cops think.'

Grimes smiled slyly. 'Do you now? We interpret lying as hiding something from us, which is usually a reliable indicator of guilt.'

He shook his head. 'Look, I didn't kill anyone. I loved Alexis Scott. In fact, I still have a soft spot for her. I would never kill her father, no matter how big a jerk he was.'

Nick leaned across the table. 'You do realize she's pressing charges against you for stalking? So it doesn't sound like Alexis shares the same affection.'

Lacey's hostile glare landed on Nick. 'Mainly because that travel writer poisoned Alexis against me. I'd love to know how she wormed her way into Alexis's life. And how exactly do you fit into this, state cop? Homicide detectives don't usually invite other agencies to consult.'

'When did you become an expert on what my department does?' Grimes sneered. 'So you were alone the night Mr Scott died?'

'Yeah, just like half the population of Kentucky.'

'But most of the population isn't holding a grudge against him.'

'You don't have a single shred of evidence against me.'

'Maybe not right now, but I plan to go over everything from your house with a fine-tooth comb, just in case the techs were having an off day.'

Lacey's smug expression faltered. 'You two are barking up the wrong tree. And since I'm basically a nice guy, I will throw you a bone.' He ran a finger around his collar. 'I'm not the only one keeping an eye on Alexis.'

Grimes glanced at Nick, then refocused on Lacey. 'You have my attention.'

'Yesterday I spotted Alexis having lunch with her lawyer in that new restaurant on E. Washington, Gardenias.' Lacey looked Grimes in the eye. 'I've been curious what kind of food they serve there. When Alexis left, I followed her just to make sure she got home safely. That still isn't the best area.'

'You realize you're incriminating yourself? I can have your bond revoked on the stalking charge.'

Lacey pounded his fist on the table. 'Yeah, and I hope you won't since I'm trying to help. There was a guy at the bar who kept staring at Alexis. At first I thought it was because she's so pretty. But when she and the lawyer left the restaurant that weirdo walked out right after her and jumped in his car. Next, Alexis met two girlfriends in the courtyard at the Omni and guess who shows up?' When Grimes failed to respond, Lacey filled in the blank. 'The same guy watching her in Gardenias. He sat on a bench against the wall and lit up a cigarette.'

'There's no smoking in public areas in Kentucky,' Nick couldn't keep from pointing out.

'Yeah, I know, but this dude was on his third before the manager told him to put it out. Alexis and her friends had two glasses of wine and talked up a storm. Then Alexis left but her friends stayed and ordered food. The guy left right after Alexis did and lit up a smoke the moment he got outside.'

'Did you happen to catch his name or maybe his license plate number?'

'Nah, that didn't occur to me at the time. If that guy had followed her home, I would've yanked him out of his car and taught him a lesson.' Lacey flexed his fingers into a fist.

'You're saying *you* followed Miss Scott home?'

'Only to make sure she got there safely. I told you, I care about her.'

Grimes tapped her pen against the table. 'At least give us a description, since you spent as much time watching him as watching Miss Scott.'

Lacey turned his focus to the ceiling. 'Pretty average, I suppose – brown hair, blue eyes, medium weight, but taller than average. His only distinguishing feature was a bump on his schnozz right here.' He touched a spot midway down his nose. 'That and the fact he was a chain-smoker.'

Nick pulled out his small notebook to jot the details.

'Do you know this guy, Lieutenant?' Grimes asked.

'No, but I have an idea who might have met him. I'll check into it and get back to you, Detective.'

'In the meantime, Mr Lacey, respect the restraining order Miss Scott has in place. If we find you within a hundred yards of her, you'll be arrested, your bail revoked, and you'll sit in jail until your trial date.'

'I've got rights. You better not set me up like the last time.' Lacey's eyes became dark slits in a contorted face. 'I told you about this guy as a courtesy and this is the thanks I get? Unless you're arresting me, I'm outta here.' Lacey pushed to his feet.

'You're free to go,' Grimes said, unruffled. 'Just remember what I told you.'

Nick cracked his knuckles one at a time. 'Lacey truly rubs me the wrong way.'

'So I gathered, Nick. So you think Jill Curtis might know the new mystery stalker of Miss Scott?'

'She might. On the phone Jill told me about a man claiming to be Alexis's half-brother who appeared out of nowhere.' Nick refilled his coffee cup, then relayed everything Jill had told him, starting with the reading of William Scott's will and ending with the bombshell about a firstborn son and Grandpa Parker's mishandling of finances over the years.

Grimes listened without interruption, her expression growing more incredulous by the moment. 'So this Kevin Scott barges into the lawyer's office, announces his plans to contest the will, namely Alexis's half, then marches into the distillery like he owns the place and just happens to be there when the new master distiller overdoses? I need copies of the responding officer's and the paramedic's reports.' She jotted a few notes on a scratchpad. 'Even though you heard this secondhand, what's your gut feeling about this wannabe heir? Do you think he caused the OD so he could look like a hero saving Rossi's life?'

Nick considered this. 'We won't know until the lab finishes analyzing Rossi's blood sample and his inhaler, but I suspect fentanyl was inside the inhaler. It's the only synthetic opioid powerful enough to kill with a single inhalation. That being said, from what Jill described, I doubt Kevin Scott had the opportunity or enough time to taint an asthma device.'

Grimes tossed her pen down. 'So someone decided to kill the master distiller before this half-brother shows up?'

'That would be my guess, pending lab results. But it doesn't let the half-brother off the hook for William Scott's murder.'

'He certainly has motive since he could end up with half the distillery. What we need is evidence. Can't anything just be straightforward?' Grimes shook her head. 'I'll see if paramedics collected anything of Kevin's that might contain DNA. Then I'll check to see if his DNA matches anything from Scott's crime scene. If the paramedics have nothing, do you think Miss Curtis could get a DNA sample from her new confidant?'

'I can ask. For some reason, Jill has talked to the mystery man more than anyone else.' Nick stood and snapped the lid on his coffee mug.

'Before you go, Lieutenant, I want you to realize Ross Lacey is a potential threat to Jill and maybe even you.' She waited as Nick sat back down. 'When we executed the search warrant at Lacey's apartment, we found plenty of evidence he'd been stalking Miss Scott for a long time. The DA will have no trouble obtaining a conviction. But we also found photos of Jill Curtis, whom I believe you're very fond of based on how you answered the phone.' Her lips curled into a smile. 'Lacey had half of one wall dedicated to Miss Curtis – some pictures taken entering and exiting her hotel, some taken on the street, a few from inside restaurants, and one even has you in the shot. One rather disturbing photo was taken with a long-range, telephoto lens while she was getting undressed.'

Nick's blood throbbed at his temples while his palms turned clammy. 'I want that creep picked up on new charges. No way should he be free to—'

'Hang on and hear me out. I'll make sure the district attorney amends the charges to include stalking and threatening Miss Curtis. But Lacey gave us a tip in exchange for not revoking his bail.'

'That tip might turn out to be totally worthless.' Nick struggled to keep his temper. 'And those charges were for stalking Alexis.

Jill has a right to expect Lacey brought in on new charges. Half a wall of photos should be enough evidence.'

Grimes held up her hands. 'I don't disagree, but I'm investigating a homicide. I recommend Jill take out her own restraining order again Lacey. Then at the first violation, he'll be arrested and his photos of Jill entered into evidence. His bail will be revoked as a serial stalker. In the meantime, let's look into this Kevin Scott.'

He sighed. 'Fine, I'll see if Jill can get something with his DNA. But she won't be meeting this new whacko without me nearby fully armed.'

Nick left police headquarters annoyed, partly with Detective Grimes, but mainly with the entire justice system which gave cretins get-out-of-jail-free cards if they provided information on bigger fish in the criminal pond. It's not that his department didn't use similar tactics, but when it hit close to home – or the heart – it really stunk. Nick called Jill the moment he reached his car in the parking lot.

'It's about time you called, buster. I thought maybe you regretted the proposal and had hightailed-it to the south of France.' Jill's voice sounded sweeter than the choirs of heaven to his ears.

'The only way I'm going to France, northern or southern, is if you pick it for our honeymoon. I took Spanish in high school, so I don't speak a word of French.'

Jill laughed. 'With all the translation apps you can download these days, we'll be fine. What are you doing? I bribed the concierge for another country club pass and paid for thirty-six holes of golf for Michael.'

'Thirty-six holes?' Nick asked in disbelief. 'That should take him until nightfall to finish.'

'That's what I had in mind. I'm all yours, baby. I believe you promised me jambalaya for dinner.'

'I stuck that in the fridge, but I'm not sure if it's still edible. Dinner will be on me, but in the meantime, I have a favor to ask.'

After they quickly deduced the mysterious new stalker was the would-be brother, Nick summarized his meeting with Detective Grimes, including the request that she obtain DNA from Kevin Scott on the sly. Knowing that Jill loved the excitement of detective work, her reaction surprised him.

'Why on earth would I do that for the homicide department when Grimes doesn't seem concerned about Lacey stalking me?'

'It's not that she isn't concerned . . .'

'Oh, because I'm not as rich as Alexis my case doesn't get priority?'

It was then that Nick realized two things: one, he'd rushed through his explanation of how Jill's complaint against Lacey must proceed. And two, he had mistakenly placed himself between two strong-willed women. Even if he wasn't in love with one of them, he'd made a serious error in judgement. 'No, no, no. We'll go down to the courthouse where you can file a complaint and request a TRO against Lacey. In the meantime, Grimes is a homicide detective, so stalking isn't her area. But if you prefer not to help in this fashion, I'm behind you one-hundred percent.'

'No, I'll help Detective Grimes,' Jill muttered after a moment's pause. 'I don't want it getting around that I don't support law enforcement.'

'Jill—' Nick began, but she quickly interrupted.

'Relax, Trooper. This will be easy-peasy. I wish you would've said something sooner. All I would've had to do was pick up one of his cigarette butts. What do you want me to do?'

Nick laid out a spur-of-the-moment plan, uncertain if it would work or if he could guarantee her safety. So the last thing he could do was relax.

FOURTEEN

Jill finished the last of her tamale and enchilada plate sitting at a brightly painted picnic table on a perfect summer afternoon. 'Lunch was superb. Thank you.' She tossed her napkin down with a smile. 'But don't think you're off the hook for dinner tonight.'

'Nothing would please me more than cooking for you.' Nick took her hand and kissed her fingers.

'How romantic you are, especially when you want something.' She pulled her hand back.

He frowned. 'You don't have to do this. Detective Grimes will solve the case without any help from us.'

'I'm messing with you, Nick. Call her. See if Grimes has Kevin Scott's phone number. Actually, I'm looking forward to seeing Mr Tall, Dark and Mysterious again. He might just be heir to a distillery.'

'And here I thought you were Alexis's friend.'

'I am. I'm hoping Kevin ends up with Mama Rose's half.'

Nick punched in the detective's cell number. 'You've already accepted my proposal. I'll fight Scott to the death if necessary.'

Unfortunately, Grimes picked right then to answer the call. 'Who on earth are you fighting to the death, Lieutenant?'

Nick laughed as he met Jill's eye. 'Sorry, Detective. An inside joke with my new fiancée.'

'New fiancée? And you're already challenged to a duel at dawn? I don't know whether to say congratulations or good luck.'

'Thanks. I was wondering if you have the police report for the distillery handy. I need a phone number for Kevin Scott.' Nick jotted the number and handed the paper to Jill.

'No questions asked as to why?' she asked.

'She's the one asking for a favor.'

'I sure hope Kevin's innocent.'

'Nobody in this world is truly innocent.'

'Not even you, Trooper?'

'Especially not me.' Nick winked with as much lewd intent as a person could inflict with eyelashes.

Rolling her eyes, Jill punched in the number. An hour later she walked to the entrance of the Hyatt Regency on Jefferson Street, twenty minutes later than their agreed upon time. As she and Nick had assumed, Kevin Scott stood under the awning, smoking beside a huge urn filled with sand.

'I'm so sorry, Mr Scott,' Jill murmured as she reached him. 'I had a bit of an emergency with my fiancée after we talked.' She smiled sweetly.

'Not a problem. Should we go inside and get a table?' Kevin pushed up a cuff to check his watch.

'Absolutely.' But as Jill hooked her arm through his elbow, her phone rang, right on cue. 'Good grief! It's my future mother-in-law. Could you find us a table? I'll join you in five minutes.'

'Would you prefer we reschedule for another time?' Scott looked and sounded irritated.

'Please, no. Give me five minutes, then I'm turning my phone off.' Jill held up five fingers.

The moment Alexis's half-brother disappeared through the entrance Jill plucked the cigarette butt from the urn with a plastic bag and sealed it shut. Luckily, the receptacle had recently been cleaned and all butts were the same brand. She gave the thumbs-up to Nick who watched from across the street, then sauntered confidently through the grand foyer of the Hyatt, knowing Nick would soon be close behind.

Soft lighting and plenty of polished brass provided tasteful sophistication in the bar off the main lobby. When Jill spotted Kevin in a leather booth, she slipped in across from him and requested white wine from the server who appeared immediately. A snifter of Parker Estate bourbon already sat in front of Kevin, condensation from the ice already dampening the napkin.

'Well, Miss Curtis, considering you're engaged to be married, I'm curious why you invited me for drinks on an otherwise ordinary Wednesday afternoon. I was hoping you'd fallen in love at first sight, but I suspect that's not the case.' He looked her straight in the eye.

It was the first time Jill had noticed his incredibly blue eyes. *So much like Alexis's.* But unlike Alexis's soft, perfect features, Kevin's face was all hard lines and angles with deep creases across his forehead that even the priciest cream couldn't help. Only his hair, combed straight back on one side while the other fell across his brow, softened his features. Then there was that nose. Nothing soft or perfect about that. Yet, all in all, Kevin Scott was oddly attractive.

'Miss Curtis?' he asked, his voice rising. 'Did you ask me here to talk or just to stare?'

'Forgive me. I was blown away by your eyes. They're . . . exactly like Alexis's. I didn't notice earlier because you're so tall.'

'So maybe you think I'm telling the truth?' As the server delivered her drink, he took a swallow of his. 'But you haven't answered my question – why are we here?' He clutched the glass with both hands.

'I wanted to ask you about Rose Parker Scott. I don't like her, and suspect she had something to do with her husband's death.' Jill took a sip of wine, remembering what had happened during her last visit to the distillery.

'There's plenty not to like with my father's wife.' His lip furled with contempt.

Jill steadied her nerves with another sip. 'When you and your attorney crashed the reading of the will, Rose acted shocked to hear that William had fathered another child. Was she?'

Kevin grinned. 'Crashed . . . I love your choice of words. But in truth, Rose-the-annihilator wasn't surprised by anything that day.'

'She knew her husband had a son by a previous relationship?' Jill asked as she spotted Nick at a table across the room.

'Not at first she didn't. But about five years ago, Rose and William's marriage went seriously off the rails. Rose and her father questioned my father's authority and tried to hobble his control at the distillery every chance they got. That was around the time William started having affairs with women at work.' Kevin looked down at his hands. 'I'm not defending his behavior. I'm just stating the facts. During one of their epic fights, William let it slip about me and my mother. Why, I'm not sure. Maybe he knew it would hurt her.'

Jill felt a queasy sensation in her gut. 'If I may ask, how is your mom? And how does she feel about you pursuing your inheritance?'

Kevin tightened his grip on the glass, then downed the remaining bourbon in one swallow. 'My mother passed of cancer a year ago. Long before she died, she encouraged me to form a better relationship with my father.' He pulled out a battered photograph of a dark-haired woman, a sandy-haired boy of around six, and William Scott in decidedly younger and happier times. 'But I didn't know anything about the distillery until right before she died.'

Jill hadn't noticed a hump in William's nose in the photos at the memorial service. 'You and Alexis obviously have the same father, but I'm curious about William's appearance. Do you suppose he had plastic surgery?' She handed back the picture.

'I never thought much about it, but maybe he did after he married Rose. That woman couldn't be any vainer about appearances. One of Dad's suits probably cost more than everything in my mom's closet put together.' Kevin tucked the photo back in his wallet.

'Despite a lack of expensive clothes, your mom was a beautiful woman. I'm sorry for your loss. I'm sure she was very proud of you.' Jill placed her small hand over his larger one.

'That's nice of you to say, Jill. And yes, she was.' Kevin reversed the position of their hands and then motioned for another round of drinks. 'Rose knew about me, all right. She demanded William have nothing to do with me, which worked for a while. Later when he started to get to know me, she tried to pay me off several times. Her last offer was for a million dollars to go away and never contact *her* family again. I would've taken the cash if there was a treatment that could save my mother. But there wasn't and she went downhill fast. Afterwards, all I wanted was revenge.'

'Against Alexis?' Jill asked quietly.

'No, not against Alexis.' Kevin slapped his palm against the polished surface. 'My lawyer insists my only hope for success is for my sister's half. But that's not what I want. I want Rose to feel the deprivation, the rejection, and the humiliation that my mother lived with for years.'

An icy chill ran up Jill's spine. Part of her wished to bolt from the room, away from an angry young man who frightened her. But another part felt sorry for Kevin. He'd grown up with the same deprivation, rejection, and humiliation as his mother, through no fault of his own. 'Alexis needs to be told the truth about the situation.'

Kevin finished his first drink just as the server delivered the second round. 'Then you'll have to be the one to tell her. Did you see how Alexis looked at me while Tony Rossi was dying on the floor? Like I was the one responsible.' He answered the question for her. 'Why would I try to kill the master distiller? I was hoping he'd take me under his wing.'

'You're serious about learning the bourbon-making business?'

'Of course I am. I want to work alongside my sister, not replace her. That's what my father had in mind. And he'd planned to change his will and split his estate between his children.'

'Did Rose know of his intentions?' Jill moved her wine glass out of reach.

'Mama Rose knew he wanted to bring me into the business, she just didn't know that William owned all of Grandpa's shares. Why wouldn't she know he'd planned to change his will? She had her father and the entire household staff spying for her, so nothing went on inside that house she didn't know about. And the fact someone murdered him before he made the change makes Rose a more likely suspect than me. Wouldn't I have waited until after I was officially named an heir?' Kevin glanced furtively around the room, then focused on the table where Nick sat. 'Would your boyfriend like to join us for a drink? He can keep you safer here than over by the wall.'

Jill swiveled around and smiled at Nick, who realized his less-than-perfect cover had been blown. He walked to where they sat and extended his hand. 'How do you do? Nick Harris, Jill's fiancé. I'm also an investigator for the state police.'

'Kevin Scott, nice to meet you. I hope your normal duties don't involve undercover work. You practically leaped from your chair when Jill touched my hand.'

'Usually they don't, but I'm afraid I'm overprotective where Jill is involved.' Nick sat down next to her.

'Understandable.' Kevin studied Nick over the rim of his glass. 'May I buy you a drink?'

'Actually, I need someone to drink this.' Jill moved the second glass of wine in front of him. 'Today one will be my limit.'

'I'm especially protective because I asked Jill to get a sample of your DNA, and we seldom involve civilians in such a fashion.'

Jill felt her cheeks flush from Nick's admission.

'Is that why you scooped up my cigarette butt?' Kevin asked her. 'I saw your reflection in the glass. I thought maybe you were an anti-litter freak.'

'Yes,' Jill admitted, red-faced. 'But I also wanted to talk to you and hear your side of the story.'

Kevin shrugged. 'That cigarette will rule me out as a suspect, but why would you care about me or what happens to my rightful inheritance? I told you I harbor no ill will toward Alexis.'

'Maybe I'm a big fan of justice. Or maybe I feel bad about how you were treated.'

'In case you haven't noticed, Jill, life isn't fair. And I don't need anyone's pity. I'll settle our tab on my way out.' Kevin downed the rest of his bourbon. 'Congratulations on your engagement, Mr Harris.'

'Wait!' Jill demanded, scrambling to her feet. 'Everyone can use a helping hand. Why don't I talk to Alexis about hiring you as a production trainee?'

Kevin hesitated, then looked back. 'Why would you do that?'

'Because it's the right thing to do, and for some reason I trust you.'

'You think Alexis would do that for you?'

'Yep, that woman owes me plenty of favors. Give her a call in the morning.'

'Why are you helping him?' Nick asked once Scott had left the restaurant. 'Kevin hasn't been ruled out in either William's murder or the attempt on Rossi's life.'

'Please.' Jill dragged the word into two syllables. 'As Kevin said, he wouldn't kill his father until after the will was changed. And what would his motive be to kill Rossi?'

Nick pushed the wine away and pulled her to her feet. 'Let's just get that cigarette over to Detective Grimes before you go making new friends. She can also check into his alibi for the Monday William died.'

Instead, while Nick took the elevator up to the homicide department, Jill stayed in the car, planning what she would say to Mrs Parker Scott. That woman probably even lied in her sleep. At the attorney's office she had acted shocked about Kevin's existence. But Rose not only knew about William's firstborn son but had known he planned to change his will. That sounded like motive for murder in Jill's book.

'Are you ready to sign a complaint against Lacey while we're downtown?' Nick asked when he returned.

Jill didn't have to think for long. 'No, that sort of thing can take hours. I'll do it soon, but not now. Today. I plan to catch Rose in one of her multitude of lies.'

Nick had other ideas for their afternoon. 'No, I don't want you going to Parker Estate by yourself.'

'Why on earth not?' Jill demanded.

'Three reasons, actually. If Mama Rose is indeed the murderer, then it's not safe.'

'I promise not to eat, drink, or inhale anything while I'm there. What's your next reason?'

'Like I explained, Ross Lacey has a wall of photos of you. If you're his new subject of fixation, you won't be safe until that creep is behind bars.'

Jill cocked her head to one side. 'Do you plan to stay with me twenty-four-seven until Lacey's trial?'

'Don't tell me you're sick of me already. We've only been semi-engaged for a short while.' Nick merged into heavy traffic.

'I'm far from sick of you, but I want to hear your third reason.'

'Tomorrow I go back to work. So I want to drive to my sister's house to see how Mom's getting along and tell my family the good news. Before Mom is too far gone to understand,' he added in a soft voice.

Jill touched his arm tenderly. 'If you had opened with that reason, the other two would've been unnecessary. I'd love to drive to your sister's house. Let me text Michael that I'll be back late, then I'm ready to go right now.'

'Such an amazingly cooperative woman. Whoever would've guessed?'

'Certainly not my partner, and I would appreciate you not telling him. I prefer to keep my current reputation at work.'

Nick's sister, Sarah, and her family lived in a picture-perfect area of fertile farmland and rolling green pastures that stretched for as far as the eye could see. Not surprisingly, even the air smelled better than around the Louisville area, so long as you didn't count the earthy tang of organic fertilizer used by Amish and Mennonite farmers. *God's country.* It was a term Jill had heard all her life, yet she had never fully understood it until she drove the backroads of Anderson County.

'Wow,' Jill said. 'It's beautiful. Your mother should love it here. I know I would.'

Nick took his eyes off the two-lane highway long enough to smile at her. 'Would you really? There are no clubs, no theaters, no four-star restaurants and no malls, unless you count Walmart plaza.'

'As long as they still have the internet, I can be happy. Tell me about your sister's family.'

Nick dropped his speed behind a slow-moving truck. 'Sarah works at a local hair salon. My brother-in-law, Bob, is an auto mechanic. They have a girl in high school and a boy in middle school. Both kids are active in sports and 4-H, so their parents do plenty of running around until their daughter gets her driver's license.'

'Good kids?' Jill asked, smirking. 'No sudden toilet-flushing when Lieutenant Nick walks into the house?'

'As far as Uncle Nick knows, they're very good kids.' He turned into a long gravel driveway and stopped in front of a rambling one-story house with a metal roof, trimmed hedges and flowerbeds along the walkway.

Jill jumped out of the car and froze. 'What if they don't like me?'

Nick slipped an arm around her waist. 'Don't be ridiculous. A travel writer who drinks wine from a cardboard box, has a nose for murder, and jailbirds for relatives? What's not to like?'

'Could we let them know the details a few at a time?' she asked, suddenly shy. But like with most things in life, Jill needn't have worried.

Nick opened the unlocked the door of a tidy and unnaturally quiet living room, considering teenagers lived in the house. 'Anybody home?' he called as they walked inside.

A young woman in blue scrubs and white leather shoes was doing paperwork on the couch, while the big screen television was on but apparently muted. 'Hi, I'm Karen Harper, RN. And you are?' She let her question hang in the air.

'Nick Harris, Julie's son. And this is my fiancée, Jill Curtis.' He pulled out his wallet. 'Would you like to see ID?'

'I don't think so, Mr Harris. I see plenty of resemblance with your sister.' The nurse stood and shook hands with each of them. 'I've been assigned to do an assessment of your mother. I'm just writing up my findings.'

'Where is everybody?' Nick asked, slipping his wallet back in his pocket.

'Let's see.' The nurse ticked off locations on her fingers. 'Sarah and Bob are still at work. Both kids are staying after school for a sports event, but your sister will pick them up on her way home. And an aide is helping your mother with her bath, while I write up my findings.'

'Jill and I would like to hear your assessment, Miss Harper, since we live in Louisville and can't visit as often as we'd like. Do you specialize in Alzheimer's patients?' When Nick sat down next to the nurse, Jill positioned herself near the doorway to the hall.

'I'd be happy to answer your questions. My specialty is all forms of dementia, even though a definitive diagnosis of Alzheimer's often isn't possible until after the patient dies.'

Nick hung his head for several seconds. 'Where is my mother in the normal progression of the disease?'

'The progression isn't always the same for all patients, but I can describe the various stages if you like.' She waited for an affirmative nod before continuing. 'In the beginning patients have difficulty remembering names or following conversations, but they are still able to perform routine activities without more-than-usual assistance. Those with mild cognitive impairment, called MCI, who go on to develop Alzheimer's may exhibit mood swings and are slow to react. They may need help with compli-cated activities and often lose their train of thought. For instance, they may wear the wrong clothes for the weather, get lost while traveling, or forget to pay bills. As the patient becomes aware of their memory loss, they may become irritable, fearful or depressed. Once patients become disabled by memory impairment, in other words unable to function safely on their own, we call this moderate or stage two. I feel your mother is entering this stage. Although a patient can still recall the distant past, recent events are difficult to remember, including the day of the week or their location. They start to forget familiar faces, and caregivers must give very specific instructions.' Harper paused to gauge Nick and Jill's reaction. 'During the final stage, patients become less responsive and no one is recognizable. They lose bowel and bladder control and require constant care. Once they lose the

ability to chew and swallow, they become susceptible to pneu-
monia and respiratory infections, especially once they become
bedridden. This stage eventually leads to coma and death.' Nurse
Harper's face filled with compassion. 'I won't try to sugarcoat
this. Alzheimer's is a hideous disease. Although some medica-
tions can slow the progression, we don't know what causes it
and we have no cure.'

'Thank you for sharing your evaluation.' Nick dropped his
face in his hands.

Jill glanced down the hallway to make sure it was still empty.
'Have you noticed Mrs Harris becoming worse as the day
wears on?'

'As a matter of fact, yes. It's referred to as Sundowner's
Syndrome. According to Sarah, your mother became hostile last
night when she tried to do a Sudoku puzzle. She threw the puzzle
book across the room and began shouting that someone had
switched her book with a harder set of puzzles.'

'Do you mean she's been able to do Sudoku in the morning?'
Nick looked up.

'Oh, no, but during the morning Mrs Harris is aware of and
accepts her limitations. She probably hasn't been able to do those
puzzles or balance the checkbook for a long time since the ability
to deal with abstract concepts like numbers is usually lost in the
early stage.'

Nick inhaled in a deep breath. 'Do you have any idea how
long she'll be able to stay with my sister's family? It's Sarah's
intention to keep Mom home for as long as possible.'

'That's understandable, but every case is different. It all
depends if Julie becomes dangerous to herself by trying to wander
at night, or use the stove without supervision, or if she makes
life unbearable for the rest of the family. Sarah and Bob will
know when the time is right. In the meantime, try to visit as
often as you can. No one knows how much quality time any of
us have left.'

As Jill signaled that people were coming down the hall, Nick
rose to his feet. 'Thank you, Miss Harper, for your insight. Jill
and I intend to take your advice to heart.'

'Nicky, I didn't know you were coming,' Mrs Harris said when
she and the aide walked into the room.

'Hi, I'm Vera, from Homecare.' The woman stretched out her hand. 'You must be the son Julie has talked so much about.'

Nick wrapped his mother in a bear hug. 'Yes, I'm Nick and this is my fiancée, Jill,' he said over his mother's head.

Jill watched his mother's face when he identified her. That tidbit of information didn't get past her.

'Fiancée?' Julie Harris asked. 'Is this the same nice girl you brought to Lorraine? When are you two getting married?'

Nick laughed. 'Yep, this is Jill, but we haven't set a date yet. I only asked her two days ago.'

His mother pushed Nick away and threw her arms around Jill. 'That boy has been dragging his feet, no?'

'Yes, he has.' Jill returned the hug cautiously as though afraid the older woman might break. 'But I finally pried the question out of him.'

'Who's getting married? Certainly not my little brother.' A pink-cheeked auburn-haired woman strolled in from the kitchen. On her heels were two teenagers, one the spitting image of her mother, the other bearing a considerable likeness to Nick. 'Nice to meet you, Jill. I'm his big sister, Sarah.' She offered Jill a warm embrace but gave her brother the evil eye. 'Why didn't you tell me you were coming? I only took one package of pork chops out of the freezer and you can eat a package by yourself.'

Nick quickly came up with a solution. 'Leave those chops in the fridge until tomorrow. Tonight this family celebrates the occasion in style, my treat. We can either go out to dinner or order up a storm of takeout food. Vera and Karen, you're both invited to join us.'

'After all, you're part of the family now.' Mrs Harris smiled at her two caregivers.

In the end, Vera and Karen went home to their families and the extended Harris clan celebrated the engagement with takeout Italian delivered to the backyard picnic table. Large portions of veal parmesan, chicken Piccata, and lasagna, along with pizza for the kids, enough for everyone to try everything with red wine for the toast. Nick and Jill drank iced tea, since they still had to drive back to Louisville.

'Jill and Nick, don't think this will be your only celebration,' said Sarah, lifting her glass. 'Since you didn't give us any notice, we have no cake. So we'll just have another party down the road when Sue and Bobbie can be here. Plus, we must buy you presents. I know for a fact Nick owns no potato peeler or a decent measuring cup.'

'And I've gotten along just fine without them,' Nick retorted.

And so the evening went – the two siblings sparring back and forth while the kids egged them on, greatly amused.

By the time Jill climbed in the car to go home, her face hurt from laughing. 'I really like your family,' she said. 'Surprising them tonight was a great idea.'

'Did you enjoy your dinner?' He arched a sly eyebrow.

'Everything was delicious, but it doesn't get you off the hook for cooking. I expect a big pot of jambalaya for tomorrow night, and you can expect Michael. No way can we get rid of my partner two days in a row. Then we can break our big news to him as well.'

'I look forward to it. No way should your new partner send your old partner home without a proper celebration.'

FIFTEEN

A Thursday seemed like an odd day for a person to return to work after a vacation, but Jill didn't press Nick into taking more time off. After all, he wouldn't approve of what she planned for the afternoon, despite Michael being her bodyguard all day. Jill appreciated Nick's concern, and it wasn't that she didn't consider Ross Lacey a threat. But she couldn't let fear hobble her ability to do a job. And now that the article on Louisville bourbon was done, Jill considered solving William Scott's murder her job. Or perhaps her obsession? Either way, she wasn't leaving Louisville until his murderer was behind bars.

Her first order of business was the temporary restraining order against Lacey. After they finished breakfast, Michael drove her to the courthouse, kept an eye on her until she was safely inside, and then jogged around the neighborhood until she was done. When she handed in the paperwork, a helpful clerk explained the process. Her request would be set for a hearing before a judge, who would determine if her complaint held merit or not. Since Nick planned to testify about Lacey's threatening behavior and collection of photographs at the hearing, most likely her request would be granted.

When Jill emerged from the courthouse an hour later, Michael was waiting at the curb for her. 'Where to now, partner?' he asked. 'Scenic ride on a riverboat? Watch the ponies race at Churchill Downs? Or maybe you'd like to learn how to play golf?' He mimed the follow-through of a golf swing.

Jill climbed in behind the wheel and turned the key. 'You're giving lessons after playing the game twice?'

'Some people turn out to be naturals at the sport.' Michael winked impishly. 'Or would you like to help me pack up to go home?'

Instead of pulling into traffic, Jill shifted the car back into park. 'You're leaving already?'

'*Already?* In case you haven't checked email in a while, the boss wants to know what's taking us so long. Mr Fleming won't keep paying expenses while you hang out with Nick, Alexis, or her new whacko brother.'

Jill made a face. 'Kevin Scott isn't a whacko. I think he's nice. And if possible, I want to mend the rift between him and Alexis.'

'You do what you must, Jill, but I'm heading to Chicago tomorrow. I don't want to get fired and I'm too young to retire.'

Jill hadn't planned to have this conversation while in a hot car on a busy city street, but she couldn't put off telling him the truth any longer. She swiveled around to face him. 'You know you'll always be my best friend, besides the best partner a person ever had, but I'm hoping I won't return to Chicago. Not tomorrow, not ever. I hope you don't hate me.'

Michael's eyes rolled back in his head. 'Jill, Jill. No matter how long we've known each other, you still underestimate me. I figured you would stay in Louisville after the assignment. You love Nick; he loves you, and now your crazy grandmother lives here with your crazy aunt. Plus they get less snow in Kentucky than up north.' He reached over to muss her hair. 'Once you signed that restraining order against Lacey, I knew for sure. You wouldn't need one of those in Chicago. Nobody stalks that far from home.'

Jill blew out her breath. 'Whew, I'm glad that's over with. I was afraid you'd think I'm crazy.'

'I'll always think that no matter where you live, but at least now I'll have a cool place to visit on long weekends. Now, which of my three suggestions did you pick – riverboat ride, horserace, or golf course for the rest of the day?'

'None of the above. We're heading to Parker Estate so I can chat with Rose Parker Scott. I'm convinced she's behind her husband's death. She wanted Robert out of the way before he had a chance to change his will.'

'What about the attempt on Rossi's life?'

Jill hesitated. 'Who knows? Anyone could have doctored Rossi's inhaler. Maybe Rose found someone who's more pliable to her bidding.'

Michael slapped the dashboard with an open palm. 'This is a bad idea. Nick trusts me to keep you safe until the TRO is served.'

Jill pulled into traffic. 'Is that what he asked you to do today?'

'Maybe. The guy worries about you. He knows how you go off half-cocked, sticking your head into one hornet's nest after another.'

'Oh, that is so sweet,' she drawled, her words dripping with scorn. 'Two strong men protecting the helpless blonde from the bad men in the world.'

Michael ignored her sarcasm. 'Not just bad men; women can be just as evil. Considering what you told me about Alexis's mother, she fits the description perfectly.'

'That's why I must get to the bottom of this before they rail-road Kevin into one count of murder, plus another count of attempted. If you're afraid to tag along, I'll drop you off at the hotel. What do you say, Emerson?'

Michael flexed his bicep. 'I'm in, but what should I tell Nick? I'm a little scared of him.'

'You leave Nick to me. I've got him wrapped around my finger.' Jill wiggled her pinkie and headed for the country, no longer needing GPS to direct her. 'When we get there, we'll simply tell the truth – we have no photos of the estate or the family matriarch for our segment on Parker Distillery. That should get us through the front door.'

'But all I have with me is one digital thirty-five-millimeter. I left the rest of my equipment at the hotel.'

'All we need is one camera to get the job done. This doesn't have to be high-tech. Stop worrying and let me do the talking.'

Despite Jill's perfect explanation, the maid who answered the front door refused to let them in. 'I'm sorry,' she murmured, not sounding the least bit sorry. 'Neither Mrs Scott nor Miss Alexis are home. I can't let you wander around taking pictures without permission.'

As the door began to close, Jill inserted her foot. 'What if I call Alexis and you could talk to her?'

The maid considered this. 'Miss Alexis could grant permission to enter her apartment, but not the main house. Good day, Miss Curtis. I'll tell Mrs Scott you stopped by.' She closed the door in their faces.

'What now, fearless leader?' Michal leaned his shoulder against a pillar. 'Sneak in through an underground tunnel built during Prohibition?'

'Something like that.' Jill stomped down the steps. 'Mrs Scott might have told the maid to say she wasn't home. Let's see if she's napping with an open book on her lap. Follow me.' She led him on a circuitous path around the house, ducking beneath windows, until they reached the glass-walled solarium in the back of the house. When Jill parted the bushes and peeked inside, she spotted Grandpa Parker not Mrs Scott. With his back to the windows, Grandpa's focus was on an array of cards spread across the table.

Michael craned his neck to see around her. 'What's that old guy doing?'

'I have no idea, but let's ask to photograph him while we're here. After all, he is the patriarch of a distillery family, even though he squandered the profits. He's been very sweet to me in the past.'

'*What?*' Michael asked.

'Never mind, you didn't hear about my visit with Alexis's new brother and potential heir. Just follow my lead, but remember,

Mr Parker suffers from possible dementia, though the extent of his memory loss is unknown. So be patient with him and prepared to repeat simple directions.'

'Thank you, Dr Curtis. When did you become a medical expert?' Michael asked.

'I'm no expert, but I'm learning,' she whispered under her breath. 'Nick's mom suffers from Alzheimer's.'

'Sorry to hear that. There's a lot you haven't been telling me.'

'I know, but we don't have time right now.' Jill backed from the shrubbery and headed up the flagstone path. She rapped lightly on the door, then pasted on a smile as though first place in a beauty pageant was at stake. 'Hello, Mr Parker?' she called. 'It's Jill Curtis. Do you remember me? I'm a friend of your granddaughter's.'

The wizened, white-haired gentleman in a cardigan sweater and cloth slippers pulled open the door, his dog at his side. 'Of course I remember you. I met you that afternoon with Alexis and saw you again the night they installed Rossi as new master distiller. Come in and have a seat.' He gestured toward the love-seat, then limped back to his table. 'Who's that with you?'

Jill was astounded that the old-timer correctly recalled both events. 'This, sir, is Michael Emerson, my videographer. I think you'll like the footage he took inside Parker Estate Distillery.'

'Pleased to meet you, sir.' When Michael stepped forward to shake hands, Grandpa's dog issued a low growl from deep in his throat. Michael took a step back. 'I see you're in the middle of a game of Solitaire. Would you like a little help?'

'No, I wouldn't.' Mr Parker swept the cards into a pile, but not before Jill noticed there were no mistakes in each column's sequence. *How could Grandpa play solitaire when abstract concepts like numbers were one of the first things to go?*

'What brings you to my humble abode today?' His smile had slipped a notch.

'We came to ask Mrs Scott a few questions.'

'I'm not sure if my daughter is back from errands yet.'

'In that case, we'd love to get a few photos of you relaxing in the solarium.'

'We like to show the comfortable, human side of people.' Michael glanced down at the man's paisley slippers.

Mr Parker lifted his chin and glared down his nose. 'I prefer to be photographed in business attire, so I suggest you take photographs only of the house and the estate, Mr Emerson.' Grandpa pointed at the door. 'Outdoors,' he added to prevent any misunderstanding. 'My dog doesn't seem to like you. And Buster has excellent judgement regarding people.'

'Of course. Nice to meet you, sir.' Michael and his camera beat a hasty retreat.

Once the door closed behind him, Parker moved to the upholstered chair next to the loveseat. 'What did you wish to ask my daughter? Maybe I can help.'

Jill hesitated, not wishing to betray family secrets to someone with spotty recall. On the other hand, this might be the best way to learn how much Rose knew about William's past. 'I was curious if Mrs Scott knew about her husband's previous relationships, including the one which produced Kevin. She seemed just as shocked as Alexis by Kevin Scott's appearance.'

'Of course she knew. William loved my daughter and she loved him. At first they told each other everything. He said he'd lived with a woman before they met, but neither had known about the son until much later. Once William found out, he wanted them to become one big, happy family.' Mr Parker released a nasty laugh. 'Could you imagine Rose going for that idea? For years she had put up with his indiscretions because she was infatuated with him, but William trying to establish a relationship with an illegitimate son? That was the beginning of the end of their marriage.'

'Why do you think he stayed in the marriage?'

'That's easy. William stayed because he wanted control of my distillery. And slowly but surely he managed to just about get it.'

'No one forced you to sell your shares or turn over control of the distillery.'

'I realize that, Jill.' Grandpa's lip furled slightly. 'At first, I overlooked William's transgressions under the mistaken notion he would outgrow his roving eye and settle down, but he never did. William embarrassed my daughter over and over. He was a liar, besides a two-timer. He told Rose the boy was illegitimate and therefore no threat to the Parker Scott legacy. William and Rose agreed to pay the mother a stipend each month, barely enough to keep her and the son alive, in exchange for no nasty lawsuit that would create bad publicity for the brand. The arrangement went on for several years.'

'So what upset the applecart?' Jill prodded.

'The woman found out she had cancer, so she told the boy exactly who his father was and gave him a copy of his birth certificate and their . . . marriage license. Turns out she had married William at eighteen and divorced him at twenty. That paper changed an unfortunate mistake from years ago into a legitimate heir.'

'A baby is blameless and deserves better treatment.'

'Apparently my son-in-law agreed with you after that upstart started visiting him and tugging on his heartstrings. Whoever thought William would develop a conscience after all these years?'

'So your daughter tried to pay Kevin off to make him go away.'

'But the creep wouldn't take the money. Kevin demanded public acknowledgement and a position in the business. My business! The distillery started by my father!' Parker crossed the room to an antique highboy, unlocked it with a key, and removed two snifters and a bottle of bourbon from the top shelf. It seemed like strong spirits were never far from reach no matter where you were in the house. He poured two fingers of bourbon into the first glass, then looked at Jill.

She shook her head. 'No, thank you, sir. It's a little early for me.'

Parker's complexion darkened. 'You refuse to have a drink after intruding on my privacy with your nosy questions? I don't drink alone, Miss Curtis.'

Playing solitaire accurately and now remembering her surname? Maybe Grandpa wasn't the sweet old man like she thought or as cognitively challenged as he wanted people to believe. 'Sorry, I didn't mean to offend you,' she said. 'Perhaps, just a smidgen?'

Parker poured almost as much in the second glass as the first.

'May I have a bit of ice, please?' Jill took the glass from his hand, but when Parker turned his back to speak into the intercom, she set the glass on the table. 'So when William began seeing his son on the sly, your daughter became furious, right?'

'William could never acknowledge Kevin, not with the current wording of the will. Where would that leave Alexis?'

'Alexis is a very capable woman. She would have landed on her feet, no matter what.'

Parker began to pace the room. 'Let me ask you a question. Do you have a family, Jill? Are you close to them?'

This took her by surprise. 'I have parents in Chicago, and a grandmother who just moved in with her cousin in Roseville about an hour away. I didn't even know this Kentucky cousin existed until recently, but I already love her. I'd say I'm closer with Granny and my new Aunt Dot than my parents. Why do you ask?'

The old man produced the saddest smile Jill had ever seen. 'Then maybe you can understand. When you love your family, you would do anything for them.'

'Even murder?' An icy chill shot up her spine.

'Yes, even murder.'

'But William became part of the family when they got married. Rose was more worried about herself and that's why she killed her husband.'

'*Rose?* You think my daughter would lift a finger against William? She would rather cut off her hand.' Parker cackled with malevolent glee.

'If not Rose, then who? Alexis was at the distillery and you were at the doctor's office. Rose was the only one home when Mr Scott died, other than the servants, and they have no motive.'

'If I told you I went to the moon, would you have believed that too? You really are a little ninny, just like my daughter said.' Parker took a gulp of his drink. 'William came home to pick up some files he'd forgotten, so I had the perfect opportunity.'

It took Jill a moment to process this. 'But why did you try to kill the new master distiller? He had nothing to do with money or inheritance.'

'Tony Rossi was Rose's first choice for the job, not mine. He was too lenient with the employees and would've allowed that upstart, Kevin, to worm his way into the company.'

'Here's your ice, sir.' A uniformed maid entered the room with an ice bucket.

'Who are you talking to, Dad?' Rose asked, following on the maid's heels. When she saw Jill, all color drained from the woman's cheeks, despite her carefully applied make-up.

'What are *you* doing here?' she shrieked. 'I swear, Miss Curtis, you're like a piece of gum stuck to my shoe.'

'I stopped in to ask you a few questions, but apparently it's your father who has all the answers.' Jill turned her attention back to Grandpa, who was filling both glasses with ice.

Rose rested both hands on her slender hips. 'Daddy has a very vivid imagination. You should know nothing he says can be trusted and certainly wouldn't hold up in a court of law.'

'I wouldn't be so sure about that, because he just confessed to murdering your husband.' Jill tried to discreetly locate her cell phone in her purse.

Rose swiveled around to face her father. 'Why on earth would you say something like that?'

'Because it's true, dear girl, and I couldn't have this busybody thinking you were the murderer. Would you like a drink?' He reached for a third glass and poured it half full.

'No, I would not. Why on earth would you kill my husband?' Rose began to wobble on her heels.

'Simply because I hated him. First he coerced me to retire and hand over control of the distillery. Next he conned me into selling him every share of Parker stock I owned. Then, according to gossip, he wanted to give Alexis's half of the estate to some ill-bred outsider because he'd married a woman on a lark? I couldn't let that happen.'

'William never would have cut Alexis out of his will. He loved her. And what did I care about the distillery as long as I keep the house, the condo, and our bank account? Alexis can have my shares if her shares end up going to Kevin.' Rose grabbed her father's lapels. 'You swore to me William had a heart attack.'

Something evil glinted in the old man's eyes. 'It sure looked like a heart attack. I just gave him something to help the inevitable along. Now that scoundrel will never make a fool of you again.' Parker turned back to Jill. 'Come, Miss Curtis. You agreed to have a drink with me if I answered your questions. I'd say you got more than you bargained for.' He picked Jill's glass up from the table.

'Don't drink that,' Rose shouted.

'It's OK, Mrs Scott. I've kept my eye on him. He didn't put anything in my glass this time.'

'My father just admitted to killing my husband, so let's not take a chance.' Rose batted the glass from Jill's fingers. Unfortunately, the snifter missed the thick rug and shattered on the tile.

'Such a waste of perfectly good whiskey, daughter,' Parker said, clucking his tongue. 'The toxin wasn't in the decanter. It was dried on the inside of the glass, my glass. I would never harm a pretty young lady like Jill, even if she was a busybody.' Parker lifted his snifter in toast and downed the contents. Within a few moments he swayed, reached unsuccessfully for the table, and fell to the floor.

'Dad, what have you done?' Rose dropped to her knees and picked up his hand.

'Let's just say I reserved the special snifter for myself,' he mumbled before passing out.

Jill punched in 9-1-1. But even if the ambulance had wings it would have been too late. Mr Robert Parker was dead before she hung up the phone.

By the time Nick finished his first day back to work as an investigator, Jill had already recited the events in the solarium three times – first to the officers who arrived with the paramedics, then to Detective Grimes, who wasn't pleased to see her, and finally to Alexis, who had been summoned by one of the maids. By the time Alexis arrived, Rose Scott was inconsolable with grief, not only from her father's death, but by the fact he had murdered her husband. When Nick walked into the solarium, Jill knew it was time to abandon her friend, Alexis, and deal with her maybe-fiancé. And judging by the expression on his face, she knew a fourth recitation would be mandatory.

'Hi, Nick. Let's talk where it's quiet.' Jill took his hand and led him to the living room, away from the dead body, two grieving women, and the forensic techs.

'What on earth are you doing here?' Nick hissed between his teeth. 'You were supposed to file a restraining order at the courthouse and hang out with Michael all day.' He pointed at her partner, who sat dejectedly in a corner listening to what transpired.

'My *bodyguard* needed more pictures for the article, and while we were photographing the exterior we ran into Mr Parker. He invited us inside the house, but then made Michael wait outside.' Jill stretched up on tiptoes. 'Who called you about the suicide?'

'Detective Grimes texted me the moment your name was mentioned as the nine-one-one caller. How do you know it was suicide?' Nick gazed down from his impressive height.

'After Mr Parker confessed to killing his son-in-law, he explained that the toxin was dried on the bottom of his glass, not mine. Don't worry. I didn't plan on drinking anything. How did your first day back to work go?'

Nick exchanged a scowl with Grimes, who had followed them to the living room. 'We're not talking about *my* day right now. You've already told your story to Detective Grimes, but please go over it again for my benefit.' Nick maneuvered her to the sofa. 'Leave out no details.'

Jill went through the story step-by-step, exactly like before. When she finished, Nick wrapped his arm around her shoulder. 'This mess with Mrs Parker Scott could've gotten you killed. Do you know how unhappy that would have made me?' He lifted her chin with one finger.

Grimes stepped forward and took over. 'My department was closing in on Mr Parker. On the night Rossi was named master distiller, Nick had a security guard collect a sample of your vomit and send it to the lab. He suspected you had been drugged and the most likely source was Grandpa Parker since he was the last person you talked to. We finally got the results back and were waiting on the search warrant when the nine-one-one came in. In other words, you didn't have to risk your life, Miss Curtis.'

Jill rubbed her face with her hands. 'You mean after I gave him Alexis's plate of meatballs that sweet old guy tried to poison me?'

'Pretty much. We only found traces of the toxin used to kill William Scott in your vomit. So most likely Grandpa only wanted you out of the picture or he would've given you a stronger dose.'

Jill pressed her fingertips to her temples, trying to make sense of everything. 'But what about Anthony Rossi? Who tried to poison him with fentanyl?'

'That would be also Grandpa. Rossi told us Mr Parker visited his office earlier that day. He spotted the inhaler in Rossi's pocket and asked to see it. He said he wanted to compare ingredients with the one he uses.'

'And he switched it.' Jill filled in the blanks.

'The police found Rossi's rightful inhaler in the trash,' Nick said, pulling her to her feet. 'You were very lucky, Jill, but now it's time to find Michael and get out of here. I have a pot roast in the crockpot and I don't want it ruined like the jambalaya.'

'*What?*' Grimes said to Nick. 'You know how to cook? You'd better hurry and marry this guy, Jill, or I will.'

Jill tightened her grip on Nick's hand. 'Nick said you've already got a husband, Detective, and only one per customer in Kentucky.'

That night the soon-to-be ex-partners ate plenty of food and talked long into the night with the man who'd soon be Jill's new partner, hopefully for the rest of their lives. Nick's dinner of tender roast beef, red-skinned potatoes and carrots in mushroom gravy was delicious. Jill also made plans to fly to Chicago before month's end to pack up her apartment and retrieve her old, but reliable, car. She would also clean out her desk at work and thank her boss, Mr Fleming, for his patience.

The hardest conversation would be with her parents. They wouldn't like her decision of a wedding in Kentucky instead of Chicago where their friends and business contacts were. After all, this was her mom's big chance to shine as mother of the bride. But a wedding at the Roseville Episcopal Church with a reception in Aunt Dot's B & B made more sense. The location was convenient for Nick's relatives and the Louisville post of fellow troopers. But she would cross that bridge soon enough.

'This is our last night at the Thurman House,' Jill said to Michael on their way back to the hotel. 'With you going home tomorrow, I can't afford that place without an expense account.'

'About that . . .' Michael grinned. 'I did some thinking while the cops kept me from the crime scene. Since the boss doesn't expect me until Monday, I decided to drive back on Saturday and paid for the suite for another night. Tomorrow we will celebrate your engagement in style in the hotel dining room. I already checked with Nick.'

'Have you lost your mind? Have you seen the prices on their menu?'

'What's money for if not to splurge on your friends? I'm happy for you, Jilly.'

'That's very nice of you, Emerson, but you still can't call me Jilly.'

Michael hooted. 'After you see how much money I shell out, you'll let me call you anything I want.'

After spending the day catching up on paperwork and packing Michael's car, Jill and Michael wandered into the bar at five thirty and ordered a round of drinks. Nick wasn't expected until six because unlike them, he didn't have the day off. But surprisingly, Nick walked into the bar before Ray had poured the first round. And he wasn't smiling.

'What's wrong?' Jill asked. 'Did something happen?'

'You could say that.' Nick sliced a finger across his throat to cancel their drinks. 'I just got a call from Jeff Adkins.'

'The sheriff of Roseville?' Michael asked, wide-eyed. 'This can't be good.'

'No!' Jill muttered. 'Don't tell me he's arrested those crazy ladies again!'

Nick slicked a hand through his hair. 'I don't know what they've done this time. Adkins just called and said to come to Roseville on the double.'

'No . . . way! Let them rot in jail for one night. Call the sheriff and say we'll bail them out tomorrow.' Jill motioned to Ray to bring their drinks. 'Michael planned a special evening for us, and we're not disappointing him.' She patted him on the arm.

'You can't do that,' Michael argued. 'Not if you want your wedding reception at their bed and breakfast.'

Jill shrugged. 'Then we'll have the reception at the VFW Hall. It's the only way those two lawbreakers will learn.'

'I didn't make myself clear.' Nick placed both hands on her shoulders. 'Jeff Adkins didn't say he'd arrested your relatives, only that we needed to come as soon as possible. Apparently, the ladies called an impromptu meeting of the Bourbon and Books Club. That's all he would say on the phone.'

A chin ran up her spine. 'As in one of them might be sick or injured or . . . worse?' Jill couldn't vocalize the third possibility.

'I don't know. Let's go find out.' Nick put money on the bar to cover the tab, along with a generous tip, but pushed the drinks away. 'Thanks, Ray. See if you can find these a home with our compliments. Sorry we messed up your plans for an engagement celebration,' he said to Michael. 'Maybe we can have breakfast with you tomorrow before you leave?'

'Absolutely, but I'm tagging along tonight.' Michael followed them out the door. 'I want to see for myself what mischief those two are in.'

So the three piled into Nick's SUV and headed to Roseville, but the closer they got, the more Jill's stomach churned. Finally she couldn't sit still another minute. 'Give me your phone, Nick. I'm calling Adkins to find out what happened. Are Granny and Aunt Dot at the police station? Or in the hospital? Or the morgue? Or did you plan to drive around town aimlessly?' Her voice had risen to near-hysteria level.

'Calm yourself, my sweet.' Nick patted her hand. 'The sheriff said to come to Sweet Dream's because that's where they're being held.'

'*Being held?*' she cried, clutching her throat.

Michael leaned in between the front seats. 'Maybe a few crazy club members are holding them hostage until Dot agrees to allow bourbon again. You know some books need a bit of incentive to reach the end.'

'Sit back, Emerson,' Nick ordered, using his cop voice. 'You're not helping. We're almost there, Jill. Try to relax.' He used a softer tone with her.

A lump the size of a tennis ball lodged in her throat, rendering speech impossible. Beads of sweat formed on her brow, even though she felt chilled to the bone. What if Granny or Aunt Dot had suffered a heart attack? Or they'd died in a car accident together? Every possible dire circumstance ran through her brain like a news banner.

Jill felt Michael grip her shoulder but she ignored him.

She heard Nick murmur words of encouragement, but she ignored those too.

Instead she concentrated on not dissolving into tears. After all, she had no idea what she was crying about. Was all this emotion due to yesterday's events with Alexis's dysfunctional family? Or was it because she'd officially talked to her boss that morning? Mr Fleming was quite pleased with what he'd seen on the bourbon tour article so far. He wanted her and Michael to do another in another Kentucky city. And the best part? He could remain in Kentucky until details of the assignment were lined up. Most likely her tears were because she couldn't stand the idea of losing Granny or Aunt Dot. Not after finally discovering one and reconnecting with the other. *Could life be this cruel?* If her new best friend, Alexis, was any indication, Jill knew it could.

The moment Nick stopped in the driveway of Sweet Dreams, Jill jumped out of the car. She heard pleas to 'hang on' and 'wait for me', but she paid no attention. Sprinting up the steps, Jill threw open the front door and saw the tanned, leathery face of Sheriff Jeff Adkins.

'Hi, Jill. You seem out of breath.' Adkins turned to the person on his left. 'I don't think you've ever met my better half. This is my wife, Jenny Adkins. Jenny, this is Jill Curtis, Dot's favorite niece.'

Being thrust into a social introduction had the same effect as a board applied to the side of her head. 'Pleased to meet you, ma'am,' Jill stuttered, forcing her lips to smile. 'What has happened, Sheriff? Where are my aunt and grandmother?'

'We're right here, honey.'

She heard Granny's voice from somewhere over Adkins's shoulder. Stepping around the larger-than-life lawman, Jill found her grandmother sitting on the couch with Aunt Dot. Granny had on her favorite Sunday dress, the one with tiny violets.

'Come sit with us, dear.' Dot patted the spot between them. 'Tonight you're the book club's guest of honor, you and that handsome Nick Harris.'

'You two haven't been arrested?' Jill squeaked like a mouse.

'Goodness, no. Is that what those men led you to believe to get you here? Look around.' Granny waved her hand through the air. 'This is your bridal shower and everyone in the club wanted to take part.'

Jill moved to the center and gazed around the room. Colorful helium balloons, streamers stretched from wall-to-wall, and a giant poster with: *Best wishes Jill and Nick from the Roseville gang*. Gang being an appropriate description for bourbon-loving rabble-rousers. One end of the dining table was filled with color-fully wrapped presents and gift bags. At the other end were several platters of canapes and a three-tier frosted cake.

Suddenly Jill caught the scent of spicy aftershave behind her. 'Did you know about this, Trooper?' she asked.

'Yes, but only for the last few hours. Your grandmother called Michael yesterday to make sure he would still be in town tonight.'

'That's why I decided to stay another day,' Michael said, walking up beside her. He pulled a festively wrapped package from behind his back. 'You didn't think I planned to spring for dinner at the hotel, did you? Not with those prices.'

'Yes, I did, you little tightwad.' Jill elbowed him in the ribs.

'Hey, I bought you a nice shower gift.' Michael added his package to the pile.

'I hope you're not giving that sweet young man grief,' called Aunt Dot, coming to Michael's defense. 'Now it's time for you to put on your corsage and open the gifts.'

When her grandmother pinned a purple orchid to her dress, Jill's eyes filled with tears. 'Thanks, Granny. Thanks, Aunt Dot. Where would I be if not for you two?'

'On your way back to Chicago and we couldn't have that,' said Granny. 'Showers are joyous occasions, so dry your eyes and stop sniveling.'

And so Jill did. She and Nick opened present after present, some from casual acquaintances like the clerk from the dress shop and the funeral director for Uncle Roger, but many were from people she didn't know at all. These residents of Roseville seemed just as happy for her and Nick as lifelong friends. Jill gushed over each set of towels, kitchen appliance, or household gadget, even those she hadn't a clue what to do with. Then the boisterous group of ladies consumed an enormous amount of food and cake and didn't leave until dusk. But not a drop of bourbon.

When the house was quiet at long last, Jill hugged each of the hostesses in turn. 'I've never been to a better shower. How do I thank you two?'

'You can start by never leaving Roseville,' Granny suggested, never one to mince words.

'Done,' Jill said.

'*What?*' they both asked simultaneously.

'When Jill agreed to marry me, she agreed to move to Kentucky.' Nick smiled from ear to ear. 'And we'd both rather live in a small town than a big city like Louisville.'

Jill picked up the story. 'So if it's OK with you, I'd like to live here until the wedding. Then Nick and I will look for a small house to rent or buy in Roseville.'

Granny looked ready to faint. 'Of course, it's OK.'

'This is even better than we hoped,' Dot added. 'We've missed you at Sweet Dreams, and Jack will be overjoyed.'

Jill looked under the table. 'Where is that old beagle? After we help clean up, I'll take him for a walk.'

'Jack's in the backyard. Go walk him now. You three aren't cleaning up anything. Emma and I need to start planning your reception. You're not having it anywhere but here.'

Thus Jill Curtis, her ex-business partner, and her husband-to-be followed Jack up and down the streets of Roseville. On a perfect moonlit night, under a sky filled with stars, each shared their dreams for the future.

'I know one thing you must be happy about,' Michael said to Jill. 'With William Scott's killer behind bars, you can forget about that crazy family and concentrate on freelance writing.'

His statement generated no response whatsoever from Jill.

'Go on, honey,' Nick prodded. 'Tell Michael how you're washing your hands of Alexis's drama.'

Jill bent down to adjust Jack's harness. 'Well, I still need to convince Alexis that Kevin has good intentions.'

Michael grabbed hold of her arm. 'Tell me you're kidding.'

She looked him straight in the eye. 'Kevin will be a great asset in the distillery once he's fully trained. And with Rose willing to give up her shares, the two lawyers can work out an agreement in accordance with William's wishes. Besides, Alexis always wanted a sibling.'

Michael shook his head. 'And here you are . . . still interfering?'

'Go on, Jill, might as well tell him everything.'

'Because I asked Alexis to be my maid of honor and she agreed.'

Lifting his hands, Michael backed away from her. 'I'm getting out of Kentucky. You left Chicago a relatively sane person and you haven't been right in the head since. Good luck, Nick, and just make sure I'm in this wedding party, whenever it takes place.' Michael winked and broke into a run all the way to the B & B, leaving Jill and Nick to walk Jack alone . . . on one perfect moonlit night.